THE REMINGTON CRUCIBLE

ANDREW SCOTT JACKSON

THM

For my father, who first encouraged me to write.

Out of every one hundred men, ten shouldn't even be there, eighty are just targets, nine are the real fighters, and we are lucky to have them, for they make the battle. Ah, but the one, one is a warrior, and he will bring the others back.
—Heraclitus

From the hottest fires comes the strongest steel.
—Chinese proverb

PROLOGUE

San Juan Harbor, Puerto Rico, 12:47 A.M.

Frank Stodd was completely lost in this godforsaken barrio he had fled into. Not a great place for an older, overweight white guy on foot in a sweat-soaked G-man suit. A warren of cinder block houses with dirt yards and the occasional chained pit bull lined both sides of the street. A toothless old woman sat on her porch, and he managed a smile, but she turned away and spat out a long stream of tobacco juice.

At the next house, two young men watched him the way hungry lions eye a wounded buffalo. He shoved the first twinge of panic back into the hole it was trying to crawl out of.

Without thinking, he rechecked the package in his jacket. Goose bumps chilled him to the core in the tropical heat. No matter what went down next, he wasn't going to give it up. His hand lingered on it for a few seconds too long.

The two men stood up and started following him, their heads swiveling back and forth, looking for witnesses. The road ahead grew darker. Half the streetlights were still out since Hurricane Irma, and the other half had been out even before the storm. He quickened his pace as the street started downhill.

He felt a gentle gust of warm air from further down and smelled the decayed low tide of the ocean. If he got back to the water and out of this urban jungle hellhole, he should be able to see the big red HILTON on the side of his hotel on the bay.

He welcomed the cover of the dark street and hugged the overgrown edge of the road. The street curved to the right, and when he arrived there, he took a quick look behind him. The two men were just starting down the hill about a hundred yards back when a pair of headlights suddenly appeared behind them, silhouetting their figures. The vehicle stopped beside them. There was an exchange of words and money with the driver, and the two pointed in Stodd's direction. Then the vehicle moved down the street. When it passed under one of the streetlights, he recognized the Escalade and began to run.

Stodd ran surprisingly fast for a big man, some lifetime imprint from his high school days of running track. He rounded another turn and saw a marina and floating docks at the end of the street. Small boats were tied up. He headed for them, hoping to hide, but had to stop as he got closer, his heart pounding. He hunched over, hands on knees to catch his breath, looking back for the Escalade. It wasn't there. There may be a way out of this yet.

He stood up, and three things happened at once. A bright orange flash from his left, a whooshing sound like someone had spit, then a sledge-hammer impact, and he was on his side, left arm and shoulder on fire.

The pavement was cool despite the night's heat; his vision blurred, and the pain took a back seat. He was tired now and wanted to rest. He closed his eyes.

When he awoke, it seemed he'd been out for an eternity. He was instantly awake, adrenaline pumping the blood out. Again, he fought off the panic as he'd been taught—slow down and think.

He heard a man's voice and saw someone step out of the shadows not thirty feet away. The man was speaking into a headset, and he listened to the metallic reply from the earpiece.

Stodd reached inside his coat and slipped the Glock automatic from its holster. It was covered with blood, and he struggled to hold on to it, thankful there was no safety to click off. He kept it hidden beneath his jacket.

Stodd forced his breathing to shallow sips. No chest movement. Staring at the pavement and trying to mimic the lifeless eyes he'd seen so many times at a crime scene.

The shooter stood over him, gun at his side. He bent over to take a closer look, and Stodd drew the Glock in one fluid motion and squeezed off three rapid-fire rounds. The slugs passed through the man's chest, knocking him backward. He landed in an expired heap and didn't move.

Stodd rolled to his good side and struggled to his feet, dizzy from lack of blood. Nothing about the man he had just shot was familiar. He looked local, but even in his half-conscious state, Stodd could see there was something about him, the haircut, or the shoes, that didn't quite fit on this side of the globe. He staggered back a few steps and heard the dead man's earpiece chatter.

Then the Escalade turned onto the marina road and accelerated toward him.

He made it to the dinghies before collapsing. He picked himself up and half climbed, half fell into one of the small boats. He must get to a hospital and call the police. He wondered if the police could be trusted. He reached into his jacket for his cell phone, but the damn thing wasn't there. It must have fallen out when he went down on the pavement. Shit. Shit!

The Escalade drove to the end of the floating dock, fifty yards from him. Stodd watched two armed men get out of the car and look around. They stared in his direction but didn't see him among all the other boats. A man in the back seat said something, and they started toward the marina building. Stodd cast off the bowline and pulled the start cord of the small outboard motor bolted to the stern. The engine sputtered to life, its staccato exhaust spitting out a blue-black cloud. The men were running toward him now, and he cranked the hand control lever to its maximum speed.

The harbor was a maze of boats, mooring lines, and buoys, the water as black as a crow's feather. The light from the dock faded as he drew away, and the darkness enveloped him until he could barely see where he was going. By some miracle, he managed to get out toward the middle of the harbor before nearly colliding with the side of a big boat. He pulled the dinghy alongside and killed the engine.

He waited for a few seconds until he heard the distant whine of an outboard engine on another dinghy. They were coming after him.

His vision blurred, but he heaved himself out of the dinghy and over the rail of the larger boat. The effort took nearly the rest of his energy, but he was able to stand at last. He staggered toward the center of the vessel and fell down a short set of steps to the cabin. The jolt made his bleeding worse. The pain came screaming back, throbbing in his left side with every accelerated heartbeat, and he bit into the padded shoulder of the jacket to keep from crying out.

Although the sound of the distant engine grew louder, they seemed to be having trouble finding him. He allowed himself to hope they would go past him in the dark. But he heard the boat throttle down as they prepared to come alongside.

He wouldn't make it through the night without a doctor, and his chance of getting to a hospital was more remote with each passing minute. Nausea and pain hit him hard again, and he choked down some vomit. The effort brought up the unmistakable iron taste of blood in his mouth. Lung shot. Then panic and shock hit him hard, and he knew he couldn't fight it.

Without hesitation, he reached into his jacket with his good arm and found the package. He couldn't let them get it. He'd rather die first.

The two men were on the boat in seconds.

He was ready for them this time. When one peered down into the cabin, he raised the Glock and fired. The man fell overboard, clutching his neck. The other ran for cover behind the wheelhouse.

Stodd took his cue and managed to get out of the cabin and over the side to his dinghy. He started the engine, fired a few wild covering rounds at the wheelhouse, and sped away toward the light of the dock.

The remaining pursuer was soon after him again. Stodd fired awkwardly behind him, his shots wild and high. The two boats wove in and out of obstacles in the crowded harbor. Neither man could get a clear shot at the other.

When Stodd saw the docks again, he was just a few hundred yards away. Three more minutes, and he would be there.

He realized too late that his pursuer hadn't fired for some time. He looked over his shoulder in horror to see the man much closer than he'd guessed. He had exchanged his pistol for a submachine gun.

The two slugs that slammed into his back kicked him like a horse. His hand flew off the throttle as he was thrown face down to the bottom of the boat. The dinghy came to an abrupt halt, and he heard the other boat come alongside. Another short blast and two more shots hit him, the others perforating the sides and bottom of the dinghy. All he could do was lie there feeling the water flowing in around him before all sight and sound faded away.

The man with the machine gun confirmed Stodd was dead and searched all his pockets. He found his wallet and gun but nothing more.

A spotlight arced over him, and an amplified voice announced, "This is the United States Coast Guard. Stay where you are and put your hands in the air."

The voice from the patrol boat began to repeat the command in Spanish, but before it could finish, the man emptied the rest of his magazine at the approaching spotlight, leaped from the dinghy, and disappeared beneath the dark surface.

1

The lee side of the tiny island was still and warm. The moon was far past its zenith, a thin, waning crescent sinking toward the western horizon to make way for the sun to arrive in an hour and burn new life into the tropical waters and land.

The sea's surface was a midnight-blue sheet of glass, and except for an occasional fish jumping here and there, uninterrupted for miles in all directions. Only the gentle slapping of the waves against rocks on the nearby island would remind an observer that something other than water covered the earth.

The island was one of hundreds between Puerto Rico and the Virgin Islands. It lay in a stretch of water forty miles long the cruise ships avoided and few of the locals ever visited. Stuck off by itself, it was more a hazard to navigation than anything else—just rocks and a few clumps of grass, the top of one of the ancient volcanoes that made up the archipelago. Before the invention of surface radar and pinpoint navigation, these rocks had claimed many ships. Through the centuries, some of their hulks had remained above water until the next inevitable hurricane washed them off without a trace. They lay in the depths just offshore until absorbed into the bottom. Pelicans and other sea birds rested on the island overnight, but because of its small size and better nesting elsewhere, they chose not to make it a permanent home.

The tugboat *Aurora* sat on the surface in stark contrast to its natural, unspoiled surroundings. Built for a variety of tasks, including towing and pushing ships fifty times its size, she had served her crews well in the thirty-five years since her keel was laid in Norfolk. Now, the sides of the hulls showed streaks of rust stains from unpainted scuppers. They trailed down like tears on the faded name and registry on the stern. The once beautiful teak decks were cracked and in dire need of repair. All about her were signs of neglect and decay. She had spent the last two years of her life in the corner of the protected harbor in San Juan, chained like a prisoner to a concrete mooring in twenty feet of water. Few had cared for the once proud ship during those years except for an old friend of the deceased owner who had visited her as often as he could.

Life had begun again for *Aurora* two weeks ago. Her bilge had been pumped out, and the big diesel engines started again. After an overhaul in St. John, she would be clean and strong again in another week.

A deckhand was asleep now in the wheelhouse, a half-empty bottle of Mount Gay rum precariously perched on the ledge by his head. He sat in the captain's chair behind the wheel, his feet propped up on the chart table. A marine radio spit and crackled into life, and a woman's voice followed.

This is St. Thomas weather service with the five o'clock report," the voice said in a heavy Island accent. "Report for this hour is sea all smooth."

The deckhand stirred, snorted, and went back to sleep.

Below deck in the forward cabin, Steve Remington lay on an old mattress staring at the ceiling, his heart racing. The radio announcement hadn't woken him, nor had the rain squall that marched over the tug ten minutes earlier, followed by the sound of the runoff trickling down the scuppers and into the sea. He'd been jolted awake by something scraping against the bottom of the steel hull directly below his bunk. He raised his arms, cursing himself in disbelief because, this time, his hands were shaking.

He knew what it was. He had just accepted it as something that was part of his life now. After telling himself not to look, he'd pulled up the NOAA website that tagged and tracked Carcharodon carcharias—the white pointer, or as most know it, the great white shark. There were three in the Caribbean as of yesterday, and he didn't know how, but he knew one of the bastards would find him. Despite his rational and logical mind telling him he was just imagining things having nothing to do with him, he was convinced the giant predator had just rung the front doorbell.

He'd been here before in the darkest part of the night. Things looked hopeless then. He spoke out loud to the ceiling above his bunk, "It's okay, it's okay," but it didn't help much. Middle-of-the-night anxieties were just a genetic carryover from the primitive days of man when the fires had died down and the beasts in the forest came in for the kill. Finally, after several long minutes of a deep breathing technique he had learned to do, he got his heart rate under control.

A slight change in the direction of the wind swung the tug gently around on its single anchor, bringing his cabin porthole to face the east, and Steve recognized the first yellow-blue glow of a sunrise beginning to show.

His mind shifted to other thoughts. At last count, he still had enough money in the bank to handle the overhaul of the tug. Though he'd tried to calculate the expenses accurately, it was like trying to put an exact price on remodeling an old house; there were bound to be hidden costs and over-runs. Yet he was optimistic. He had his military retirement now—not a great amount but enough to keep him going. He would have her in shape in no time and then start a small towing and salvage business in the islands.

His seagoing uncle, whom he had loved like the father he never knew, had taught him about the sea and all its mysteries and beauty. He had willed the boat to Steve along with the old beach cottage on St. John. The rusted tug and the run-down cottage were the sum of his inheritance in life, but they had become treasures to him, especially in the challenging years after his wife's death.

He thought back to the man who had approached him that morning at the marina in San Juan, wanting to buy the tug. He said he represented a man with a lot of money who wanted a tug to add to his fleet of ships and that the man would pay well over what the tug was worth. Steve explained that the boat had been in his family for a long time, and he could never sell it. Besides, Steve told him, it needed a complete overhaul and wasn't seaworthy except for short distances.

Steve loved the islands. He had spent the summers of his youth down here. The cottage was a special place in a remote section of St. John. He was grateful to have it. He would never have been able to buy it after the earlier real estate craze that had spread over the world like a virus, driving prices out of the reach of most people. Steve and his wife had always planned on living here in their later years. She would have loved seeing the old tug and hearing his plans. She had always supported his ideas, no matter how crazy they were. He wished he could talk to her now. But he forced the thought from his mind and began to think of the boat again and which repairs must be done first.

Another rain squall was approaching. There was no thunder or lightning, just a wall of freshwater moving across the sea like a giant wandering car wash. He listened intently as the wind picked up, and the squall passed over the tug and moved on.

The approach of the trawler was executed with precision. The engines were reduced to a low murmur for the last half mile and shut down when within earshot of the tug. The vessel glided on silently toward the tug long after its propellers had stopped. The squall had been the icing on the cake. The white noise from the rain covered the approach the last few hundred yards, and the strong breeze that followed became the final accomplice that nudged the trawler forward the last few yards needed to close the gap. It lay alongside the tug, still not touching but an easy step away.

Three men stood on deck waiting to board. Slung over the shoulder of each was a 9mm machine gun equipped with a suppressor. Their dark clothes hid them in the shadows of the trawler in the moonless night.

A fat older man at the wheel, silhouetted against the predawn sky and highlighted by the glow of his cigar, spoke to the three on the deck.

"Let's get this done and get out of here," he said in a loud whisper. "And make sure you scuttle the boat."

The men nodded to placate him, then crossed one at a time to the other boat.

Steve felt the gentle sway of the tug to one side, followed by an odd sound from the rear deck area. He didn't realize at first what he was hearing above him. The muffled sounds of the machine guns reminded him of the IBM electric typewriters he had grown up with, except that someone was typing at a thousand words a minute.

Then he heard, all in the same nightmarish cacophony, the distant sound of glass breaking, followed by a heavy thud on what sounded like the wheelhouse floor.

Then, silence and the electrifying realization of what the typewriter sound had been. It had just been a few years since he had heard it.

The telltale squeak on the last step of the stairway to the stateroom from the wheelhouse told him someone was coming.

The Beretta was buried in his duffel bag at the foot of his bed. He rolled off the bed and tore open the bag.

In what seemed like slow motion, he ripped clothes out until he reached the soft, zippered pistol case. He had just put his hand on the gun when he saw the man standing in the doorway. He had given him too much time.

The burst from the machine gun was short and merciful as it swept across him in its venomous arc. One bullet cut into Steve's midsection and vaulted him backward, and another caught him in the left arm, breaking and deflecting off the ulna. Steve found himself in a dreamlike fall that ended when he hit his head on the iron bunk railing. He landed on the floor and lost consciousness.

The sound of flowing water brought him out of his dream of carelessness and death. In his waking mind, he saw it as crisp, cool water—not running as in a mountain stream or from a faucet but flowing evenly. The sound was relaxing, and for a long moment, he listened, reluctant to open his eyes. If he was dying, it might not be so bad. But when the water reached the spot where he was lying, the pain let him know he was still very much among the living. The saltwater lost all its seductive qualities when it bit into his wounds and stung him awake as if he had fallen into a school of jellyfish.

He opened his eyes and found himself face down on the cabin floor. Seeing his blood gave him the impression that it was all blood on the floor. His blood. His heart rate started up again, adding more to the soup on the floor.

Then old training kicked in, and he calmed himself and cleared his head. Take a moment, assess the situation, and move on. Words to keep living by.

He knew where the water was coming from. They had opened the stop-cocks to flood the tug. Steve's anger rose through his dizziness, galvanizing him to survive. He grabbed the bunk above him with his good arm like a wounded prize fighter, down but not beaten, and tuned in to voices above on the main deck.

He heard a chorus of shouts and laughter. He guessed they must have found the case of assorted alcohol he had bought before leaving San Juan. This was followed by a shouted demand from the leader to hurry up, and the laughter faded away.

Steve steadied himself against the bunk. One bullet had passed through the extreme right side of his abdomen with what looked like minimal damage, but the other had made his left arm useless. At least it appeared to have missed an artery. His whole arm was numb now, but he could move his fingers freely, though with intense pain.

His vision had started to clear, made more acute by the adrenaline pumping through his heart, willing him to survive. The water was now up to his calves in the cabin, and the tug was starting to list to one side.

He saw the Beretta and grabbed it, held the handle between his knees, and with his right hand, fed a round into the chamber. He now had fifteen rounds in the double-stacked magazine and barrel. More than enough.

Moments later, he froze when, not ten feet from where he stood, Steve saw the legs of one of the gunmen descending the vertical ladder from the deck to the small galley adjacent to the cabin where he was standing. He took a step back, raised the Beretta, and waited. The gunman jumped the last few steps and landed squarely on the floor with the machine gun in both hands and his back to Steve. He began searching the galley systemati-cally, going through the cabinets and drawers. When he finally turned to face Steve, he reeled back, dropping a bottle of rum he had found, and stared open-mouthed at the bloody apparition in front of him, pointing a pistol at his chest.

The two men outside on the rear of the tug froze when they heard the shots. The man at the wheel of the trawler nearly dropped the cigar from his mouth. They weren't the syncopated, muffled sound of the machine guns but the deafening double-tap blasts of a pistol fired in a confined space.

One of the remaining gunmen motioned for the other to investigate. The man checked his magazine and carefully descended the stairs from the tug's wheelhouse to the main stateroom. Peering through the open door-way, he could see the entire room but stood by the entrance until he was sure no one was waiting just inside. Light came from the galley down another flight of stairs at the far end of the room. He waited a while longer, raised his gun, and crossed the stateroom to the stairway, descending three steps to the flooded galley. A bulkhead blocked his view of the interior of the small space. He turned quickly around the corner, burst into the room, saw a figure, leveled his gun, and fired.

Muffled fire spat out of the barrel, but instead of falling, the figure shat-tered into a thousand pieces and fell to the floor. Too late, the gunman real-ized he had shot at the reflection in a full-length mirror in the corner of the galley, a common fixture on boats with cramped quarters.

He turned to meet the real man and caught three bullets in his chest and neck. He collapsed to the floor, the saltwater covering him instantly. Steve waded through the cramped galley, stepping over the dead man to the foot of the galley stairway leading to the elevated stateroom. Loss of blood was beginning to catch up with him; he felt light-headed. If there were any more of them, he hoped they would come soon.

He managed the first step up the short stairway. The tug listed a little more with the nightmarish sound of metal being stressed to its limit that accompanies a dying ship. At the top of the stairs, he leaned against the bulkhead, pointing his pistol toward the far end of the stateroom and the door to the wheelhouse. He didn't have long to wait.

The third gunman dove into the stateroom, rolled like an Olympic gymnast, and landed upright in a crouched attack position. He leveled his machine gun in a deadly room-clearing maneuver, from left to right, blowing out windows and shredding walls like paper. The occasional slug that hit something too hard to penetrate ricocheted furiously within the cramped, steel-walled chamber. Nothing at waist level was spared.

Steve fell to the floor the instant the barrage started, and the bullets slammed into the wall above him harmlessly, though some only missed him by inches. The one-man machine-gun offensive ended in a hollow click when the last bullet in the thirty-round magazine was spent. The gunman was already ejecting the empty magazine and taking a new one from his belt.

But Steve was standing over him before he could chamber the first round. He made a quick mental note. Caucasian, like the others, European definitely, probably Eastern European, based on the bits of conversation he'd overheard. The man had no chance to raise his weapon before Steve pulled the trigger.

Steve cleared his way to the main deck behind the Beretta, expecting another gunman, but found nobody. He studied the trawler next to the sinking tug and saw a heavy older man forward, hurriedly untying the trawler's bowline from the sinking tug. He waited until the man returned to the wheel, and stepped onto the boat just before the man pushed up the throttles and turned the trawler back to the west toward Puerto Rico.

Steve crept up behind him and watched the man light a cigar. As he lowered his hands to the wheel, Steve pressed the still-warm barrel of the Beretta on the back of his neck and pulled the hammer back slowly. The unmistakable multiple clicks of the hammer being cocked and its vibrations echoed through the base of the man's skull.

"That was my uncle's boat," he said to the back of the man's head. "It was one of the few things he had in his life, and he left it to me for safekeeping."

"Look, pal, this is nothing personal. Just business," the fat man said.

Steve heard a quiver of fear in the man's voice. He was trying to make a deal.

"Who sent you and why?" Steve said, trying to control his anger.

"I don't know who they are, but it's worth a hundred grand to me. I'll give you half. You can just disappear for a while."

Steve pushed the gun harder into the man's neck.

"Some foreign guy. He sent his three friends with me to do the job. They just needed me to guide them to you. Swear to God, that's all I know. Jesus, those guys were professional grade; how the hell did you take 'em all down?"

Steve recognized the man now. His name was Bancroft. He had seen him in the weeks he'd spent around the marina getting the tug seaworthy. Rumor had it he was heavily in debt, a blowhard who always talked a big game. All hat and no cattle, as they said out west. He relaxed the pressure on the back of the man's neck.

The boat suddenly lurched ahead, throwing Steve off balance. The man had jammed the throttles forward all the way to the stops, bracing himself and throwing Steve backward as the trawler's bow responded to the twin diesel's full power, lifting high in one motion like a maverick stallion. Steve landed on the transom and was saved from going over the stern by a wire stanchion. His gun fell out of his hand on the deck. The fat man produced a knife and lunged across the slippery deck quicker than a man his size should be able to. Steve groped for his gun and found it just as the man was on him.

He got off four quick shots at point-blank range. The man turned, holding his great stomach, and fell halfway over the stern. He was struggling frantically to right himself when Steve grabbed his belt and the seat of his pants.

"Nothing personal, just business," he said, launching the man over the rail with one motion.

He walked up to the spinning wheel, eased the throttles back, and turned the boat around. There was no sign of the fat man. He made his way back to the little island where the *Aurora* had been anchored, but the tug had vanished. Nothing on the surface, not even a piece of paper. But then the single large, ragged dorsal fin of a giant shark surfaced for a few seconds and disappeared.

He managed to staunch his bleeding with crude bandages from the trawler's meager first aid kit and made a sling for his broken arm. He cleared the island and turned the boat to a heading for St. John. As he did, he remembered the now dead deckhand—an old rummy with no home or family. The man had proved to be a good helper these last few weeks, and Steve would miss him. He didn't even know his last name.

The sun was starting to peek over the horizon. The Virgin Islands, still miles ahead in the distance, were outlined against the morning sky. A pair of dolphins joined him and swam just beyond his bow wave. He dismissed going to the hospital in Charlotte Amalie. Whoever was after him would inquire at the local medical facilities when the men did not return. He would get his friend Doc to look after him instead.

He searched his mind for clues about who would want to kill him and why but came up empty-handed. He'd had an extensive military career but, as far as he knew, had made no enemies that would go to this extreme. Who was he kidding? Any number of people might want him dead.

He looked at the trawler a little closer. It might do him just as well as the tug. He would repaint and rename it, of course. He glanced down at the fuel gauge.

Hell, it still had a full tank.

2

Commander Jim Oliver banked the Navy P-3 Orion into a sharp right turn to a southwest heading, beginning the patrol of their assigned section of the Atlantic thirty miles southeast of Key West, Florida. They had arrived on station ten minutes before, and the crew quickly settled into their assigned tasks, which would occupy them for the next six hours. Oliver had made a gradual descent to two hundred feet above the water to get below a thick cloud layer. As he wrapped the plane into a high angle of bank in the turn, the crew braced themselves instinctively until the plane was once again in level flight.

Their target that day was a small freighter out of Venezuela bound for Jacksonville with a load of limestone it had picked up in Cartagena. The US Drug Enforcement Agency had tracked the boat from its home port, where it had confirmed the loading of a record quantity of high-grade cocaine that had been transported overland in Colombia. Tons of limestone was then carefully placed on top of the drugs, making them virtually impossible to detect during a boarding by the Coast Guard at sea or by customs officials in Jacksonville. The DEA would wait until the freighter reached Jacksonville to make their arrests, but they were concerned because they hadn't had a position on the boat in over twenty-four hours. A tropical depression had blanketed the northern half of the Caribbean with extensive cloud cover that made satellite reconnaissance difficult, so the Navy had been tasked with finding the ship.

The crew was given a search pattern based on dead reckoning from the ship's last known position and launched at 0400 to be on station at first light. Oliver thought about the day's mission, a slam-dunk compared to his regular job of finding subs. But the curious part of the operation today was the order to drop a sonobuoy every hour and report anything unusual. Spitting out random sonobuoys that looked for underwater contacts was not standard protocol when searching for surface ships. When Oliver asked in the briefing what that was all about, the intelligence officers had just looked at the floor as if checking their shoeshines. He knew better than to press the issue with them. He had certainly done crazier things in his career that didn't make sense.

Years ago, Oliver, then an ensign fresh out of Navy pilot training, had joined his squadron just days before it left on its scheduled six-month deployment to Keflavik, Iceland. As luck would have it, they had been thrown into one of the last great deployments of submarines by the former Soviet Union. He and his squadron had successfully located, tracked, and executed simulated kills on no fewer than eighty-four submarines traversing the GI-UK Gap, the strategic choke point in the North Atlantic between Greenland, Iceland, and the United Kingdom. It was a new squadron and fleet record, the planes and crews performing flawlessly the job they had been trained for.

That had launched Oliver's career, but shortly after the unprecedented Soviet buildup, the empire collapsed, their submarines were parked, and the world of Navy anti-submarine warfare shrunk. He had been lucky to stay in a flying billet. Still, after years of slow promotions at remote locations with thankless jobs, he had been selected to take over as a squadron commanding officer. The replacement aircraft for the P-3, the P-8 Poseidon, was a modified Boeing 737. A fine machine, but not the old reliable Oliver flew today. In just a few months, the P-3s would be gone, and he relished every chance he got to fly one.

Nowadays, the mission included more and more drug interdiction flights such as this one, but the Chinese had become the new threat, and there would be plenty of work ahead. He and his crew all liked these missions, wandering around the Caribbean at low level with lots to see, including the occasional yacht with topless girls waving to them as they roared by overhead.

He rolled back to wings-level above the now choppy blue sea and glanced at his tactical scope in front of the throttle quadrant. The screen showed under twenty miles to the waypoint that would begin the search. The radar operator, a specialized enlisted man near the back of the plane, had taken a good digital snapshot or picture of the search area on their descent, marking each surface contact on his scope and eliminating obvious non-targets like oil rigs and cruise ships to concentrate on those that met the target ship's profile. It would be just a matter of visually identifying their target among the traffic in the area. By the looks of the snapshot, it would be a short day because only three or four ships were around.

"Let's loiter number one, guys," Oliver said to the other two crew members in the cockpit. The flight engineer, Chief Murphy, leaned forward in his center seat, and the copilot, Lieutenant Junior Grade Peter Cooper, pulled out the checklist. As Cooper read it aloud, Murphy went through the series of procedures that would prepare the engine for shutdown.

The cockpit crew had done this thousands of times, and the procedure was firmly fixed in their minds. Finally, Murphy turned to Oliver with his hand on the number one engine emergency shutdown handle.

"Check me on number one, sir."

"You've got number one," Oliver replied.

Murphy pulled the handle out its full travel of about a foot. The port outboard engine simultaneously shut down, its propeller brake slowing the now unpowered four-bladed prop and feathering it into the wind for the least amount of drag in the wind stream.

Oliver glanced through his side window and saw the blades had stopped in the ideal position, which would produce the least amount of buffeting over the wing during their long patrol and was favored by the crew for the smoother ride.

"Good X, Chief," he said.

It was pure luck; no one could predict where the blades would end up, but Murphy somehow managed to stop the blades in that position nine out of ten times.

The plane flew toward the waypoint on three engines, burning significantly less fuel and allowing them to stay in the air longer if necessary.

"Radar, Flight," Oliver said over the intercom. Each crew member was hooked into the system with a headset. The radar operator, Petty Officer Second Class Jacobs, had just adjusted his screen for atmospheric conditions and sea state. Satisfied, he set the radar on its 60-nautical-mile scale.

"Go ahead, Flight," Jacobs replied.

"What's your best guess?"

"There's a guy about thirty miles at your two o'clock," Jacobs answered, referring to a large surface contact that met the profile of their target. "I think it's a good place to start."

"Roger that," Oliver replied.

Behind Jacobs sat the aft observers on each side of the airplane. They stood a constant watch for anything Flight or Radar missed. On the starboard side, Petty Officer Third Class Montoya swiveled his chair around to get a better view of his search area. He reclined the chair and propped his feet on the bulkhead by his window.

Staring out at the vast expanse of ocean, he took out a pack of cigarettes from the sleeve pocket of his flight suit. He lit one and drew in deeply. Smoking was allowed only in the back of the plane near the outflow or exhaust valve. He settled into as comfortable a slouch as he could for the next few hours.

Across the aisle from him, Seaman Apprentice Carter, an eighteen-year-old from Daphne, Alabama, fresh out of boot camp, called over to Montoya.

"Hey!" he shouted over the steady drone of the engines.

Montoya turned to look at him.

"Just one more, and I swear I'll pay you back with a whole pack when we land."

Since taking off, Carter had begged for a cigarette every time Montoya lit up.

Montoya shook his head.

"Try somebody else. I'm running low as it is. You need to bring your own smokes for a nine-hour mission."

Carter frowned and stared out his window.

They were in the search area now. Oliver was flying directly toward their first contact. Chief Murphy settled back in his seat and continued work on the fuel log he had started on preflight.

They ruled out the first contact. It was the right size and shape but clearly the wrong color; the ship they were after was painted white. This one was black with the typical red oxide paint below the water line to thwart the inevitable rust. Oliver flew a course parallel to it and read the name across the stern.

"Nope, not it," he said over the crew intercom system. Then he banked away toward the next target on his tactical scope.

After about five minutes on their new heading, Jacobs made another adjustment to his radar to compensate for the increasing wave height brought on by a stiff breeze that had accompanied the sunrise and atmospheric low-pressure system. He was studying the image of their next ship when suddenly, a previously undetected surface image appeared only three miles ahead. It differed from the hard image he most often got from surface ships. It was fuzzy and undefined: there one sweep and gone the next, only to reappear again. Large waves or, sometimes, surfaced whales could cause such anomalies. Jacobs had erroneously chased them when he was new, much to the chagrin of his instructors, who'd taught him to ignore them. But just for a few seconds, this one looked like it might be something. It was the part of his job that he enjoyed the most: creative interpretation of what his purely mechanical device was showing him.

He adjusted the gain, and the image disappeared. An actual surface contact would have remained on the scope. He shrugged it off and went back to the freighter.

Montoya finished his cigarette and extinguished it in the ashtray at his seat. He was listening to the exchange between Radar and Flight and knew that sooner or later, they would find the drug boat, and he would be called up to the cockpit to take pictures. One of his many collateral duties was photographer. Sometimes, drug missions allowed him to get some great shots of cargo being transferred or thrown overboard after they surprised a ship. One of his pictures had even made it to the cover of a Navy magazine featuring the role of the military in what the politicians liked to call "the war on drugs."

"C'mon, man," Carter pleaded again from across the aisle. Montoya gave in and tossed him the pack. Carter was jubilant, quickly sticking a cigarette in his mouth.

"Lighter?"

Montoya fished the lighter out of his pocket, an old metal Zippo that had belonged to his father. He tossed it across the aisle.

But the lighter never made it to Carter's hands. It seemed to take on a power of its own, defying gravity and abruptly flying up to the ceiling before clamoring back down to the floor.

Montoya stared at it uncomprehending. The lighter was bent in two. Then he noticed the holes in the floor and ceiling of the cabin. Two holes in each, about the size of a quarter. Daylight streamed in from those above.

He looked at Carter. The kid was covered with blood, eyes wide open as if studying the bulkhead in front of him, the unlit cigarette still stuck to his lips.

Frantic, Montoya quickly looked out his observers' window. Not until he saw the tracers did he understand what was happening. Several rounds were now finding their mark in the wing and engines. The shots were being fired from the surface directly behind them, but he couldn't see their source.

"Flight, Aft!" Montoya shouted into his microphone.

"Go ahead, Aft," Oliver answered immediately.

"Someone's shooting at us. Carter's been hit, and I saw tracers from behind us."

"See what you can do for Carter. We've got problems up here," Oliver barked. Chief Murphy was looking at the gauges for the number three engine. Its typical rock-steady indications were beginning to waver. To complicate matters, they were losing fuel from the right-wing tank at an alarming rate.

Oliver had begun a turn toward the nearest emergency field, Boca Chica Naval Air Station just north of Key West.

"Chief, start number one," he said, but the seasoned enlisted man was ahead of him; the previously feathered prop had already begun to turn in the airstream. After a few more seconds, he turned on the fuel, and the engine spooled to life, temporarily yawing the aircraft with its additional thrust.

"Nav, Flight," Oliver said over the intercom.

The navigator and communications officer sat directly behind the cockpit on the copilot's side, separated by a bulkhead.

"Go, Flight."

"Get Base on the line. Tell them we're declaring an emergency and heading for Key West."

Things had stabilized somewhat, even though they were still losing fuel. However, the number three engine was still shaky. Oliver made a decision. He turned the plane around and headed back toward the position where they had taken the hits. He had to see what had shot up his plane, possibly killed one of his crew, and put them all in jeopardy. He switched his microphone to PA so he could be heard throughout the plane.

"Everybody on the port side except Radar. I'm going to give this guy a good offset to keep our distance so he can't hit us again. It'll only take five minutes, and we need to ID this asshole."

"Flight, Radar."

"Go ahead!" said Oliver.

"I've got a surface contact, but it's barely visible on the scope. I saw it before, but I thought it was just a big wave or a whale," Jacobs said, trying to explain himself.

"Pass it up to my scope," Oliver said, and Jacobs relayed the exact geographic point from his scope to the cockpit.

The contact appeared on Oliver's scope a little over a mile ahead. He banked the plane to the right to maintain some distance and looked for a long moment at the choppy surface. The sea state was high, producing waves up to six feet. A brisk thirty-knot wind blew the crests of the waves off, forming thousands of whitecaps.

Then he noticed a shape partially hidden in the trough of a wave. As the trough became the crest of a swell, it was in clear view as if on a pedestal for display, a mile off the port wing.

They all saw it at once. No one spoke until Oliver broke the silence.

"Montoya, are you getting this?"

Montoya was too busy to answer. He held the heavy two-handed surveillance camera up to the window and squeezed off the last of thirty-five frames.

The entire cockpit was looking out the portside windows when the number three engine RPMs began to flux. Oliver felt the vibrations instantly. Within a few seconds, the entire engine and wing were vibrating badly. One of the rounds had penetrated the non-self-sealing fuel tanks in the right wing before slamming into the number-three engine gearbox. The gearbox, an extremely complex set of gears and fluid that controlled the prop, was beginning to break apart. More significantly, however, was that a tiny sliver of the round had separated on impact with the gearbox and nicked the heavily bundled wiring connecting the plane's electronics compartment to the engine. Fuel vapors from the wing tank had already reached the bundle.

After a few more seconds, the entire right side of the airplane began to shake like an unbalanced washing machine with a bad bearing.

"Shut down number three, Chief," Oliver shouted above the noise. The cockpit shook so violently they couldn't read the gauges.

"Check me on three!" Murphy shouted back, his hand already on the emergency shutdown handle.

"You've got number three."

Chief Murphy pulled the handle. Immediately, fuel was cut off to the engine, the prop began to slow, and an electrical signal was sent from the plane's main electrical center in the fuselage to the number three engine to trip the generator field as part of the shutdown process.

When the current moved through the nicked wire bundle on its way to the generator, it ignited the fuel in the right wing and blew the P-3 from the sky in an enormous fireball. What was left of the plane and crew hit the water and sank within seconds.

The crew was killed instantly, except, of course, for Seaman Apprentice Carter, who had died shortly after the first round fired at them had pierced his heart.

3

The small, fully loaded Indonesian freighter *Inshallah* squatted next to the dock in a remote, dark corner of the port of Jakarta. It was 3:58 in the morning, and the cargo and fuel loading for the fifty-five-day trip to Miami had been completed just an hour before. As the last of the cargo was loaded, the lower half of the steel hull, painted red with anti-fouling paint, disappeared below the water line, and the freighter took on its intended balanced design for transporting goods across thousands of miles of often treacherous oceans.

The loading crews were gone now, and the docks were empty. Most of the ship's crew were down below, getting some rest before an early morning departure. The captain stood on the bridge and looked at his watch. The second hand struck twelve. Four o'clock, and the dock lights went out as planned.

A flatbed truck pulled up to the dock in the next minute, and two men got out. The passenger carried a small suitcase. The driver went to the back of the truck and pulled a tarp off a black rectangular container. One of the ship's smaller cranes lowered a steel cable and hook to the back of the truck. The driver quickly attached the hook to the container. In the next minute, the container was brought on board the ship, the truck drove away, and the man with the suitcase began walking up the gangway to board the freighter.

4

Treacher walked down the crowded sidewalk just before noon in Miami's central business district. It was August, with the humidity in the high nineties, and the ocean breeze off Biscayne Bay choked and lost by the time it reached the confines of the inner city. Sweat ran down the middle of his back, but he marched on as if in a military parade, eyes straight ahead.

He wore pair of Armani Ferragamos, not his usual military boot, and they clashed with the olive-green army fatigue pants he always wore. A tropical shirt, Panama hat, and sunglasses completed the disguise. It would shield his face from the ever-growing number of surveillance cameras that constantly compared the images they captured with a worldwide database. His walking gait was also in the database, so he had glued a pebble inside his right Armani, which produced a convincing limp. Under his hat, Treacher's hair was oddly out of place with his wardrobe. He kept it cropped short on the sides in military fashion with a flattop that made him look like a retired general who had made it big with a defense contractor rather than the wanted international criminal that he was.

He carried a small black bag which held a Makarov, the older-model KGB and Russian police pistol that he was never more than a few feet away from, especially when he was back in the States.

He had attained the rank of major in the United States Army, where he had received his training. But that was really where his former life had ended. He and a handful of his fellow Rangers had been surprised and captured in a sanctioned but unofficial and highly illegal foray outside of Grozny at the start of the first Chechen War. Treacher and his platoon were there to help thwart the Russian takeover of Grozny, and it was in their makeshift POW camp that he showed his true colors. After only a few days of captivity and interrogation, he had sold out his men and everything he knew to the KGB military advisor who had paid the camp a visit.

Treacher knew quite a bit about US Special Ops plans and intelligence in the region, and that made him very valuable. He was offered a job with the Russian war effort to retake Chechnya. He quickly accepted with one condition: the rest of his men would all be killed to ensure his cover.

The Russians were more than happy to oblige him, if not a little startled by the request. On a rainy morning two days later, they lined the ragged and wounded men up in front of the mass grave the prisoners had dug for themselves the day before and shot all of them. The Russians made Treacher watch the mass execution as a further test of his new loyalty to them. He looked on with indifference. They'd never liked him anyway, he reminded himself.

After the war in Chechnya, he was offered a position in the KGB. His ambition and ruthlessness fueled his way to a position as one of their top operatives in record time, but after the collapse of the ruble and the cutbacks that followed in the late nineties, he was cast adrift as a liability the Russians no longer needed.

He had seen it coming and strengthened his ties with his KGB colleagues, now profiting wildly from selling everything the former empire had to offer—primarily weapons. Still, he had struck gold in recent years in the ever-increasing international drug trade. He had again become known as a man who could get things done, and his intimate knowledge of America fit perfectly into his new line of work. He was, however, and always would be, still just a lieutenant to the real power players. He preferred it that way.

He was glad to be leaving Miami on this day. He never felt safe in his home country, if one could call it that. He stopped in front of one of the taller buildings on the street and lit a Nat Sherman. It was the last one in the pack, and he twisted the empty wrapper with both hands to form a crude origami bow tie and tossed it to the sidewalk just a few feet from a trash can.

He looked up at the green-tinted glass front doors that matched the rest of the building in front of him. Above the doors were the words WELLS FARGO CENTER in large black letters. Over the noise and confusion of the busy street, his ears picked up a sound that was long familiar to him. Cocking his head to one side, he looked up as a corporate helicopter appeared briefly in the ionosphere of microwave towers, construction cranes, and high-rise office buildings, its rotors spinning freely amongst the concrete-and-steel surroundings.

He watched intently as the craft slowly disappeared over the top of the building and landed on the helipad thirty-eight floors above him. He entered the building and walked directly to the elevators. An attractive woman in her late thirties was waiting by the doors. She smiled as he walked up, and he glared back at her with contempt.

The elevator opened, and Treacher stepped inside. He punched in a four-digit code beside the letters PH on top of the panel of buttons, and the penthouse button lit up. The woman pushed a lower-floor button and stepped to the opposite corner of the elevator, eager to get out of his way. The elevator ascended rapidly to the exclusive top floor of the building, stopping briefly to let the woman off at an office floor.

The doors opened into a plush lounge area. There was a small waiting room with a door leading out to the helipad. The helicopter was waiting there, its rotors still spinning slowly after the engine shut down.

The pilot was signing a receipt for the use of the pad. A young woman at a desk who handled occasional corporate helicopter traffic asked the pilot if he needed anything further, but he appeared not to understand. Treacher watched him, amused. He always pulled this stunt when they were in the States. She tried again in Spanish, but the pilot answered her in a language she had never heard. She looked confused and began to repeat her question in English, only louder this time, as if the extra volume would aid in the translation.

"That will be all we require," Treacher said, walking up to the desk.

The woman looked relieved. The pilot took his copy of the receipt and followed Treacher to the waiting helo. Within minutes, they were airborne and flying low over the bay and the Art Deco buildings of South Beach, the pilot talking to the local air traffic controllers in a practiced Texas drawl.

"Departing to the east VFR," he said. "We'll stay at five hundred feet. Y'all have a great day now."

"Bimini airport is fifty-two miles," the pilot said. "The G-650 will meet us there for the trip to San Juan."

"Good," Treacher replied.

He sat next to the pilot with the black bag on his lap. He opened the bag and took out a small package, no bigger than a soft drink can, wrapped carefully in bubble wrap. Removing the bubble wrap, he inspected the electronic component he had just picked up from the manufacturer of the delivery vehicle, then placed it back in the bubble wrap. The device was a critical part they needed and would make the vehicle completely autonomous. The next step was recruiting a qualified technician to install it, but that was well underway.

Alfred Hilbert couldn't believe his luck. He watched Monica pull the black lace panties up and put on the matching bra, then slip into the clothes from the night before when he'd first met her by chance in the hotel bar. The sex had been mind-blowing, and she had been so nice to him. No woman had ever been that nice to him. Not even his wife.

In the morning, she woke him up by straddling him and taking him inside her for another round, then leaving him in bed to take a shower.

She picked up her small purse and walked over to him on the bed.

"Here's my number," she said. "Call me if you ever get to San Juan again."

She gave him a long, passionate kiss, then walked to the door, raising a hand and waggling her fingers goodbye without turning around, and left the room.

He looked at his Casio. Shit. Ten thirty already. He had an appointment at eleven with his potential clients downstairs in the lobby. He sprang out of bed and headed for the shower, his head aching from the multiple rum and Cokes the night before.

At five minutes after eleven, Alfred took the elevator to the lobby. Two men sat in chairs near the front doors. One was an older, distinguished-looking man looking at his watch, the other younger and more casually dressed.

The younger one popped up when Alfred approached.

"Mr. Hilbert?" the man said, smiling like a salesman.

"Yes. Please, call me Alfred." They shook hands.

"I'm Ray," the man said. "And this is Ruslan."

The distinguished-looking man remained seated and nodded. Alfred bent over as if bowing, which was the point, and offered his hand to Ruslan, who shook it and smiled.

"Please," Ray said. "Have a seat."

Alfred sat.

"We understand you are a very knowledgeable and skilled electronics engineer," Ray said. "And that you worked on the development of our little toy."

"I did most of the electrical design and oversight of the installations. It was designed for Special Forces, but I understand there have also been other buyers."

"Ruslan likes to take his clients for a ride in it," Ray said. "We added the viewing windows when we bought it."

Alfred nodded, realizing the kind of money these people had and what he could charge.

"And now we'd like to install the autonomous option you designed."

Alfred perked up a bit. It was his crowning addition he'd added.

"I call it the Tesla addition," he said. "Once engaged, it does anything you ask it to—within its parameters, of course."

"Excellent," Ray said. "We'll need you to make the installation in about six weeks. We have your email where we initially contacted you. Is that a good one to use?"

"Here's my business card with my cell phone and personal email," Alfred said. He wrote his quote on the back of the card, which was inflated for his estimate of Ruslan's net worth.

Ray looked at it and handed it to Ruslan, who put it in his shirt pocket. When Alfred was gone, Ray took out an iPad and checked his email.

"What do you think?" Ray said.

"He'll do," Ruslan said. "Of course, he won't get paid his six-figure price until the job is successfully completed. Do you have the insurance we purchased in case he has second thoughts?"

"Oh, yes," Ray said. He started the video and handed over the iPad.

One camera was outside Alfred's hotel door, showing him entering the room with Monica. The two other cameras had been well positioned inside the room and showed the rest of the night and morning in the best resolution money could buy.

"It's amazing how technology has come along," Ray said. Ruslan simply nodded and smiled again.

5

Steve finished his hour-long run and clasped his hands together on top of his head while his breathing quickly returned to normal. His course took him through the confined tropical forest under a lush canopy of mahogany, kapok, and palm trees to the foot of the small hill on his corner of the island. There, he had left the protective shade of the trees and run along a goat trail that wound up the mountain and down to the shoreline on the other side. He had sprinted down the beach until the familiar pain in his side and arm returned. He waded out into the lagoon in front of the cottage; the cool water refreshed him instantly. He swam out to the reef and back, exhausted as he staggered onto the beach but revitalized and satisfied with the strenuous workout after months of healing. He strolled up the path to the cottage and found the doctor sitting there with his first drink of the afternoon, looking at him sternly and shaking his head.

"When did you take your cast off?" he asked in the clinical, businesslike tone he reserved for his more stubborn patients. It was the same tone of voice he used when talking to a misbehaving child.

"Hi, Doc," Steve said, trying to ignore the question. He collapsed on a nearby hammock strung between two palm trees. A pleasant sea breeze was picking up and began to rustle the sea grape leaves around them.

"I'd like to know when you got your MD," Doc continued. "That arm of yours needed at least another week before it was fully healed, and you're running up and down the beach like a madman."

"It was itching again. Besides, it's been six weeks since you put it on, and I could tell it was ready to come off."

"What did you take it off with anyway, a machete?" Doc said, still trying to maintain his professional advantage.

"Actually, I asked Joseph to cut it off with a hacksaw," Steve answered, closing his eyes and waiting for the rebuke.

"Oh, hell, not that witch doctor! Did he cast some chicken bones and tell you your fortune while he was at it? Where is he anyway?"

"He went into town to get a few things. He'll be back shortly," Steve said, glancing at his watch. Offshore, he heard the echoing grind of diesel engines. He lifted his head to see a big Bertram trolling in the deep water just outside the reef and recognized it as a charter boat from Cruz Bay.

Doc took another sip of his drink.

"Listen, you really should take it easy for another week or so," Doc said. "We thought you might die on us after you came in that morning all shot to hell. It's a wonder you're here at all. I needed a hospital that day, not this shack on a beach."

But Steve had insisted they stay away from hospitals. Although Doc had vehemently opposed the idea initially, he finally agreed. Steve's intuition and their long-standing friendship had convinced him that whoever wanted Steve dead would have finished him in the hospital. He was safe here, it seemed; either they had no idea where he lived or, more likely, didn't know that he was still alive.

"Still can't figure it out, Doc," Steve said, gazing up at the cloudless blue sky through the palm trees. "Bancroft said they were paying him a hundred grand to get rid of me. Didn't know I was worth that. They must have had the wrong guy. We'll probably never know."

Doc stared out across the water. They had turned over the possibilities many times. Nothing made sense.

"Something popped into my head today on my run, though," Steve said. "That morning in San Juan, before I took the tug out, I saw a spot of what looked like dried blood on the floor of the wheelhouse. I didn't think much of it at the time. It was just a small spot about the size of a half dollar. I was busy getting the boat ready and forgot it until now."

"Are you sure it was blood?" Doc said.

"No. Not really. And I guess if it was blood, it could have been from a fish the deckhand caught. The galley is just below there. Anyway, thought I'd mention it."

"I'll put it in the evidence locker," Doc said. He tapped his finger on the side of his head and smiled.

Steve had piloted the trawler into the lagoon in front of the cottage the morning after he was shot, driving it through the dangerous narrow opening at high tide. It was a tricky maneuver at best. There was a gap in the reef only twenty feet wide, barely deep enough to admit a boat of its size. Depending on wind, current, and the surge through the gap, one could easily wind up on the reef, as many had. He had anchored the trawler there near the beach, and in the weeks that followed, Joseph had painted her topsides and disguised her the best he could while Steve recovered. They both set to work on her, doing as much as possible to hide her identity until the day came to take her back out of the lagoon and over to Cruz Bay for engine work.

It was good therapy for Steve as his body healed. The cottage was surrounded by the Virgin Islands National Park, never to be developed. The park was a gift from the Rockefellers when they owned most of the island. Steve's grandfather had been one of Rockefeller's fishing guides, and they cut out his cottage and a few acres when they formed the national park. Few visitors or tourists were around; most confined themselves to the resorts on accessible beaches that could be easily driven to. As he worked, Steve often thought about his grandfather and uncle. Merchant Marines, they had taught him everything he knew about the sea. They had seen all of what the sea had to offer through the perils and triumphs of the previous century.

He heard car tires on the gravel in front of the house, and he and Doc turned to watch the old Land Rover Defender pull up. A tall black man as broad-shouldered as an NFL lineman got out of the vehicle. The full-sized paper grocery bags he carried looked tiny against his massive frame.

"Looks like your man Friday is back," Doc said, loud enough for the man to hear.

"Good day, Doctor," the man said in a hybrid British and Island accent. "Getting ready for surgery?" he added, nodding toward Doc's drink.

Steve smiled at the beginning of their friendly bantering that could go on indefinitely if left unchecked. "Hello, Joseph, did you see the trawler?" He interjected before Doc could utter the insult already forming on his lips.

"Yes, she's in fine shape. Charlie says her engines are tuned and ready to go." They had left the boat with their trusted mechanic in Cruz Bay.

"Very good," Steve replied. "Doc was just complimenting you on your expertise in removing my cast."

Doc groaned loudly. "Did you get the Beefeaters?"

"How could I forget? You only asked me seven times," replied Joseph. "And I suppose you want one now with tonic and lime while I'm here."

Doc looked at his watch. It was a few minutes past four.

"Well, maybe a small one, my friend."

Joseph turned to enter the house, mumbling something about modern-day slavery, when he stopped and turned back around as if reluctant to speak.

"There's something else," he said in a lowered voice. "Charlie said two men he didn't know came around this morning looking at the boat and asking who owned it."

"What did he tell him?" Steve asked.

"You know Charlie. He told them some guy from San Juan owned the boat, and he was just working on it. But he said he was pretty sure they didn't believe him."

6

The cooling-off time of day in Cruz Bay was punctuated with remarkable regularity after the daily afternoon rain squall passed by, and the sun was only a hand's breadth above the horizon. The people at the marina and boatyard began to appear like fiddler crabs crawling out of their holes in the sand.

Steve had parked well away from his boat. After the warning from Joseph, he immediately drove over to do a thorough surveillance of the area to see who was out of place or new in the marina other than the steady influx of tourists.

He looked first at the outdoor bar, but there was no one else of interest in there. The usual tourists wandered around, easy to spot. The fishing charters were beginning to come in, and most of the customers headed to their hotels after the obligatory dockside photos and monetary settlement. A few locals he recognized were working on their boats, and he made sure they didn't see him for fear of having his name hailed for all to hear.

He walked toward the slip where the trawler was docked, keeping out of sight as much as possible. He had been fearful this day would come when whoever it was that wanted him dead began to suspect that he wasn't. The islands were a small community; sooner or later, someone would recognize the trawler and start talking. But he had grown fond of it, and as far as he was concerned, it was a reasonable replacement for the loss of the tug. Another reason he hadn't gone to the authorities, because they would have confiscated the boat long ago.

He stopped when he got close enough to get a good look at the trawler. He stood in the shadow of a utility shed near the fuel dock, where he was unlikely to be noticed. He felt a swell of pride. The transformation of the trawler had been complete and thorough, and he looked forward to taking her on a shakedown run to St. Martin in a few days.

He felt the beginnings of the evening breeze, right on time most every day, and he decided to stay by the shack a little longer. He had a clear view of most of the marina. Besides, a sailboat was coming in—one that he didn't recognize, and he always loved seeing a new boat.

He watched the Leopard 50 sailing catamaran entering the crowded marina under power from the boats' twin Yanmar diesels. Its sails were neatly tucked away and ropes coiled. Evenly spaced bumpers hung over each hull, strategically positioned to protect the hulls and gelcoat from scraping the concrete piers. As it drew closer, he noticed the layers of salt spray on the mid-cabin windows, suggesting the boat had been long at sea.

A single woman at the elevated helm above the starboard hull seemed to be the only crew on board. Steve did his long-practiced assessment of people automatically. About his age, mid-forties, maybe a tad younger. Hard to tell precisely because she'd been in the sun a lot. More handsome than pretty, with a bit of the hard, wiry look of a tuned-up athlete, but in a good way. Strikingly handsome as he got a closer look. Her hair was in a ponytail, dangling out the back of a sun-bleached baseball cap.

He scanned the available side-by-side slips. There was only one left between two much more expensive multimillion dollar yachts. Steve thought the catamaran could just fit in the slip with minimal room to spare on each side.

The harbor master, a crusty older Virgin Islander, sat outside his shack, practically lying in an upright plastic chair, and watched her approach. He had assigned her the spot when she called on the radio and told her to back in. There were no dockhands in sight. A moderate breeze had picked up as fodder from a nearby squall swirled around the marina.

Steve watched with fascination as the woman expertly reversed the starboard engine while simultaneously leaving the port engine in forward idle. The catamaran swapped ends obediently, making the 180-degree zero turn in the minimum space of the marina as graceful as a ballet dancer's half pirouette. Now, with both engines at reverse idle, she turned around backward on the helm to face the slip, reversed her hands on the throttles, and made the minute corrections for the fickle wind to fit the cat into the slip. The big boat eased into the space with less than a foot clearance on each side. She put the engines in forward for a second to stop the backward momentum, then into neutral. The boat sat perfectly still, becalmed in the minimal space like its long-lost home. The woman threw out four lines, one from each corner of the boat. They landed on the decks of the slip, each near a tie-down cleat. She stepped off the boat, paused for a second with her eyes closed, perhaps to give thanks for a safe journey or just glad to be back on land, then tied each rope to its respective cleat.

The harbor master got up now. Steve saw that he had been nodding in approval to the task he had assigned the boat. He approached the catamaran, and there was an exchange of papers showing the boat had departed from the United States and was still in the United States territories, so customs and immigration were not an issue.

Steve watched the harbor master return to his chair. Looking back at the boat, he saw the woman holding a freshwater hose over her head. She had removed the hat and was soon completely wet from the hose. Her long, dirty-blond hair, naturally highlighted by days in the sun, streamed down her back and stopped just below her shoulder blades. She wore only a T-shirt and gym shorts, which clung to her lean, fit body, revealing nearly every detail. Then she grabbed a towel, and the unintended show was over.

Next, she washed down the entire boat with fresh water, scrubbing the caked salt spray off with a deck brush and wiping down all the brightwork until the boat shined like new. She disappeared below the decks for a few minutes, then appeared again after changing clothes, carrying a long MARPAT duffel bag with a zippered top and placing it on the deck just below the helm where it would be hidden from view. Steve recognized the desert digital camouflage of the US Marine Corps and made another mental note. She looked around quickly, then went below again, returning seconds later with a soft black bag. Steve raised his eyebrows. It was a soft case for an M4 assault rifle with a collapsible stock. He had one like it back at the cottage. She placed the bag inside the zippered duffel, then added a large silver revolver in a shoulder holster before zipping the duffel up. She easily picked up the duffel with one hand and placed its strap over her shoulder.

When she turned to leave the boat, she saw Steve and stopped. She held his gaze for a good five seconds, then stepped off the boat onto the deck of the slip and started walking toward him. As she approached him, she nodded to him slightly. Steve nodded back as if the two of them were now complicit in what she had stuffed into the duffel. As she came near him, she stopped.

"Do you know if there's a payphone around?" she asked. Steve noticed a strong voice with a slight Southern accent. She had a smile in her eyes, but it was not on her face yet.

Steve pointed to the outside bar. "There's one in that little bar there if it's still working."

"My cell phone died a few days ago," she said. "Never know when you might need backup technology."

"That's the truth," Steve said. "Long trip?"

"Not bad. I left Government Cut ten days ago."

"Which way did you come?"

"Anguilla Cays, then the Old Bahama Channel."

Steve nodded. He had taken that route from Miami with his uncle once in the tug when he was fifteen.

"Thanks," she said and hesitated momentarily, her smile breaking out now. Then she turned to walk to the bar.

As she turned, Steve read the name patch Velcroed to the duffel. Philipps, K.

Leaving the protection of the shed, Steve walked away from the marina and then turned toward the opposite side of the marina parking lot, carefully studying the other side of the trawler for any sign of something out of place. Again, nothing, no one.

He was about to retrace his steps back to the Land Rover when his eyes caught movement from the second floor of a small hotel less than a hundred yards away. There, facing the marina, a single window was open. Steve watched as a cloud of blue-white cigarette smoke drifted out, shining like a beacon in the afternoon sun. Anyone in that room would have a perfect view of his boat.

Coincidence, maybe, but after a few more minutes, he watched a man walk into the hotel's front door, carrying two Styrofoam takeout containers. Steve was instantly alert. The man was the out-of-place link he was looking for. He had the same look as the guys on the tug. Ex-military, foreign, Slavic descent.

A few minutes later, he saw the man from the street closing the window. Another man stood behind him, and Steve could see them arguing inside the room, probably about the open window. Then a shade was drawn to within a few inches of the sill, and a window air conditioner was started nearby.

They were in for the night. A couple of Eastern European tourists? Not likely. He was convinced they were looking for him, staking out the boat for his inevitable return. It wouldn't be long before they found out who he was and where he lived.

He needed to call Doc and Joseph and let them know. A plan was starting to jell, but he wanted to bounce it off them first. Keeping out of sight of the hotel window, Steve made his way back to the outside bar and called his home on the payphone. He and Doc had decided after the attack on the tug to keep their cell phone use to a minimum. He had just heard Joseph say hello when he heard movement behind him. He turned quickly. It was the woman from the boat.

"I'll call you right back," he said and hung up.

"Hi, it's me again. I hate to bother you," she said, "but could you tell me where the Driftwood Hotel is?"

"It's on the other side of the island," he said. "But it's been closed since the last hurricane."

The news had an immediate impact on the woman; she seemed to deflate but then got a look like she wanted to kill someone. He glanced at her duffel on the floor across the bar. Still zipped up. That was a good thing.

"Thanks," she said and turned away.

He stood there for a few seconds watching her gather her things, then picked up the phone to call Joseph to get back to the matter at hand. But he surprised himself by replacing the phone in its cradle.

Something about the woman made him want to help her. She was obviously ex-military and military people tended to look out for each other; but there was something else, something familiar. His plan for dealing with these guys could wait until he got back to the cottage. He walked over to her table.

"I can give you a lift to another hotel if you want," he said.

"Oh, that's okay," she said. "I can get a taxi." She turned to walk out the bar.

"You're ex-military, right?" he said. "I'm guessing Marines." She glanced at the duffel.

"Yep."

"Just trying to help out a fellow service member," he said. "I'm retired Navy."

She took a deep breath. "I was supposed to meet the owner of the boat I delivered and get paid. The number he left for me to contact him was at the Driftwood Hotel that he owned. Now I know why the recording says the line has been disconnected. I'm sorry to bother you with this," she said, looking at the floor.

"It's no bother," he said and gave her a minute, sensing there was more she wanted to say.

"I took this delivery job from a friend in Miami who's a yacht broker. He sold this boat to this guy down here, and he is supposed to pay me. I went through a bad divorce about a year ago; it turns out we had no real savings, and what we had went to paying off loans. After that, I kind of reinvented myself. The trip gave me time to think about where I've been and where I want to go with my life. I needed the delivery money to start over—maybe here in the islands. And now this thing with the boat owner doesn't look good. I'm sorry," she said, closing her eyes and shaking her head. "That's a lot to unload on a stranger."

"Maybe your friend, the yacht broker, could help you out," Steve said.

"He just started his business," she said. "I'm pretty sure he doesn't have it either."

"I'm Steve, by the way."

"Kelly. Do you live here, or are you just a tourist like me?"

"I have a small cottage on the other side of the island."

Just then, Joseph's wife, Martha, walked up. She helped Joseph once a week, taking care of Steve's cottage. The other reason he had come into town was to pick her up at the ferry from St. Thomas. Steve introduced her to Kelly and explained the situation.

"Steve is good people," she said with a slight nod to Kelly. It was her highest compliment, and Steve had never heard her apply it to him.

"I've been cleaning houses all day, Steve," Martha said. "I'm ready to go when you are."

"Tell you what," Steve said, nodding toward his boat. "I'm taking that trawler over there on a short cruise to St. Martin in a few days. I might need someone who can handle a boat if you're interested. I will pay you for your time, of course."

Kelly stared off in the distance for a while, then said, "Give me a number where I can reach you. If I don't get paid by the owner, I'm going to need some cash."

Steve looked at Martha, who shook her head and produced a pen and paper. Steve wrote down the number of the cottage landline.

"Do you think your sister could put Kelly up for the night?" Steve asked Martha.

Martha considered it, looking at Kelly again.

"I think so," Martha said. "She owes me a favor anyway."

Steve saw Kelly shaking her head, and before she could protest, he said, "Martha's sister has a few rooms she rents out on Airbnb. It's clean, quiet, safe, and about five minutes away."

"And she has one available tonight," Martha said. "I just helped her clean them."

Steve and Martha gave Kelly a ride to the Airbnb. When they arrived, Martha got out and talked to her sister at the door, gesturing to Kelly.

"By the way," Steve said, "who was the boat owner you were trying to call?"

"His name is John Cockerel," she said, and Steve winced. "Do you know him?" she asked.

"I know who he is. He doesn't own that hotel. He used to work there as a security guard. His main job now is second-in-command of the St. Thomas police force."

"A cop?" she said.

"Yeah," Steve said, "and as crooked as they come."

"That's an expensive boat for a cop."

Steve and Martha left Kelly at the house, picked their way through Cruz Bay, then started the ten-minute drive back to Steve's cottage.

In the hotel room overlooking the trawler, there was a soft knock on the door. One of the men moved from his position by the window and walked over, his gun drawn. He stood to one side of the locked door.

"Yes?"

"It's Cockerel," the voice replied. "I've got the information you want."

7

The antique Bakelite telephone rang in the cottage the next morning just before noon. Steve had just returned from his run and picked it up.

"Hi Steve, it's Kelly."

"Hi. How are things going with Cockerel?"

"I finally tracked him down after leaving several messages at the St. Thomas police department. Turns out he's been on St. John since yesterday. I think the only reason they told me where to find him was because I told them I wanted to talk to him about a serious crime I had witnessed."

"That crime being trying to cheat you out of your boat delivery payment?"

"Exactly."

"Well done. Did you talk to him."

"Oh yeah. I went to the local police station and found him sitting at a desk with his feet propped up. He said he didn't know anything about any boat or delivery fee and threatened to arrest me if I didn't leave."

"I'm sorry," Steve said.

"Yeah, me too. I'm out five grand, so if you still need some help over there, I guess I'm in."

"Sure. Need a ride?"

"Martha's sister is insisting on bringing me over later today. She's been really good to me."

"Okay, sounds good. See you then." Steve hung up the phone. He didn't want to capitalize on her bad luck, but he was glad she was coming over to join the cruise down-island. It was only a day or so trip each way and he could use the help, but he also wanted to see her again. She intrigued him, they had a few things in common, and truth be told he'd been thinking about her since they'd met.

Joseph was helping Doc move some newly donated equipment into the clinic on the island's north side and wouldn't be back until late, so Steve made a trip to nearby Coral Bay and picked up barbeque at Johnny Lime's for everyone that night. Kelly and Martha's sister arrived around five, and they all watched the sunset while devouring one of their favorite foods in the islands.

The next morning, Kelly woke slowly to the sound of waves on the shore of the lagoon. She stretched out on Steve's double bed and gazed out sleepily at the palms swaying in the morning breeze, their fronds rustling quietly together in unison with the wind. The cottage was not air-conditioned, but the breeze was so cool she actually had to pull up the bedspread to supplement the single sheet in the early morning hours. The windows were all open and screened, and the tropical breeze, born on the sea and purified across countless miles of open water, filled the room. The sun was just starting to make its way over the tops of the palms to the southeast.

She stared at the ceiling for a moment, unconsciously took a deep breath, and let it out. She was reluctant to assess her current situation in such serene surroundings. Steve had given her a tour of the secluded property the day before, and she had become friends with Martha and her sister. Doc and Joseph's absence made them cannon fodder for a string of stories.

"Steve's as good as they come," Martha had whispered in Kelly's ear. "He just can't keep a clean house."

Steve had slept last night on the old rattan couch out on the screened porch that ran the length of the southern end of the cottage next to the bedroom where she had slept. Kelly felt guilty when a rain shower in the middle of the night drove him into the house, but the shower had ended quickly, and he settled back on the couch and seemed to have fallen asleep again immediately.

She looked around the room and noticed a collection of photographs and plaques she had missed before. Instantly, she thought of her father. He had been a Marine Corps pilot, and a wall in their house he called the "I love me" wall had been dedicated to his accomplishments, appointments, and awards while serving in Korea and Vietnam.

Steve had a similar wall. Not ostentatious or overdone, just a section in a corner of the room set aside to document a military career whose mostly routine memorabilia were interspersed with the extraordinary. She recognized the oversized Navy/Marine Corp pilot wings carved from monkey pod wood from the Philippines that every military pilot who'd served there had somewhere in his possession, framed letters of appointment to various ranks in the Navy from ensign to commander, and photographs of Steve standing beside different aircraft with people in a wide variety of locations throughout the world.

There was a black-and-white photograph taken at his graduation from Aviation Officer Candidate School in Pensacola; several from the air, including an incredible close-up of a Soviet Bear turboprop; and finally, a picture of a much younger Steve with five other men, all dressed in desert camouflage and heavily armed.

Then, on the dresser, away from the collection, she saw a simple framed photo of one of the most beautiful women she had ever seen. The woman looked like she was as happy as anyone could be. Behind her, Kelly thought she recognized New York's skyline. It was an old picture with the Twin Towers still standing. Draped across one corner of the frame was a medal Kelly had never seen among her father's things. The ribbon was simple in design, with a single white vertical stripe down the middle of a royal-blue background. Suspended from it was a gold cross with a ship under sail engraved in its center. Kelly studied it for a few seconds and looked again at the woman in the photograph. She caught a glimpse of herself in the mirror and grabbed her hairbrush.

She slipped on some clothes and opened the bedroom door after a quick makeover. A waft of cooking smells hit her immediately. Someone was making breakfast, and it smelled delicious. She walked through the small den and past a large macaw on a perch. The bird squawked like an alarm on a motion detector, and a man's deep baritone voice hailed her from the stove.

"Good morning," he said. "I'm Joseph."

A large black man stood in the kitchen, an apron that looked like it would fit only a child tied around his waist. He was breaking an egg into a bowl with one hand and holding an omelet pan with the other. The pan looked like a miniature in his enormous hand, the egg as if it had come from a pigeon. Steve had told her about Joseph and that he'd be around during the day, but the last thing she had expected was to see a big, powerful man performing such a delicate task in the kitchen.

Joseph looked at her inquisitively, then smiled broadly.

"Oh, I'm Kelly Phillips," she said finally.

"It's a pleasure to meet you, Kelly. Would you like some breakfast?"

"Sure, it smells wonderful." She saw a plate of sausages grilled on the stove, and she was suddenly famished.

"Coffee?" he asked, holding up a freshly brewed pot.

"Thank you. Do you live here too?" she said, suddenly regretting being so nosy.

"About half the time. Martha and I have a house on St. Thomas. She likes it over there, and I like it here."

"Oh," Kelly said, now really regretting the question.

Joseph handed her a plate, and they went out to the porch and sat at a table. Again, she noticed the sea breeze, so different from the inner city. She ate the omelet, sausage, and fresh papayas quickly.

"Steve's gone into town; be back soon," Joseph said, reading her thoughts.

"Oh, all right," she said. "Guess I'll need to find a place to work and live if I'm going to stay in the islands."

"Steve said you might be staying awhile until you figure out what you want to do."

"That was very nice of him to say."

"He has a habit of helping people out when he can."

Joseph leaned back in the chair with his coffee and told her about growing up in the islands and working in various places in the tourist industry. Most of his friends worked in hotels and restaurants, and he'd done that for several years, but he was never satisfied with it. He wanted to be a fisherman and finally saved enough money to buy a boat. He had known Martha all his life, and they were married. He gave up his job at a large resort on St. Thomas catering to the whims of ungrateful tourists and decided to pursue his dream. He was successful from the start, and he knew the ocean, the places the fish were, and when they were there. He and Martha were happy, and they began to talk about having children.

"Then the hurricane came. I had taken my boat out and put her on dry land and, in the traditional way, filled her hull with water so she wouldn't blow away. All the island people had done the same, but the marina next to us was full of big yachts in the water. The storm surge lifted them with a giant hand and tossed them together with my boat like an angry child who throws his toys into a pile. I found what was left of my beautiful boat. It was completely ruined. I just sat down right there and cried. I had everything in it."

"I'm so sorry," she said.

"I sat there all day with my head in my hands, not knowing what to do, when Steve walked up. He must have thought I looked pretty bad off. He said he was looking for someone to help him repair his cottage, which was damaged by the storm. He hired me on the spot."

Kelly looked around the place. Things looked like they had not been moved in years.

"This side of the island didn't get much damage. There were a few trees down, but no real work though. I think he was just giving me a break. I've been here ever since." He took a last sip of coffee. "It was one of the kindest things anyone has ever done for me."

Kelly sensed Joseph seemed a little embarrassed, having told so much to someone he had just met.

"Well, I guess he took me in too," she said. "At least until we get back from the shakedown."

"We've got a saying down here," Joseph said with a smile. "You can work for the tourists, or you can fish."

Kelly contemplated that for a moment. Somehow, she would get her life back on track. She had known hard work all her life, but it hadn't gotten her very far. A bad marriage and a few bad relationships had left her searching for happiness back in the States and now here on St. John. There was nothing to do but keep trying and keep moving forward.

"I'll do the dishes," she said, standing up abruptly.

Joseph nodded and helped her clear the table.

Steve started the Land Rover and picked his way through the crowded streets of the open-air market. It was just before noon on Saturday and the busiest time of the week for the village. Most of the locals had just been paid their week's salary and were busy spending it on groceries and supplies in a variety of shops and stores. The shuttle boats and ferries to St. Thomas had begun their trips, bringing tourists over for the day to snorkel or stay in one of the small hotels, and he had dropped Martha off at the shuttle boat landing. A rental car company added to the traffic, as well as several goats and chickens wandering through the yards and streets.

At last, he reached the edge of town and accelerated on the open road toward the cottage. He had checked on the two men in the hotel, only to find the window closed and the blinds drawn. He deduced the room number, and when he called the hotel clerk from the payphone, he was told that the room was vacant. The men had apparently decided to call it quits for now. Perhaps if the trawler disappeared for a few days, they would lose interest altogether, though he doubted it. He was convinced they must be drug dealers and had somehow mistaken him for someone who'd stolen from them or owed them money. It would be tricky to convince them other-wise, but he would have to try.

And, of course, he had paid a visit to the trawler before he left. After long minutes of admiring her, he felt it was as if she was a restless thoroughbred just waiting to be released. It was time to let her out.

He started up the hill's switchbacks, negotiating the curves, driving on the left-hand side in the English way. Occasionally, he would meet a tourist in a rental Jeep going down the hill on the wrong side of the road. But, over the years, he had avoided any major accidents. When he reached the top of the ridge, he pulled off the road as he frequently did to take in the view to the west. Below him lay the village he had just left. The olive-green trees of the island ended abruptly at the ocean, separated thinly by the white sand of the beaches. In the distance, he could see Red Hook on the eastern end of St. Thomas through the increasing haze of the day. A score of sailboats and powerboats dotted the water, their paths crisscrossing in the channel between the islands. Well south in the deeper waters offshore were several cruise ships and cargo ships.

Looking back to the east and his own private paradise, Steve gulped in the warm breeze as the wind hit him full in the face. It raced along the tops of the trees unchecked.

He was about to get back in the Rover when he saw an enormous yacht appear around the southern shore of St. Thomas. It cleared the last spit of land, and as it turned toward Red Hook, he saw it was a catamaran, easily the largest he had seen anywhere. Its dual hulls gave it the appearance of a leviathan ready to swallow the smaller boats in the channel. He watched for several minutes while it slowed and finally anchored at Red Hook. He was unable to estimate the size of the ship, but he had seen smaller corvettes when he was in the Navy.

He put the Land Rover in gear and started down the other side of the ridge. In ten minutes, he had turned off the main road onto his gravel driveway bordered by dense bamboo and driven the quarter mile toward the water down to the cottage.

He saw Kelly at once. She was working on an old outboard motor clamped on a stand near the house. She had the cover off with tools spread around her on the ground. Ancient grease and dirt from the motor were smeared on her arms, and Steve noticed that this actually added to her beauty somehow, in a curious way. Her hair was neatly French braided into a single ponytail, and she wore a pair of shorts and an old T-shirt he vaguely recognized as one he had donated to the rag bin. It could have been a scene out of a magazine ad, where the model pretends to actually know something about the complicated task she's been carefully posed with. She smiled at him as he got out of the Rover.

"No one has been able to start that thing," Steve said, remembering the hours he had spent working on it while Doc and Joseph looked on.

She glanced at him, concentrating on a wire she was replacing deep in the engine. When she was finished, she pulled the starter cord. The engine turned over, coughed twice as if spitting up something foul from its gut, and then sprang to life.

"You mean like this?" she shouted, adjusting the throttle linkage and choke until the engine was running smoothly at idle, sucking up the water in the tub the foot sat in and spitting it out in a steady stream as if it were fresh out of the box from the factory.

Steve just stood there staring at the motor.

"How?" was all he said when she turned it off.

"There was a broken section in the coil wire. I fixed it and made a carburetor adjustment," she said matter-of-factly. "It wasn't getting power to the plugs," she added to fill Steve's continued silence.

"I was going to try that next," he said, still staring at the motor in disbelief. "Actually, I had no idea how to fix it."

"Hope you don't mind. I thought it was the least I could do for letting me stay here."

"I don't mind at all," he replied, very much intrigued.

"My Dad used to work on his in the backyard; sometimes, he worked on friends' motors too. I hung out with him and watched when my mother wasn't around. I guess I just picked it up."

"Yeah, I guess you did. Thanks again. I've got a small boat to put that on."

"That one?" she said, pointing to a wooden dinghy upside down on sawhorses.

"Yeah, it needs a coat of paint, but otherwise, it's okay."

"Been shopping?" she asked, looking at the paper bag full of groceries he held.

"Just picked up a few things in town."

"I'll take them inside." Before he could object, she took the bag from him and carried it to the cottage.

He watched her walk away, got another bag and a six-pack from the back of the Rover, and followed her inside. He was sure he had never met a woman quite like this before.

8

Steve touched the freshly painted hull of the dinghy and nodded to Joseph. The two of them had sanded and painted the small boat the day before and were ready to mount the outboard motor Kelly had repaired. They lifted the boat and carried it to the beach. Steve bolted the newly repaired outboard to the transom and hooked up a portable gas tank. The motor caught with the first pull of the cord and, after a minute or so, was idling nicely.

It was amazing to Steve that the dilapidated motor could run at all. He was still a little in awe. Kelly had gotten it to run so smoothly, and just then, she and Doc showed up.

"We heard the motor running and had to come to take a look," Doc said.

"I thought you might like to go with me to get dinner," he said to Kelly. "We could take the boat out in the lagoon and see what we could find."

"Okay," Kelly said. "Give me a minute to change, and I'll be right back."

When she returned, Steve had the boat in waist-deep water. She carried a set of professional-grade mask fins and a snorkel. He turned the dinghy away from the beach and jumped in behind her.

"Bring back dinner!" Doc shouted as they headed out, and Steve held up a Hawaiian sling spear and gave him a thumbs-up.

The lagoon in front of Steve's cottage was protected from the surf by a reef just visible above the water at low tide. There were a few openings to the sea, but only deep or wide enough for a large boat if you were intimately familiar with them and timed your entry or exit perfectly at slack tide, as Steve had done with the trawler months ago. Even then, the current surge through the small opening could put a boat on the reef and tear the bottom out. The reef's security and a lack of easy access to the lagoon from the road made it especially private. The depth of the water at high tide was only twenty feet at the deepest point, providing an idyllic protected environment for marine fishes and animals of all kinds.

Steve anchored the dinghy over some grass beds in fifteen feet of water and turned the engine off.

"You okay with snorkeling?" he asked Kelly while adjusting his Rocket Fins.

"I've done some," she replied. "Mostly on vacations. I've got an open-water certificate, but that was twenty years ago. Had to bring these though, because I was coming down here. Also, handy sailing because sometimes you need to make a repair under the waterline."

"Amen to that," he said, smiling.

Steve put on a mask and snorkel, then showed her how to back roll off the side to enter the water without upsetting the dinghy. Within a few minutes, they were snorkeling together side by side.

They swam on the surface as if suspended in air, the water so clear they could see the coral reef wall hundreds of feet away. Rays of sunlight streaked through the shallow blue water and lit up lime-green turtle grass on the white sand bottom. The long, graceful blades of grass danced endlessly in unison as they were moved by the constant underwater current flowing in and out of the lagoon with each surge from the sea. Schools of brightly colored reef fish patrolled the bottom. Steve pointed out a small school of Caribbean reef squid seemingly motionless as they treaded water and held their station in defiance of the current.

Kelly tapped Steve on the shoulder and pointed up. They lifted their heads above the water and pulled out their snorkels.

"This is amazing!" she said. "It's so beautiful."

"It's a good day for this," he said. "The water is perfect. Stay here for a minute."

Steve dove to the bottom, clearing his ears to equalize the pressure as he descended. He reached into the grass, picked up a large shell the size of his outstretched hand, and brought it back to the surface. The shell was the same color as the sandy bottom on top, but a brilliant sunburst orange lined the underside.

Treading water, Kelly removed the snorkel from her mouth again, and Steve handed the shell to her. "What is it?" she asked.

"Conch," he answered. "Or the first course of our dinner, whichever you prefer."

"Yum. I always wondered where they got the conch in conch chowder."

"This is it," he said. "We need another one though."

He put the conch in the boat, and they both began searching the grass beds again from the surface. After a few minutes, Steve dove down again. This time, he picked up two conchs, looked them over, and put one back.

Kelly watched the light-tan shell blend in perfectly with the color of the sand.

"That will do," he said after surfacing. He put the second conch in the boat. "We'll leave the rest for another day."

"How do you see them?" Kelly asked. "They blend in perfectly with the bottom."

"You look for their eyes," he answered with a straight face.

"Yeah, right," she said, and he broke into a large grin.

He took off his gear and put it in the dinghy. Then, using the engine's weight to counterbalance his own on the small boat, he pulled himself out of the water at the bow and swung his feet over the gunnel while shifting his weight with his arms—his fit body working in unison like a gymnast on the parallel bar. Kelly watched him intently.

He lifted her into the boat easily, and despite the breeze cooling her salty, wet skin, she felt incredibly warm and soft. It was the first time they had been close to each other. Just then, a swell lifted the dinghy a little, and she lost her balance for a moment. Her hand reached instinctively for his chest, and as soon as she regained her balance, she drew it back.

"Oh, sorry," she said.

He looked down at her, and when their eyes met, he recognized something he had not allowed into his life for many years. She looked away quickly.

"Thank you," she said, carefully seating herself in the gently rocking dinghy and gathering up the conchs to look at them closer. She turned one over, and they saw the foot with its hard bottom retract back into the shell in defense.

"Here, put them in the dive bag, and we'll hang them over the side in the water to keep them fresh," Steve said, handing her the mesh bag.

He hauled up the anchor and started the engine. "Now for the main course."

He guided the boat over to the narrow opening in the reef. After carefully maneuvering into a position safely away from the rocks, he stopped the engine and dropped anchor in the much deeper water. The boat swung into the current of the incoming tide, holding them safely away from the backside of the reef. Again, they donned their snorkel gear and entered the water.

This time, Steve took the spear with him and swam toward the reef, with Kelly following. They could feel the flow of the water through the channel. As they swam closer to the opening in the reef, the current grew much stronger as the water that fed the lagoon surged in. About thirty yards from the opening, Steve stopped and pointed to the bottom. There, strewn along the sand, were the rusted, barnacle-encrusted remains of a forty- to fifty-foot steel boat. A few of its pieces lay around it, but the hull was broken in half, lying on the bottom and open toward the surface.

Kelly pulled the snorkel from her mouth. "How did it get here?"

"The locals say it was caught in a storm in the 1960s. As the story goes, it was trying to get into Hurricane Hole when it was blown into the reef. It hit right here, tearing that trench in the coral. That ripped a hole in the bottom and it sank, but it gave us this nice little channel to get in and out of the lagoon.

"But they're the reason we're here now," he said, pointing to fish darting in and out of the wreck. At least twenty red snappers, each about ten pounds, were looking for smaller reef fish to eat.

He took a deep breath and quickly descended to the wreck with his spear. Most of the snapper fled, but one large one stayed in the open, hovering above the sandy floor next to the rusted hull of the ill-fated ship. Steve slowly stretched the surgical rubber attached to the butt end of the spear with his right hand while holding the business end with his other hand. Then, with his right hand holding the restrained surgical rubber, he grabbed the shaft near the three-pronged spearhead. He now had an accurate, close-range, lethal weapon to aim with his outstretched arm.

His lungs began to ache, and his heart pounded to extract the last bit of oxygen from his system as he inched forward for a good killing shot. Suddenly, the fish turned away, ruining the shot but allowing Steve to move a foot closer. Every fiber of his being told him to push to the surface for air. However, he held perfectly still, letting the surge and current sway him gently back and forth, waiting for the fish to turn and offer him a better angle. If he tried to maneuver this close to it now, he would surely spook the fish. Finally, the big snapper turned back, pivoting with its dorsal fins and rotating an eye to get a closer look at Steve.

He let go simultaneously of the spear's shaft and its taut rubber sling. The released tension drove the barbed tips into the snapper's head just behind the eye. At last, Steve swam to the surface with the fish impaled on his spear.

Kelly was ecstatic. "Wow, what a great shot! You must have been down there for three minutes! I thought you were never coming back up."

"I was beginning to think he was never going to turn and give me a shot," Steve said. He took some slow, deep breaths, wondering how long he had been down; it might have been one of his most extended free dives ever. And the dumbest.

They swam back to the boat, and Steve pulled the snapper from the spear and put it in the dive bag. He winced a little with a new pain in his chest brought on by the dive, a result of one of the bullets that had ripped through him just months ago. As they returned to shore across the lagoon, Kelly in the bow with her drying hair streaming behind her, Steve admitted to himself how intent he had been on winning her admiration. As if reading his thoughts, she turned around and looked at him, holding his gaze as long as she dared. Then she was waving at Joseph and Doc, who had just walked out from beneath the palm trees to greet them. She held up the snapper with one hand and the conchs with another and let out a victory whoop.

9

Joseph took the conch shells and snapper into the kitchen and began preparing them for dinner. Kelly watched as he made a cut in the top of each shell with a small knife and expertly cut the conch away from the shell where it was attached. After cutting the undesired parts away, he was left with a piece of meat he cut into bite-sized chunks and began to make his chowder.

Hours later, the delectable aroma from the kitchen drifted down to the water where Steve and Kelly sat with Doc in beach chairs, sipping Mount Gay rum and Coke. They had showered outside after their day in the salt-water, with warm freshwater from a small cistern Steve had made after experiencing the island's intermittent water supply. Water in the cistern heated up during the day to an ideal temperature for an afternoon shower in the enclosed area to which it was connected.

Steve finished his drink and stood up. "I'm going to help Joseph," he said. "Would anyone like another drink?"

"No thanks, I'm fine," Kelly said.

Doc, who had made himself a strong double to begin with, showed Steve his half-full glass. After a few minutes, Kelly and Doc could hear Joseph's deep voice giving Steve directions in the kitchen.

"It's lovely here," Kelly said. "As close to paradise as I've ever seen."

"Yes, it's quite nice," Doc agreed. "This place has been in Steve's family for over two hundred years. His ancestors were planters here. They grew sugarcane and other crops for sale in America. I think they once owned this entire end of the island, but only this cottage and a few acres remain. The cottage was built by Steve's uncle, who lived here for nearly fifty years."

"Where is he now?"

"He died about five years ago. The place fell into disrepair, as any place will quickly do in the islands in this salt air."

"Then Steve moved in?"

Doc took another sip from his drink, gazing out across the lagoon. Kelly sensed either he was gathering his thoughts, or she had asked the wrong question.

"After Steve's wife, uh ... died, his friends urged him to come down here and fix the place up. He'd fallen dangerously into a deep depression over her death. He continued to do that when he got a chance on active duty, and more so when his uncle got sick. He's only been retired from the Navy for a few years. It turned out to be a good idea because the cottage had been lived in for all those years by his uncle, who never married and was a bit of a hermit. Steve had his work cut out for him, but it gave him a new sense of direction and purpose."

"So, you came down here with him?"

"I guess you could say that. I'd been thinking of retiring from the British Army. Steve's postcards and letters describing this place made my decision much easier, plus the local clinic here needed some help."

Kelly thought about the photograph of the woman in Steve's room. She had died young, in the prime of her life.

"You were a doctor in the British Army?" Kelly said.

"Thirty-three years," he answered and sat up a little in his chair.

"Where's Mrs. Doc?"

"Oh, she left a long time ago."

Kelly had grown fond of Doc and didn't want to harm their growing friendship. She changed the subject to something she was a little more interested in.

"I guess you met Steve in the military?"

"We first met in Diego Garcia."

"Oh yeah. We called it Dodge when I was in, but I never got there."

"Right, it's a small atoll in the Indian Ocean, one of the last remnants of the British Empire. We met again in Riyadh during the Iraq War. Steve had managed to get himself shot, but not before carrying out one of the most critical missions of the war. He carried the only other survivor on his back six miles across the desert at night to the extraction point, where they were picked up by helicopter."

Kelly thought of the photo in the desert.

Doc finished his drink and then continued. "I ran the field hospital in Riyadh. We became good friends while he recovered."

"What was his mission—are you allowed to say?"

Doc hesitated for a moment, considering her question. Kelly saw him shrug his shoulders as if to say, "What the hell."

"He went in a hundred miles behind Iraqi lines with five other members of his SEAL team. The target was the hardened bunker that controlled Iraq's Southern Air defense sector. Their mission was to get close enough to laser designate a small soft spot in the bunker for a smart bomb delivered from our aircraft. Air superiority was critical for our invasion from Kuwait."

"As you would imagine, the place was heavily guarded. The mission began to fall apart when they stumbled into a minefield that wasn't supposed to be there. Most of the team was killed and cut down by machine gun fire from the target."

"How did they finish the mission then?"

"Steve was wounded, and so was the commanding officer of the team, the only other survivor. But they defended their position long enough to allow Steve to crawl in and designate the target. The bomb leveled the place, killing most of the soldiers guarding it. Steve carried the CO back to safety."

Kelly listened intently, picturing the scene in her mind.

"It reads like a book," she said.

"You should have seen Steve's award recommendation, written by the SEAL commander," he said. "It was ten pages long."

"That's an incredible story. Is that where he got the medal I saw inside?"

"Yes, the Navy Cross. The attack on the air defense operations center was a turning point in the war. Once the Iraqis' air defense was destroyed, we could attack at will from the air."

"I saw his scars from the battle today in the lagoon. The one in his side looked bad."

"Well, those are a little more recent," Doc said, avoiding her eyes.

Kelly was stunned by that answer, but Steve called to them from the house before she could form a question.

"Anybody hungry?" he shouted.

"Famished!" Doc yelled back, winking at Kelly. "We were wondering what was taking so long."

Joseph and Steve had set the table on the screened porch at the end of the cottage where Kelly had breakfasted the first morning. The four of them settled in. The sun had just disappeared below the horizon, and the cooler evening breeze had set in. A trio of candles in the middle of the table flickered in their hurricane holders and cast a soft glow.

The conch chowder in cream and sherry sauce was superb. Kelly assured them she had never eaten better in the finest restaurants. It was followed by an even better dish of baked stuffed snapper and an avocado and olive salad that Joseph said was his grandmother's secret recipe. They finished a bottle of an excellent Napa Valley white wine and opened another. Although Steve jokingly pretended to share credit for the meal, he admitted it was all Joseph's doing as soon as he got the rise out of his friend that he'd intended.

"Where did you learn to cook like this?" Kelly asked.

"My mother worked as a chef at Caneel Bay Plantation—one of the luxury resorts on the island. I grew up helping in the kitchen. Some of it stuck with me."

"I guess so," Kelly said, delicately scraping the last morsel she could off her plate.

Doc pushed back from the table and produced a pipe from his shirt pocket. He carefully packed it with a British brand of tobacco. He lit it, drawing on it carefully until the tobacco's spiced smoke filled the air. Kelly's father once smoked a pipe, and she still associated the smell of it with him.

It was quite dark around the cottage now, with no moon or light pollution on their end of the island; the stars lit the distant white sand beach. Kelly could easily see the dinghy sitting above the high-tide line.

"Did you check the weather?" Doc asked, looking at Steve.

"Yes. Looks like a good forecast for at least a few days. No fronts or big winds in sight."

"That'll mean fairly calm seas," Doc added. Kelly saw them exchange glances.

"Steve said he told you about the cruise to St. Martin to check out the trawler," Doc said. "Really, just an excuse for a boat trip."

"I'm looking forward to it," Kelly said.

"Then it's settled," Doc said, standing up with his dinner plate. Kelly stood, too, and began clearing the table.

"We'll leave tomorrow afternoon," Steve said, looking out at the ocean beyond the reef. "Looks like a great time for a shakedown cruise."

10

The trawler cleared the point of land that protected the harbor on the southern end of St. John and crashed into the heavier seas of the Caribbean. Her bow plunged into the deep swells and parted them into blue-white spray and foam, making her own highway through the open sea against the southeast trade winds.

This was what she had been designed and built for, and Steve sensed an energy and force in her keel that longed for the open ocean after being tied to the dock in the calmer waters of the island.

The twin Cummins six-liter diesel engines performed flawlessly after extensive renovation and fine-tuning. Steve inched the throttles back and synchronized their RPMs, impressed with the power and the smooth ride the boat produced at twenty knots. Then he took a reading from the Garmin global positioning system he'd mounted to the instrument console in front of him and turned to a new heading for St. Martin. He cross-checked the heading and course a second time with a chart of the area that displayed all known hazards to navigation. Satisfied with the new course, he turned on the auto helm. The electronic controller would now steer a course, making constant minute adjustments as necessary to compensate for drift caused by wind and current.

As a final precaution, he adjusted the surface search radar, setting an alarm that would sound for converging traffic or unknown hazards to navigation, and sat back in his chair.

He contemplated the two men he had seen in the hotel room when he met Kelly. There was no sign of them around the marina when they arrived to take the trawler out.

Joseph had made a few inquiries from his friends at the ferry, and they confirmed that the men had not been back. But Steve was convinced they would return and was still working on the best way to deal with them. When he brought the trawler out of the marina less than an hour ago, motoring past the buoys and the no-wake zone, he'd glanced across the channel and seen the massive catamaran, still at anchor off Red Hook.

Filing the problem away for now, he scanned the horizon ahead. The open sea always gave him a sense of euphoria and freedom that he never tired of. Kelly, who had been on the bow, riding the seesaw movement through the swells, walked back to the wheelhouse, carefully holding on with at least one hand. Doc sat in a chair on the stern, rigging a trolling line on two big fishing reels.

"You'll be able to see the cottage in a minute," Steve said as Kelly walked into the wheelhouse. He handed her a pair of Steiner Military-Marine binoculars.

"There's our lagoon," he said, pointing to the island a few miles away. "And you can see the house now through the trees."

Steve watched her squeeze the binoculars closer together to fit her smaller face better and carefully adjust the focus. Then the view was gone, blocked by a tiny offshore island as the trawler moved further south.

"Did you see it?" Steve asked.

"Yeah. Joseph must still be there; I saw your Land Rover," she said, lowering the glasses. "It's really a beautiful spot."

"The best spot on the island," Steve said. He maneuvered the trawler to avoid a fish trap marker and returned it to its course. Then he glanced back at Kelly, who had been silent. She sat on a small couch in the wheelhouse, behind his left shoulder, the binoculars in her lap. She held his gaze for a moment, then quickly looked away.

Suddenly, they heard a commotion at the stern. One of the trolling lines had detached from its outrigger, and its reel was clicking line off as the fish ran for the cover of the ocean depths.

Doc was frantically trying to put down his drink, put out his pipe, and get the rod out of its holder on the stern before the fish stripped off too much line. Steve throttled back to maintain a few knots of forward momentum, and Kelly rushed back to the stern. Once the rod was out of the holder, Doc sat and jammed the butt into a smaller holder built into the chair. He began pulling upward on the rod while reeling in line on the downstroke in a gradual pumping motion. He shot a glance at Steve, and they nodded in agreement that it was a good fish, though not one of the monstrous marlin or swordfish they had battled here before. If it had been, Doc wouldn't have been able to take in line at all until the fish finally tired after several grueling hours.

Just then, the other reel's bait clicker sounded its alarm and began paying out the line. Simultaneously, the line detached from the outrigger, and the rod bent over under the strain of the new fish.

"You take that one!" Steve yelled, motioning to the rod. He saw her hesitate. The rod was like a living thing, bent nearly double under the strain and jerking sporadically as the fish tried, again and again, to free itself from the line.

"Get ready," he said.

He pulled the throttles to idle to give the line some slack, and the tension on the rod abated.

"Now," he said.

Without a word, she took the heavy rod from the transom and transferred it to the chair like she had seen Doc do. A second later, the rod bent over as the fish tightened the line. She gripped the rod with both hands, using the butt in the rod holder as a fulcrum and giving her much more leverage.

"Like this," Doc said. He showed her how to pull the rod up, pulling the fish toward him, then quickly reel in as much line as possible while lowering the rod and starting the process again.

"Pull up, reel down," he said.

"It's so strong," she said, but she kept at it and slowly began to reel the fish in as it zigzagged wildly back and forth beneath them in the dark blue water.

Steve stayed at the helm, looking down on them as he monitored the boat's position. He was glad to see no other boats around to worry about. It wasn't long before Doc's fish broke the surface and disappeared.

"Dolphin!" Steve shouted.

"Oh no!" Kelly cried and stopped reeling, a troubled look on her face.

"Not the mammal," Steve said, "the fish."

"Mahi-mahi," Doc added.

"Well, why didn't you say that in the first place? That's my favorite seafood!" She began to reel in with new vigor.

Though they couldn't see them, the dolphins were part of a large school of the sought-after game fish that had meandered into these waters only a few days before. They were following an immense school of baitfish, numbering well into the thousands, that had hatched together in the shallow-water nurseries near shore. They had instinctively made their way into deeper waters to begin their pelagic adult life.

After feeding on the baitfish for a few days, the school had taken up position under a multi-mile-long floating weed line formed by wind and current. The trawler had passed just parallel to this sinuous line, presenting the artificial bait to the waiting fish beneath it. Now, as the hooked fish struggled in vain against the lines, their schoolmates swarmed around them in a frenzy, perhaps looking for an easy meal.

Doc's surfaced again—this time much closer to the boat.

"Nice fish," Steve said. When it saw the boat, it dove again, stripping off a new line to start the process all over.

Then Kelly's fish showed itself, much further from the stern than Doc's. It immediately dove and started stripping line.

"Did you see that?" Doc said, speaking over his shoulder toward Steve.

"That's a bull," Steve said. "And it's a big one." He had seen the high, blunt forehead of the male mahi. "Just let him run," he said. "He'll get tired."

When the run was over, Steve noticed the spool of the big reel was only half-full. He estimated there was at least a hundred yards of line out.

Undaunted by the setback, Kelly began to reel again with renewed determination.

After a few more minutes, Doc got his fish up to the boat, and Steve produced a gaff, expertly hooking the fish under the gill plate and hauling it aboard. The brilliant colors glistened against the deck: iridescent greens, blues, and yellows stood out, intermixed with the white and silver scales that had earned it the Spanish name Dorado, meaning gilded. It slapped its tail frantically against the deck, trying to swim where there was no water, then lay still. Steve opened a large cooler and placed the fish in a frigid slush of saltwater and ice he had prepared.

They turned their attention to Kelly, still struggling with the big bull. It was nearly twice the length of Doc's. When she finally got it up to the boat, and it rolled over on its side in the water, Steve and Doc gasped at its size.

They had never seen one quite this big. Its pronounced male head made it look like a different species of fish.

Steve repeated the gaffing, and Doc helped him haul the fish out of the water, on top of the gunnel, and then onto the deck. Kelly was ecstatic. She hugged Doc and Steve, saying she was so relieved she had not lost the fish. Steve put Kelly's mahi into the cooler and added more ice. It was so long that its tail stuck out of one end of the oversized cooler.

Doc produced a bottle of champagne and plastic glasses for everyone from his ice chest and popped the cork.

"I was saving this for later, but now's as good a time as any. Here's to a successful shakedown cruise and the biggest mahi I've ever seen come out of these waters!"

They congratulated one another, and Steve pushed up the throttles. The induced wind dried the sweat on their skin, cooling them instantly.

Steve watched Kelly raise the lid of the cooler to take another look at her mahi, now lifeless in the cooler's ice.

He was grateful that the sharks had not shown up, like they often do, and taken her fish.

11

They passed smaller islands on the horizon to the north as they continued their easterly course to St. Martin. Steve explained these were the southernmost of the British Virgin Islands and showed Kelly a nautical map of the area. After another hour, there was no land in sight.

A glorious sunset found them forty miles southeast of St. John, and Steve told them they would easily make St. Martin by dawn the next day. The trawler continued to perform flawlessly; the rebuilt twin diesels never skipped a beat. Steve and Doc took turns standing watch all night, and Steve woke Kelly, as she had requested to see the first lights of St. Martin's western shore in the predawn sky. They had made good time, and he decided to wait until sunrise to bring the trawler into the harbor at Marigot. They stayed there all day, napping, eating, and exploring the French side of the island. They bartered most of their fish for diesel fuel at the local marina restaurant, keeping what they wanted for their dinner. Their catch fetched a handsome price; apparently, fresh mahi hadn't been plentiful there for some time.

Later in the afternoon, Steve checked the weather forecast for the area. Contrary to the earlier report, a new low-pressure system was coming in from the west and would arrive in a few days. It would stir up the seas and bring with it rain and thunderstorms. Although they had planned to stay longer, they decided to return that evening. By sunset, they had cleared the harbor and were in deep water. Once again, Steve set his course, hooked up the auto helm, and went below to the galley.

Kelly made a salad with fresh local fruit and marinated the mahi in olive oil and spices for the grill. She had cut some potatoes into wedges, and they were baking in the gimballed gas oven. She was glad she'd gotten this chance to show her own cooking skills in the galley. As she sprinkled some lemon garlic on the fish, she thought back to earlier in the day when she sat in the wheelhouse with Steve's binoculars in her lap. He was busy at the helm, and she had suddenly become transfixed. He stood barefoot in shorts and a faded T-shirt, his sandy-brown hair blowing wildly. His face revealed the maturity of his age and the lines and creases that came from living a full life—far different from the soft, pasty corporate faces she had grown used to from the men she had known lately. Steve was a sharp, refreshing contrast. What you saw is what you got. An open book with a few hidden chapters that made him even harder to resist. She shook her head in an attempt to slap herself back into reality and out of some silly schoolgirl infatuation pit she stood poised to jump in.

Just then, Steve walked into the galley. Like most boats, it was a small, cramped galley that only left enough room for one person to cook. His sudden appearance startled her, and she hoped he hadn't seen her shaking her head at herself.

"Smells good down here," he said.

"Just a little something to keep the scurvy away," she replied.

He moved toward the refrigerator at the end of the galley, and as he did, he had to squeeze by her, their hips just touching. "I thought I'd open some of that French wine we bought in the market today," he said.

She handed Steve a glass of the white wine she had just poured. "Beat you to it," she said.

"Thanks."

He looked down at her, a full head shorter than he. He reached across her and set his glass on the counter behind her, their cheeks almost touching.

Then there was a loud noise as Doc came crashing down the stairs from the deck. They jumped apart like errant children caught by a parent.

"Need some ice," he said, opening a small cooler on the floor. "Smells delicious, Kelly."

"Thanks, just the potatoes," she said, glancing up at Steve.

"I'll start the charcoal," Steve said and climbed the steps to topside. After a few minutes, he had a nice fire in the new grill he had installed on one of the stern stanchions.

They dined in the wheelhouse. Kelly thought the fish was the best she'd ever tasted, and she said so. "All I did was marinate it," she said. And she was glad to see that the potatoes and colorful fruit salad were perfect complements.

"Something about being on the water in a boat and eating fish you caught that day," Steve said. "My grandfather used to say God doesn't count against you the days you spend on a boat."

"The merchant marine?" Kelly said.

"Yes."

"Or maybe we are just working up an appetite out here in the tropics with the sun and the stars all around us," Doc said, looking out on the frothy wake off the stern.

After dinner, Doc cleaned the dishes while Steve and Kelly took the first watch. Another postcard sunset and the stars came out one by one until the night sky was filled with them. The moon hadn't risen yet, and with no artificial light from houses or streetlamps, the panorama was spectacular.

After a while, Doc came up smoking a Cohiba he'd purchased on St. Martin.

"Beautiful evening," he said, gazing back at the phosphorescent wake churned up by the propellers.

A falling star lit up the sky behind the boat. It was followed by another, then four or five more.

"Look," exclaimed Kelly. "There's a bunch of them."

"Must be a meteor shower," Steve said, and they watched until they lost count of them. Doc stayed a little longer, put out his cigar, carefully placing the unburned half in his shirt pocket, and bade them goodnight.

"Wake me when you need me," he said, absently waving as he negotiated the stairs down to the galley and his cabin.

Steve followed him to discuss something about the boat, leaving Kelly alone for a few minutes. The night air was starting to chill her. She moved up to the protected area of the wheelhouse and felt warmer instantly when she stepped in out of the breeze. The soft glow of the instruments gave the room a cozy atmosphere. She studied them for a moment.

When she heard Steve behind her, she turned to see him with two small glasses.

"Thought you might like a little after-dinner drink," he said, handing her a glass. "It's a white port from a favorite vineyard in the Napa Valley."

She felt the strong wine immediately. "Wow, that's really good," she said.

The surface radar collision warning at the helm gave its first alert of a potential threat. A single ping from the unit accompanied a yellow dot on the screen, indicating the threat. The audible warning grew louder and more frequent unless a change of course was made. Steve looked ahead. There on the horizon was a freighter, barely visible. He programmed the auto helm to change course to pass well behind the freighter, then return to course after it was clear.

"Those things are handy," Kelly said. She was sitting on the small couch in the wheelhouse.

"And a little annoying sometimes," Steve replied. He stayed at the helm to keep an eye on the freighter.

"What did you do in the Marines?" he said.

"I was a ground pounder with the 1st Marine Division," she said. She looked at the port glass in her hand, now half-empty.

She didn't want to make him pull it out of her. He must have made some calculations by now. He'd probably guessed her age, plus the well-worn desert camo duffel, meant she had probably done some time in the sandbox within the last twenty years.

"I was in Iraq for most of 2004," she said. "I was enlisted, an MP—something I just wanted to do at the time. I was pretty young. Women weren't allowed in combat roles then, but MPs saw plenty of it, which was a way of getting in the fight. I happened to be in Fallujah when it got crazy after the mutilations of the civilian contractors."

Steve didn't say anything.

"Doc told me you were there too. Actually, he told me the whole story."

Steve hung his head and shook it from side to side. "Doc talks too much sometimes."

"I know it's none of my business," Kelly said. "If you'd rather not talk about it. Doc told me your wife died. I'm very sorry."

"She died when I was on a ship in the Navy," he said, "I was halfway around the world in the Indian Ocean on a mission. It took me three days to get back."

Kelly waited for him to continue if he wanted to.

"She was in the first tower hit on 9/11. She had a good job there, working for a nonprofit trust fund that—of all things—placed Middle Eastern orphans in American homes. She never had a chance. The plane hit the North Tower several floors below her. I should have been there with her. God, we were just kids. Newlyweds."

"Oh my," Kelly uttered in a small, faint voice, and she was surprised to feel a tear run down her cheek.

She swallowed hard to maintain her composure. Innocent lives had been extinguished by powerful, evil forces in the world. An overwhelming sadness began to engulf her like a dark cloud. Steve did not deserve the pain he had suffered. She had opened an old wound, but she was sharing his pain and had assumed the grief with him. She hoped the burden was just a bit lighter for him now.

She didn't want the night to end like this. She took a deep breath, sat up, and dried her tears, smiling rather sheepishly, although she wasn't at all embarrassed by her show of emotion. She sensed the difference in Steve, too. It was all becoming a little too much to deal with right now.

"How long was Doc married?" she asked abruptly.

Steve smiled.

"Only a few years. It ended when she came at him with a knife one night. He deserved it, by his own admission."

"I can't imagine that!" Kelly replied.

They both laughed, considering possible scenarios that might have led to the knife scene crescendo.

"Doc's a great guy, but I'm not sure he's the marrying type," Kelly said. "But we're becoming great friends."

"He likes you very much," Steve said. "Now tell me about you."

"Not much to tell, really. After my enlistment, I used my GI Bill eligibility and got into the University of Virginia, majored in political science, then went to work on the campaign trail with a candidate for lieutenant governor from my hometown in Virginia."

"Just jumped right in," Steve said.

"My father knew him," she admitted a little shyly.

"Your father?"

"John Phillips," she said.

"Not the Senate Armed Forces Committee member and state senator John Phillips?" Steve asked incredulously, stiffening a little.

"Yep, that one," she said matter-of-factly. She hated telling people about her father. "Anyway, the guy won the race, and I went to work for him full-time on his staff."

"Sounds like you were well on your way."

"Yeah, I guess, but then I began to see the way politics really work. The campaign platform sounds great—you know, change the world and all that. I really got behind it and believed it and we did do some good things, but the paybacks, favors, special-interest groups really got to me. After a year or so, I realized that nothing ever gets accomplished unless it's already been bargained away to the other party or has something to do with reelection. I finally got disgusted and quit after the lieutenant governor tried to rape me in his office one night."

"Ah, the subtle approach."

"Right—and it's surprising how a knee in the crotch can ruin the whole moment."

They both laughed, and Kelly continued.

"I got out of the whole thing. I tried to explain it to my dad—left out the rape attempt—but he's been wrapped up in it for so long he can't see out."

"We had a bit of a falling out. Then I married a guy who worked with me and played housewife for nearly eight years. That ended by mutual consent a year ago. Unlike me, he embraced the whole political scene. He used to say politics isn't for everyone. It wasn't for me, that's for sure."

"Too many power-hungry people in it for all the wrong reasons," Steve said. "You just didn't fit the mold. It's hard to find the few good ones. Somewhere along the line you learned how to sail and navigate a big sailboat."

"My dad taught me. A lot of our vacations were on sailboats all over the world. I loved it all from the beginning. Got my captain's license during college."

The moon was up now just above the horizon behind them. Kelly stared at it, lost in thought.

"I'm glad we met," Steve said. "It's always good to have a capable friend on your side."

"Who says I'm on your side," she said, then broke out in a grin.

"I can handle this middle watch if you'd like to catch a nap. I'd feel better if you were there for Doc's morning watch."

"Okay," Kelly said. "That makes sense."

"We can hot bed my bunk. I made sure it was a good one when I redid the boat."

She got a wicked grin on her face and started to say something but stopped, then said a quick goodnight and disappeared below.

12

They woke to gray skies just after dawn. The swells were larger now, with an occasional whitecap blowing off their tops, and the wind was in their face at twenty knots. During the night, under the thin veil of sleep, Steve sensed the sea changing and felt the boat struggle more against the wind and current. As he went on deck, the picture in his mind matched what he saw. The trawler was still running smoothly, but her bow cut deeper into the swells, pitching the boat up and down more than before.

Doc was in the wheelhouse, smoking the rest of his Cohiba.

"See anything yet?" Steve asked.

"Our island just a few minutes ago."

Kelly came up with coffee for Steve and a cup of tea for Doc.

"Morning," she said to Doc, handing him his tea.

"Good morning, my dear."

"We'll be home in two hours," Steve said, reading her thoughts.

She settled into one of the padded chairs behind the windscreen.

An hour and a half later they were abeam their end of the island. Kelly found the binoculars and began scanning through the trees for the cottage.

"There's the cottage," she said. "I don't see the Land Rover. I guess Joseph has already gone to meet us."

Steve had emailed Joseph before they left St. Martin, telling him when they would be back. She handed the binoculars to Steve, and he took a cursory look while keeping an eye on a converging sailboat. The traffic had increased significantly within five miles of the island.

The cottage looked the same, but something seemed out of place. In another few seconds, it would be out of view. Then he saw the screen door, and the next moment, the house was gone, obscured by a thick palm grove that choked the shoreline as they made their way around the southern point of the island on the way to the dock at Cruz Bay.

Something wasn't quite right. There was only one standing order at the cottage: the screen doors must be kept closed at all times. Not necessarily locked since break-ins were rare on this side of the island. But Steve had the misfortune of being prime mosquito bait. He could be standing in a group of ten people and be the only one bitten. One of the screen doors would occasionally catch on the steps if it was swung open too far, and Steve had been meaning to fix it. Still, he had never known Joseph to ever leave it open.

Kelly studied Steve's face as he lowered the glasses.

"What is it?" she said.

"Probably nothing," he answered. "The screen door is open."

"Oh. Well, that doesn't sound too bad," Kelly said, relieved. "I thought you'd seen something serious from the look on your face."

"Yeah. I guess Joseph left it open. He owes me a beer if he did."

Out of the corner of his eye, Steve saw Doc looking at him from where he stood on the stern. Their eyes met in understanding, and Doc gave him a slight nod.

Steve gave way to the sailboat as required by maritime custom, passing behind it, and turned toward the marina. He saw the ferry in the distance heading back to St. Thomas on its midmorning run from Cruz Bay.

When they pulled into their slip, the Land Rover was waiting for them, as Kelly had surmised, but with no sign of Joseph. Steve and Kelly went through the routine of washing the trawler down with fresh water and tucking it into bed. An hour later, there was still no sign of Joseph. Steve and Doc speculated he might be over in Charlotte Amalie with Martha, whom he jokingly called his part-time wife, perhaps in the throes of some new crisis. Still, it was unusual for him not to leave a note. They climbed into the Land Rover and headed for the cottage.

They made quick time getting through the village and up the mountain road. As they neared the top of the ridge, Steve pulled over to the scenic overlook and stopped underneath a parasol-like guanacaste tree.

"What's up?" Kelly said quickly. No one had spoken since they left the boat.

"There are some things we need to tell you," Steve said, glancing in the rearview mirror at Doc.

Kelly suddenly looked alarmed.

"Don't worry," Steve said, seeing the expression on her face, "but there's something going on that you need to know about—and maybe take the next boat out of here."

He told her everything he had told Doc about the attack on the tug at night, the assassins on the trawler, the men in the hotel watching the boat, and the real possibility that these people were still after him for some unknown reason. He also told her about his suspicion of the local police force, that even if he came up with some hard evidence about the attack, he would have to go to other authorities when the time came.

Kelly listened intently. As Steve told her the story, he was surprised at how calmly she took the information. Doc gave her a reassuring nod or two from the back seat as Steve talked, occasionally adding his comments. She was silent for a few minutes, but instead of wanting to distance herself from the whole affair, as most people would logically do, she said she wanted to help in any way she could.

"When my uncle died, the tug was left in San Juan for three years," Steve said. "I was bringing her back over here for a complete overhaul when this guy Bancroft showed up that night. I knew him from buying marine supplies in San Juan. He ran a parts store there, and I figured he was into something illegal, but I never expected he would try to kill me.

"Maybe your check bounced," Doc said, attempting to ease the tension.

"Why didn't you go to the police then?" Kelly asked.

"As Steve said, the police down here are a mixed bag," Doc answered for him. "Some are good, honest cops. Others are corrupt, at the highest levels. Whoever's behind this either has Steve mixed up with someone else, or they're looking for something they think he has or maybe something he knows. They're sure to have law enforcement in their pockets."

"And knowing this guy Cockerel," Steve added, "it's best to keep quiet for now."

"What about your deckhand?" Kelly said. "The one who went down with the tug. His family must be wondering where he is."

"Joseph knew him; he was from West Africa. His family was wiped out in one of the coups over there. He fled here to find work," Steve replied. "But we couldn't find anyone who knew much about him. No one even knew his last name."

"We think you should get on the next ferry to Red Hook, take a taxi to the airport, and get the hell out of here," Doc said.

Steve started to say he would buy her a ticket home and she cut him off.

"I'm staying," she said. "You need me here."

Steve saw the resolve on her face.

"Okay, that's settled," Doc said, chuckling to himself.

Steve hesitated a moment, looking at Doc in the rearview mirror, then at Kelly. He gave her a tight smile and started the truck. They came to their driveway off the main road, and Steve drove past it without slowing down. He turned off the road a few hundred yards past the drive onto a narrow, unpaved switchback that snaked up the small mountain behind the cottage. After a few minutes, they had climbed several hundred feet, and the dirt road ended abruptly at a microwave relay tower. Steve stopped the Rover and got out with the binoculars from the boat.

"This is part of my jogging route," he said. "It's the only place I know of with a view of the cottage from any side other than the ocean."

Kelly and Doc got out and looked over the edge of the road. Far below them, Kelly could see the roof of the cottage, part of the driveway, and the front porch.

"Take a look," Steve said, handing the binoculars to Doc.

"Uh-oh," Doc said and gave the glasses to Kelly.

The screen door was closed now.

Steve was back at the truck when she lowered the glasses. He unzipped a small green aircraft mechanic's tool bag in the back, pulled out his Beretta, checked for a full magazine, and inserted it into the pistol. He checked that the safety was off, chambered a round, and holstered the gun in a black nylon shoulder harness. With the harness on, he was ready to start down the hill to the cottage.

"I'll wave to you from the porch when it's all clear," he said, and before either Doc or Kelly could say a word, he turned and jogged down the road toward the highway.

Kelly started to speak as he disappeared around the first switchback, but instead, she just stood there and watched him go. Doc placed a hand on her shoulder.

"Steve's very careful," he said in a reassuring voice. "He knows what he's doing."

"I believe that—I really do," she said. "But a little backup might be a good idea if it goes south down there."

Her duffel was in the back of the Rover. She unzipped it and pulled out the Smith & Wesson Model 66 .357 Magnum in its shoulder harness, checked the cylinder of the pistol for a full load, and put the harness on— the big pistol resting under her left arm. She unzipped the rifle case, pulled out a Windham Weaponry SRC M4, checked the safety, and visually inspected the rifle to ensure it was empty. Then she picked up a full magazine and inserted it into the rifle, giving it a firm push and than a pull to make sure the magazine was properly seated. Next, she pulled the charging handle fully back and chambered a round, tapped the forward assist to ensure the bolt was fully forward and locked, closed the ejection port cover, rechecked the safety, and then placed the rifle sling over her right shoulder in a low carry.

Doc stared at her, his mouth slightly open.

"Don't worry," she said. "I'll stay well out of sight near the road—just in case."

She began a slow walk down the road to give Steve enough time to get in place.

Doc shook his head, then raised the binoculars slowly like an eager, engrossed fan at the Super Bowl.

13

_____

Steve crossed the main highway and jogged back toward the cottage a short distance before slipping into the stand of bamboo. The nearly impenetrable stand towered over him, some of the stalks as big around as his arms, and it grew too close together to walk through in places. Steve had left it there to provide a natural screen from the road, and he or Joseph had to get the old tractor and mower out a few times a year to keep the stuff from taking over the drive and cottage.

He stood motionless in the bamboo for a few minutes. He listened, watching a large garden spider catch and wrap a grasshopper a few feet away. After another minute, he chose a path through the stalks that would keep him hidden from the house and quietly stepped forward.

He moved a small step at a time, deliberately placing each foot with no sound and stopping every thirty seconds to "let the jungle settle down from his movement" as he had been taught many years ago. He was a natural at it, drawing on some unknown ancestor who had passed it down through genetic code. He constantly checked his flanks, occasionally studying the area behind him. After a few more minutes, he could see the back of the cottage and changed course to approach the corner farthest from the drive.

He reasoned that if someone was waiting, they were probably inside, listening for his Land Rover to approach, most likely positioned with a view of the gravel drive. There was a window by the screen door on the side of the house where a sentry could sit well hidden inside, watching.

He noted this while continuing to sweep the grounds outside the cottage, but as he drew nearer without seeing anyone, he concentrated on the house itself. A short detour in his approach allowed him to view most of the yard on the side of the lagoon. Again, no one.

Just as he began to take his next step, he heard the unmistakable sound of a muffled belch from the kitchen, where a window was partly open.

One in the kitchen, more than likely another somewhere in the house. He drew a mental picture of the interior and concluded that the logical place was the front living room with a clear view of the driveway.

Leaving the bamboo, he quickened his pace through the yard to the back of the house, then around to the side porch overlooking the lagoon where they had eaten dinner several nights before. He crept up the short steps to the screened porch door, opened it carefully, then crossed the porch and peered in a windowed door that led into the living room. There, at the other end of the room, just as he had predicted, a man lay asleep on the couch, a machine gun lying across his lap. Another Russian, like the ones that night on the tug. Steve had seen enough of them in his Navy career—ex-military turned mercenary. The world was full of them.

He took a few more seconds to look around the room. They had killed his parrot, either out of practicality to keep him from squawking or because they were assholes. Probably both. He lay at the bottom of the cage, his neck twisted at an odd angle. The bird had been a gift from his wife for their future life together on the island. Killing the bird only strengthened his resolve. These people were really beginning to annoy him.

He reversed his steps, went to the back of the house, and looked into his open bedroom window. Nothing. Without hesitating, he cut through the screen, unlatched and removed it, then raised the window enough to pull himself up and into the room. Opening the window was tricky; the sash stuck a little as he tried to lift it, but he managed to get it open without making a sound.

He waited a few more seconds, studying the old pine plank floor. Several spots in the most traveled areas creaked when walked upon and would sound an instant alarm to the men in the other room. As carefully as he could, he moved to the wall on the balls of his feet as if tiptoeing through a minefield and then made his way to the door by walking against the wall, where the floorboards were less likely to make a sound than near the center of the room.

Peering around the corner of the living room door, he saw the man on the couch still asleep. He crept silently down the short hallway and checked the other bedroom. Unoccupied. Convinced that there were only the two of them, he returned to the living room doorway.

From here, he could see the second man in the kitchen seated at the table, looking at his phone. His pistol lay on the table beside his left hand. The man would have no trouble getting a good shot at Steve if he was left-handed. But he was turned away from Steve to look out the kitchen window, his feet propped on another chair. That would help.

There was no good way to do this. The most sensible thing would be to shoot the man with the machine gun first, then cover the one in the kitchen. After all, the machine gun was the greater threat. But he could not bring himself to shoot the man as he slept. He would try plan B.

He slipped off the thumb safety on the Beretta and approached the man in the kitchen, leaving himself an easy field of fire for the man on the couch.

When he was within ten feet of his target, he slowly pulled back the Beretta's hammer to accentuate its distinctive sound. The man in the kitchen froze.

"Put your hands on your head," he said. But before he could say another word, the man had snatched up his gun, stood, and was turning to shoot.

Startled by his speed, Steve fired instinctively, catching the man in the upper chest just below the neck. The man got off one round before he went down, and Steve heard the bullet fly past his left ear like a supersonic hummingbird, so close he thought it had grazed him. It slammed into the wall somewhere over his left shoulder and sent something hanging there crashing to the floor.

Seeing movement to his left, he turned to find the man on the couch raising the machine gun. Steve fired twice, and the weapon flew from the man's arms as one of the bullets struck his right forearm. He ran panicked for his gun, lying now near the front door, and Steve fired again, this time intentionally lower. The man fell to the floor, screaming and clutching his leg with his good arm. He began shouting in a Slavic language Steve couldn't identify. He checked the man in the kitchen. He lay unmoving in a growing pool of arterial blood. Approaching the man in the living room, Steve could see the leg bone sticking out through his clothing, but the lack of much blood told him the femoral artery was intact. He calmly pointed the Beretta at the wounded man's head.

"Who are you, and why are you here?"

The man replied loudly and angrily in the same language.

"Who sent you?" Steve shouted.

The enraged man continued to babble, making no attempt to answer the question. Steve pressed his foot on the man's wounded arm. He screamed and stared wildly at Steve. His eyes rolled back in his head and then refocused on Steve as he began to go into shock. Steve pressed down on his arm again, and the man grimaced and stared at the ceiling, on the edge of consciousness.

"Where is the boat?" the man suddenly asked in plain English before closing his eyes and passing out.

Steve contemplated the question as he took a Glock 19 from a belt holster on the wounded man. Then he slipped his Beretta into its holster under his arm, the adrenaline rush from the last sixty seconds leaving him light-headed.

The boat. They were after the tug, not him. He was relieved, but the revelation only brought up more questions. Who would care about an old rusting boat that had been sitting for years at anchor? What could possibly be so special about the tug that would keep these guys coming back? He needed time to sort it out.

He checked the wounded man's pulse. It was weak but steady. Then he went out to the porch to motion for Doc and Kelly and found the fully loaded Kelly standing fifty feet away in the driveway next to a mahogany tree. Steve gave her a thumbs-up, and she returned it. He realized she intended to use the tree as cover if need be.

The next minute, Doc drove up in the Rover and got out.

He shrugged as if to say, "I couldn't stop her," and Steve frowned back at him. They had taken a significant risk assuming he had won the gunfight.

"How many?" Doc said.

"Two. One's still alive," Steve replied.

Doc walked briskly into the cottage as if he were making rounds at triage. After a few seconds, he hurried back to the Rover, retrieved the small medical bag he always carried with him, and went back inside without a word.

"I'd better go help him," Steve said. "Stay here and intercept any nosy neighbors who might have heard the shots."

"What'll I tell them?"

"Make up something," he said, knowing no one would come. "Tell them we shot a snake in the house." The closest neighbor was over a mile away. She began to unload her weapons and put them back into the duffel.

He helped Doc bandage the wounded man, and Doc gave him a shot of something from his bag. Then they carried him to the Land Rover. Kelly removed her duffel from the Rover and helped Steve drag the dead man from the kitchen and put him in the back of the truck, covering him with a tarp. Doc jumped in the driver's seat, assuming the role of ambulance driver.

"I'll take them to the clinic," he said, starting the car. "They'll handle it from there."

Steve watched him disappear down the driveway and out of sight. Doc had a good friend who ran the clinic and who would try to keep as much of the incident under wraps as possible. Steve had searched their pockets before Doc drove them away. He was not surprised when he found no iden-tification other than fake driver's licenses from the United States.

He went inside and called Joseph's house, but there was no answer. He'd expected to at least get the answering machine and hear Martha's familiar singsong voice, but instead, the phone just continued to ring.

Suddenly, he had a very bad feeling. Joseph and Martha would be in danger too. He had to get to St. Thomas to warn them.

"Come on, we're getting on the next ferry at Cruz Bay," he said to Kelly. "We'll try to catch a ride. You can put your pistol in my day pack if you want."

They had a surprisingly short wait. A honeymooning tourist couple who had rented a Jeep for the day picked them up. Soon, they were at the dock with the next ferry due in fifteen minutes. It would leave from the Red Hook marina on the east side of St. Thomas, completing its final run for the day.

While they waited, he called Doc at the clinic. Everything had been kept quiet so far, but Doc told him several of the staff were beginning to ask questions. They would all be going home for the day soon, and news of the two white men, one dead and the other with two gunshot wounds, would spread around the island like wildfire.

"I'm trying to get some ID on these guys, but so far, nothing has come up," Doc said.

"Okay. Kelly and I are going over to Charlotte Amalie to warn Joseph. I tried to call but didn't get an answer, not even the machine. I'll call you from there. In the meantime, you know what to do. And be careful; they may be looking for you too."

"Already thought of that. I'll be in Road Town."

"Good. Talk later," Steve replied and hung up.

Road Town was in the British Virgin Islands on the island of Tortola, a short ferry ride away. Doc had a girlfriend there, and he visited occasionally. He'd be safe until they knew more, or this thing cooled off. If it cooled off.

He tried Joseph's number again without success. A few people had gathered for the ferry. They could see it now, barreling across the channel from Red Hook, a large white bow wave in front of its blue hull. Steve noticed an islander friend standing nearby who had done some work on the trawler. He was highly regarded as the best boat electrician in the islands.

"Hello, Jonathan," he said, approaching the man and shaking his hand.

"Steve," the man answered. "How's the boat?"

"Good. No problems. She did well on her cruise the other day."

The mechanic smiled, acknowledging the compliment. But before Steve could say anything more, the man lost his smile, and his expression turned serious.

"There were some tourists here today, looking for you."

Tourists was the term for anyone not from the local community of the islands, whether they were on vacation or not.

"I know. How many?"

"Four. One was dressed like an army man," he said, adding, when he saw the confused look on Steve's face, "You know, army pants and boots."

"He was in uniform?" Steve asked.

"No, not really. But he had short-cut hair, and the way he ordered the others around, maybe he thought he was in the army. I thought they might be friends of yours from when you were in."

"Not hardly. I think they're from the IRS," Steve improvised, trying to come up with a cover story. He glanced at Kelly from the corner of his eye and was pleased to see no reaction from her.

"Well, I didn't know. I told them where you lived—sorry. Man, I better pay my taxes."

"Yeah. Have you seen Joseph?"

"He went to see his wife yesterday. I rode the ferry with him. I'm doing some work on that big boat at Red Hook."

"What boat?" Steve asked.

"The one that anchored two days ago. Your IRS boys were on it," he added, winking at Steve. "One of the diesel generators had a bad bearing."

The ferry was close now. The three of them watched as the pilot expertly reversed the engines and eased the big boat into its slip, its rubber bumpers just touching the dock. Several deckhands tied the hawsers to large cleats, as they had done hundreds of times before. The gangway was lowered. Passengers streamed off, followed by their bags and light cargo for the island, and then the passengers waiting on shore filed on. Since it was the last ferry to St. Thomas, quite a few tourists went aboard.

A few minutes later, the pilot blew the warning horn and eased away from the dock. After they were safely out of the harbor and clear of the no-wake zone protecting the anchored boats, it quickly accelerated to its maximum speed for the short trip across the channel.

They spotted the big yacht as soon as they cleared the harbor. It was the largest boat around, over two hundred feet in length, too large to dock at any marina in the area. It was anchored a half mile out, and as they drew nearer, Steve noticed the waves in the channel lapping harmlessly against its hull. The ship seemed to be attached to the bottom as a permanent fixture rather than floating on the surface. Smaller yachts and sailboats nearby bobbed like corks on their moorings. They were like toys next to the colossal catamaran.

As the ferry drew closer, passing off the big ship's stern, Steve saw that a formidable superstructure connected the identical twin hulls. He had rarely seen private boats this size, noting a floatplane and high-speed launch perched amidships with an attached crane to handle them. There was also what looked like a large retractable skirt between the two hulls. It hid the area between the hulls, and he surmised it was to provide privacy when the ship was in port.

He saw the familiar Cayman Islands ensign on the stern as with many boats in the area, registered there for tax purposes, and across the back of the ship, between the hulls, the name *Conquest*. But it was the jack flying from the bow that gave him concern. He'd seen the flag before but couldn't place it. Green, white, and red stripes below a circle of stars enclosing a wolf lying on a pedestal before a full moon. He knew only that it was the flag of one of the many not-so-friendly nations somewhere in the world.

"It's the largest catamaran in the world," Jonathan said. "At least that's what they told me when I was on board. Just under two hundred and fifty feet."

Steve didn't answer. He watched a man on the stern who appeared to be part of the crew, casually coiling a rope as he kept an eye on the ferry. Once the ferry was past, the man turned to enter the cabin, and Steve spotted a pistol wedged into the small of his back.

"I know where I've seen that flag," Kelly said while they waited for a taxi. "The one on the front of the ship." Steve hadn't mentioned it and was surprised and pleased she'd brought it up.

"I remember a diplomatic dinner the governor held at his mansion when I worked there," she continued. "There were people from all over eastern Europe. It was right after the breakup of the Soviet Union, and lots of countries had declared their independence and were looking for business opportunities in the United States. The governor was trying to get them to consider Virginia as a possibility. I like flags and what they represent, and that one stood out. It's the flag of the separatist independent Chechens."

Of course—he remembered now. On one of his tours at the Pentagon, he'd read a brief on the new nation of Chechnya, which had declared its independence from Russia only to be denied due to its strategic location in the Caucasus and its geographic link to the rich oil fields to the south. Two brutal wars followed over the next decade, and Russia finally secured the region, but rebel forces continued to fight. They were spurred on by centuries of atrocities between the two nations, most recently after the Second World War, when Stalin sent more than a million Chechens to the work camps of Siberia for allegedly helping the Germans. The region had been punctuated by a thousand years of strife and ethnic hatred. It seemed as hopeless to Steve as the Arab and Israeli impasse.

"Can you remember anything else?" he asked.

"No, I didn't attend the dinner. I just remember the governor being excited about it. There were several countries represented there. I know we spent a ton of taxpayers' money on it all."

The ferry docked, and they made their way onto the dusty street in front of the terminal. After a short wait, a taxi pulled up from the queue, and they got in.

"Charlotte Amalie," Steve said to the driver. "I'll show you where when we get closer."

14

The taxi was a twenty-year-old Chevy van with rusting sides and an engine hitting on maybe five of its eight original cylinders. It made a string of stops on the way to Charlotte Amalie, the main port, hotel, and cruise ship location on the other side of the island. Steve knew from past experience and the way the new passengers greeted the driver that he would be one of the few paying riders on the trip. He noticed that the driver, an old Virgin Islander, was using his left foot to work both the gas and brake pedals. His right leg, shriveled and much smaller than the left, lay to the side.

By the time they had started up the steep ridge line separating the two sides of the island, the van was close to exceeding its gross weight limit. It slowed to a crawl as its underpowered engine struggled to carry its load to the top. Traffic backed up behind them, and horns started to blow. At last, by some miracle of physics, the van reached the crest, and those who were brave enough to look out got a breathtaking view of the harbor below. Several cruise ships were in, their passengers flooding the streets downtown looking for duty-free bargains.

Kelly shot an anxious glance at Steve as they picked up speed down the mountain and around hairpin turns of the switchback. He put a reassuring hand on her knee but silently wondered if the brakes were in the same shape as the engine.

"We'll get off here," he said to the driver as they approached one of the side streets. The vehicle took a long while to come to a complete stop; the driver, standing on the brake pedal with his good leg, left them in a cloud of oily blue smoke on a street of concrete block houses overlooking the busy harbor. Built on the side of the mountain, each house was painted a bright island pink, coral, lime green, or plain white. Clothes hung to dry at most, waving in the breeze that rushed up the mountain. A variety of dogs sat in whatever shade they could find under the bougainvillea, and children played in the narrow street.

"When we get to the house, I'll go to the front door," Steve said. "You stay outside and back me up—just like the cottage."

"Sure. Should we check out the back of the house?"

"There's no door to the back. Joseph hasn't gotten around to installing one yet."

"That makes it easier," Kelly said.

Joseph's house was at the end. Steve had helped him qualify for the loan to buy it. He remembered vividly how proud Joseph and Martha were to finally own a home. It stood out in contrast to the others—neatly kept, no trash in the yard, and a perfectly manicured landscape with an eye for detail that could only be Joseph's. Steve had last been here to celebrate the housewarming when the house and yard had been packed with hundreds of their friends. It was quiet now. The breeze seemed to have stopped as they approached the front door.

"Doesn't look good," Kelly said, whispering.

The curtains were drawn all over the house like the owners were on vacation. Steve only nodded, then stepped onto the front porch. Behind the outer screen door, he could see the main door was ajar. He opened the screen door slowly and went in, Beretta in hand.

"Joseph?" he called. "It's Steve."

No answer.

"Anybody home?"

There was an unnatural stillness inside the house. Steve noticed at once that all the windows were closed, which was most unusual at this elevation, where the primary cooling source was the trade wind breeze.

He found Joseph in the kitchen. He was tied to a chair with an electrical cord, his head thrown back from the impact of a single gunshot wound to the forehead, but not before he had been systematically tortured. Several of his fingers had been cut off; others had been smashed with a hammer. His lifeless eyes stared at the ceiling, and Steve closed them as best he could. His loyal friend had held out to the end.

Steve felt completely responsible. This fine man had died for no apparent reason, killed by ruthless and nameless people. Rage began to grow inside of him, and he fought to control it.

Steve cleared the rest of the small house as he went to the master bedroom. He found Martha there spread eagle on the bed. Her throat had been cut, and the mattress beneath her body was soaked with blood. They would have kept her isolated from Joseph in the kitchen, threatening all types of atrocities if he did not cooperate with them. It was hard to tell what they had done to her other than the obvious.

He returned to the front door, opened it, and motioned for Kelly to come up.

"They're both dead," he said.

She turned away with an involuntary gasp and closed her eyes.

They left at once, but Steve stopped at the old woman's house next door to ask if she'd seen anyone. The woman said she had gone into her house early the previous night and thought Joseph and Martha were home because she saw a light in the kitchen. But in the morning, she noticed that all the windows were closed and the curtains drawn. Steve thanked her and joined Kelly on the street. It was clear, the windows had been closed so neighbors wouldn't hear the screams. Neither of them spoke for some time as they walked down the mountain into town.

"There must be someone in the police department we can trust," Kelly said, finally breaking the silence. "It's the only logical thing to do. We've got to go tell them what we know," she added when Steve didn't reply.

"I know a few good people in local law enforcement," he said. "But there are probably crooked cops I don't know. And that concerns me. Whoever these guys are, they've paid the right people in all the right places. It doesn't take much to turn some low-life stuck in a dead-end job, and judging from the size of that giant yacht, they have plenty of cash. My gut instinct is to try to figure this out on our own, and when we have some hard evidence, then go to authorities like the FBI. If we go to them now, the whole thing will get covered up or lost, and Joseph's killers will go free. I owe it to him to prevent that from happening. We're off the grid here, Kelly," he said. "You can still get out."

Steve had considered her situation on their walk down the mountain. It had quickly gotten out of hand.

"Forget it. I'm staying, and that's final," she said. "I can't explain it, but I feel this overwhelming desire to stay here with you. I've made many hard decisions in my life, but this one is easy. I hope you'll understand, and I have the qualifications to stay."

Before he could protest, she added, "They probably know I've been with you these last few days. They'd kill me the first chance they got. It's my neck on the line now, too."

He was impressed with her again and her strength to see this through and justice served. She'd be a good person to have on his side. She might look at things from a different angle than either he or Doc would.

"Okay," he said. "But it's going to be a rough ride."

"I'm your man," she said.

The streets turned to the original cobblestone used as ballast in the hulls of the empty merchant ships sailing to the colony from Europe hundreds of years ago. The cobblestones were offloaded and used to pave the first streets closest to the waterfront.

They stopped at a side street in Old Town in front of a quaint two-story building that had been converted into a hotel and restaurant. A historical marker on the front of the building dated it to the 1700s and briefly described it as a former government official's residence. A sign hanging above the arched double doors read Twins Courtyard Restau-rant/Hotel. Steve explained it now belonged to twin sisters who had come down from the States and bought it a few years ago. They completely reno-vated the colonial mansion, and the place had become an instant success.

Inside was a lush courtyard with a few tables set up, and more tables and a small bar in a secluded covered dining area. Rooms opened onto a second-story balcony lined with a wrought iron railing wrapped in a variety of tropical vines and flowers. A pair of Australian finches chirped from a nearby bamboo cage.

Steve went to a corner of the courtyard where a sign that read OFFICE hung. When the two women inside saw his face, they both jumped up and greeted him warmly, eyeing Kelly as they hugged him. "I hope you'll be staying awhile, Steve," one of them said, selecting a key from a pegboard behind the desk.

"No, just overnight." Then a thought occurred to him, and he added, "We're flying out tomorrow morning." If they managed to track him down here, a little disinformation could go a long way.

Kelly sat on one of the double beds and Steve on the chair in their air-conditioned room, a welcome relief from the heat and humidity of downtown. They had emptied the bottled waters in the mini frig.

"I need to go out for a bit," he said.

"Why? We just got here."

"I'm going to call Doc and the police."

"The police?"

"Just an anonymous call so someone knows about Joseph and Martha."

"Oh. Why don't you use this phone?" she said, pointing to the one in the room, then realized her mistake.

"No big deal. I'll be back in less than an hour. Lock the door and leave the TV off. I'm sure you'll be safe here. But if anyone tries to force their way in and breaks the chain on the door, don't hesitate. That hand cannon of yours will make anyone think twice. Are you okay with that?"

She nodded. He started to get up and she caught his hand.

"We had a word of advice in the Marines," she said.

He raised his eyebrows.

"Don't fuck up."

"I think you guys borrowed that from the Navy," he replied.

"But seriously, be careful."

"Always," he said. He waited outside the door until he heard Kelly bolt it and slide the chain into its track. Then went downstairs and outside to the busy side street. A two-minute walk brought him to the main street in Charlotte Amalie. He spotted a phone, then thought better of it and hailed a cab. He told the driver to take him to the airport terminal on the west end of the island. If his call to the police was traced, they might think he was catching a plane to leave. He gave the officer who answered his brief message and hung up immediately.

Next, he had another cab take him to the cruise ship docks on the far side of the harbor, where he called Doc's girlfriend from a payphone.

Doc answered.

"You made it," Steve said.

"Yeah, no problems. What have you found out?"

"Joseph is dead, so is Martha."

"Oh no." The grief in Doc's voice was instantaneous. Although he had played a teasing game with Joseph that they both enjoyed, they had grown fond of each other's company through the years. Nothing would be the same without Joseph and Martha.

"They tortured him, Doc," Steve continued.

There was a pause before Doc said, "We need to deal with these bastards," an anger in his voice Steve had heard only once or twice in all the years he had known him.

"The key to this has something to do with my uncle's tug," Steve said. "I'm sure that's what they wanted from Joseph, just like the gunman at my house. They want to know where it is."

"That old rust bucket couldn't be worth anything," Doc said, thinking aloud, then corrected himself. "Oh, sorry, I know it had sentimental value to you."

"How's the patient?" Steve said, changing the subject.

"Gone. So is the deceased. A bunch from that big yacht at Red Hook came to get them after I left, against the protests of the clinic. They said they had their own surgeon on board."

"Yeah, they're going to deep-six them first chance they get."

"Probably," Doc said. "Oh yeah, another thing. Neither one of them had any fingerprints."

Steve didn't understand for a moment, then remembered Doc had seen mercenaries who'd had their fingerprints surgically burned to insure anonymity in the event of their capture. Dental work was another marketing ploy to increase their value as guns for hire.

"Okay, I'll check on the boat's registry," Steve said. "It was flying the flag of independent Chechnya but registered in the Caymans."

"Interesting," Doc said. "Long way from home."

"Yeah. See what you can find on your end. The name of the boat is *Conquest.*"

"Will do," Doc said.

"And, Doc."

"Yeah?"

"Don't do anything foolish on your own. We've been lucky so far. We'll pick the time and the place."

"Right," Doc replied, his British accent rising a bit to the surface. "See you soon."

Steve rode back to the hotel through late afternoon bumper-to-bumper traffic, thinking of a plan for the next day.

Kelly let him in to the room thirty minutes later, the .357 in her hand. A delicious wave of grilled meat invaded the room. Steve had two large Styrofoam to-go boxes in his hand and a bottle of wine in the other.

"There's a guy who sells the best grilled chicken and rice in the islands out of a stand on the main drag along the waterfront," he said. "Thought you might be hungry."

"Famished," she said. She put the pistol on the bedside table between them.

Exhausted by the events of the day, they pounced on their plates and shared the wine.

At the end of their emotional and physical reserve, they were both asleep as soon as they crawled into their beds.

15

In the morning, they took a cab ride to the public library. It was small, just a few thousand books, but Steve found a single new-looking computer with internet access, and after a few minutes, he had located a list of ship registries for the Cayman Islands. The big yacht was listed as belonging to a Swiss holding company, which to Steve meant it could be anyone. He tucked the information away for now.

Another cab ride found them at the small seaplane operation on the west side of the bay near their hotel. There was a scheduled passenger service there and a few private charter planes. Steve had noticed a Lake Buccaneer seaplane that would be perfect for what he had in mind.

He talked to the man behind the counter and chartered the Lake for the day. Steve told the man they'd be back in an hour, and he and Kelly took a ride to a dive shop at the other end of the bay, where he rented a tank, regulator, and buoyancy vest as well as mask, fins, and snorkel. They put them in the trunk of the cab and got in the back seat together. Steve told the driver to take them back to the seaplane base.

"Do you think we can find the tug?" Kelly asked as the cab drove along the road that followed the Charlotte Amalie waterfront.

"Yeah," he said. "It's just a little rock of an island, but I was there a lot with my uncle when I was a kid. We used to take a few days and fish all over that area. We'd always anchor there for the night."

"What do we do once we've found it?" she asked.

"Well, that's the hard part. I guess I'll look it over from top to bottom. Maybe there's something I missed, although I went through her pretty well before I took her out of Puerto Rico."

Neither of them spoke now as the cab drew closer to the seaplane base ahead. Then Steve heard Kelly say something. It was more like an exclamation than a word. She was staring straight ahead and then turned to him, her eyes shining like a new convert.

"They're not looking for the boat, Steve," she said with certainty. "They're looking for something on the boat. Maybe something they lost there. You said it was anchored for several years. There's no telling what that boat could have been used for. Maybe a drop point or a hiding place."

Steve considered it for a moment.

"Of course, he said, nodding in agreement. "That makes more sense than anything we've come up with so far." Kelly's epiphany instantly erased any lingering doubt he might have had about bringing her along. He might never have figured this mystery out without her.

"And it must be essential to them if they're willing to go to this much trouble to get it."

But he knew there were many people, especially like those they were dealing with, who would kill for little or no reason at all to make a point. He and Kelly couldn't be too careful, and as they pulled up to the seaplane base, he wondered if they had been careful enough.

———

When Steve and Kelly left the library earlier that day and went to the busy intersection to get a cab, one of over two hundred facial recognition cameras recently installed on the island matched their faces with a world-wide database. An APB had been issued for Steve the night before. He was now wanted for, among other things, the murder of Joseph and his wife. The digital imaging camera had scanned the photo with the one on file and made a match. The appropriate people had been called. One of them pushed a button on his secure satellite phone and was instantly connected.

"They're returning to the seaplane," he said into the phone.

"Return to base," the voice on the other end said.

The man put the phone away and took one last look at Steve and Kelly as they paid the cab driver and walked inside the seaplane terminal with their dive gear in tow.

16

They loaded the dive equipment on board the seaplane and climbed into the seats. Steve sat up front with the pilot after making sure Kelly was securely strapped in the back. The taxi and takeoff were short, and the small plane climbed and turned over the mouth of the bay to the southwest toward San Juan.

Steve found the approximate location of the island on a chart and showed it to the pilot. Thirty minutes later, they were approaching it—a minuscule sliver of rock no more than a hundred yards long. Deep blue water driven by strong easterly trade winds surged against the perimeter of the tiny island and exploded into a white lather as it struck the rocky shore.

The water around the sheltered southwest corner was turquoise above a steeply sloped sandy bottom, which offered a landing spot.

A lighted beacon nearly forty feet tall towered over the treeless island as a warning for ships at night. In addition to the light, the beacon's sheet metal sides had been designed to reflect a solid return to ship surface radar. Seagulls, pelicans, and frigate birds—called scissor birds by the Islanders because of the shape of their tails—fought for limited perches on its horizontal girders.

"That's it," Steve told the pilot through his headset. "Let's circle above the south side."

The pilot nodded and put the seaplane into a turn to circle the area while losing altitude. Steve explained to Kelly that he had anchored the tug on the edge of a shallow area about two acres in size that stood out like an oasis in the depths around it. He tried to catch a glimpse of the tug's murky form on the bottom but, after a few minutes, gave up as the pilot set up the downwind leg for his intended touchdown spot.

They landed on the smooth water of the leeward side of the island and taxied to the edge of the shallow area where Steve thought the tug had gone down. The pilot cut the engine and fished an anchor from a compartment near the back seat. He opened his gull-wing door and dropped the anchor to hold their position while Steve struggled to get into his dive gear in the cramped cabin. He managed all but the tank, which Kelly helped him put on when he was in the water.

"I'll watch you from the surface," she said after putting on the smaller set of mask, fins, and snorkel Steve had rented for her. He waved to her after inserting the regulator in his mouth and disappeared below the surface.

The water was warm, about eighty degrees, and Steve estimated the visibility at forty feet. From past experience anchoring here, he knew that the depth was closer to eighty feet. He stayed just under the surface for a minute, adjusting his buoyancy vest to remain suspended and scanning the water below him for any sign of the tug. He was disappointed he couldn't see the bottom. He had hoped that once in the water, he could pick out some sign of the boat—instead, he saw nothing but the opaque depths of the ocean.

He surfaced to take his bearing from the island and was astonished to find he was well behind the plane. A strong current, probably created as water flowed around the small island, had pushed him at least fifty yards away from the plane and the island in the short time he was submerged. He was now well out into deep water. Well, that was dumb. He knew better. Just rusty, he told himself. He waved to Kelly, who was hanging onto the wing pontoon in the water, her body language telegraphing some concern. Turning onto his back, he swam with effort to the plane. After five minutes of hard work, he arrived at Kelly's side, a little winded.

"Good current here," he said, removing the regulator from his mouth and holding on to the pontoon with her.

"I could tell," she said. "Another few minutes, and you'd have really been out there. Did you see anything?"

"No not yet. I'm going to swim toward the island, following the plane's anchor rope. If I can see the bottom, it'll be a good start."

"Okay. I'll follow you."

Steve descended again and found the anchor rope. This time, he kicked hard, consciously fighting the invisible current pushing him away from the island. After a few minutes, visibility increased significantly as sunlight filtering through the water above reflected off the sandy bottom, which was now considerably closer to the surface. But there was still no sign of the boat.

He could see the anchor on the bottom below him, its tines clawing into the coarse sand. He rolled upside down, scanning the surface for Kelly. She was directly above him, her slim body silhouetted against the sky like a photo from *National Geographic*. She gave him a thumbs-up.

He completed the roll and resumed his search of the bottom. The current had subsided now that he was in the shallow, protected water of the island. He had anchored the tug somewhere in here that fateful night and was surprised he couldn't see it yet.

He swam back and forth over the area, suspended by his buoyancy vest about fifty feet from the bottom. The visibility was much better now.

There were a few fish here and there, but he was in an underwater desert offering no food or cover for any marine life. He took a look at his pressure gauge. The tank was already half-empty. He would have to conserve his air from here on out.

Suddenly, he felt something touch his shoulder and spun around to find Kelly twenty feet below the surface with nothing but her snorkel gear and a big breath of air, pointing frantically down and to the right. He looked but saw nothing. He handed her his regulator, and she took several deep breaths and then pointed again in the same direction before making the free ascent to the surface.

He began to swim in the direction Kelly had pointed. From her position on the surface, she must have seen something he couldn't, hopefully the tug. The first thing to come into view was an enormous school of ballyhoo. Thousands of them. They hung in a silvery gray cloud in the water, an undulating mass of marine life in a seemingly deserted ocean. They were each about three inches long, probably hatched together weeks ago in the shallow-water nurseries around the island, now clinging to one another in this massive school and playing out nature's law of averages. Many would be eaten, but others—stronger, faster, and luckier—would survive, protected and hidden by those around them.

The cloud parted like a curtain on a stage as he drew closer. He saw the bow of the tug first, as a large part of the school moved away, and then he saw the rest of the boat.

It was sitting upright on the bottom with a slight list to starboard as if it had been placed there carefully for display. Seeing the tug there, a pang of remorse hit him out of nowhere. He had learned everything he knew about boats, fishing, and the sea on that old tug. His uncle was an excellent teacher. An anger welled up in him, and he stored it away for later use. The anchor chain was still attached to the bow, and he followed it toward the island, spotting the big anchor still biting into the sand where he had dropped it several months before.

He swam over the tug from bow to stern. The baitfish had attracted a variety of larger fish, which darted in and out of the wreck nervously as Steve swam above them. He could see several large grouper and snapper hiding inside. A quartet of barracuda poised motionless in formation just above the bottom, their long, straight bodies shining in the noonday sun as they rested between feeding frenzies on the baitfish.

He glanced at his pressure gauge again. It read a little under nine hundred pounds. The depth gauge beside it read fifty-five feet. He quickly estimated he would need to leave the bottom for a slow ascent to the surface with no less than four hundred pounds. He began to try to slow his breathing to conserve air.

He looked at the surface and saw Kelly. Again, she gave him a thumbs-up, and he returned it, then swam closer to the tug.

Releasing air from his vest, he let himself sink slowly to the deck and hovered on the stern just outside the wheelhouse. He carefully swam through the door to the stateroom. The machine gun wielded by the last would-be assassin lay on the floor, covered with a layer of slimy rust. An array of tarnished brass shells the gun had ejected were scattered nearby.

Then he saw the gun's owner, or what was left of him. Several large fish, probably sharks or big grouper, had torn the body to shreds. All that remained were remnants of cloth and shards of bones—picked clean by a variety of efficient marine life and scattered throughout the cabin.

He surveyed the rest of the cabin without a clue of what he was looking for. He avoided looking at the pressure gauge again and instead shallowed his breathing even more. His plan had been to look for something missing or out of place, but of course, everything was out of place. Charts, books, splinters of wood, and cushions floated everywhere, some stuck against the ceiling. Exasperated by the volume of loose material, Steve decided he would need another trip with more air tanks when he noticed the fire extinguisher.

It was a large commercial type, installed when the tug was new. Its bright-chromed body, rusting and tarnished by the saltwater, was still attached to the wall of the cabin where it had been for years. But as he stared at it, alarm bells suddenly went off in his head.

The large spot of dried blood he'd seen the morning he took the tug out of San Juan was directly below the fire extinguisher, not in the middle of the cabin on the way to the galley, but over here against the wall.

He started to put the pieces together. Someone had dripped a large drop of blood on the floor the night before he took it out. He had been working on the boat every day for a week before that, and he would have seen the blood if it had been there. He recalled the homeless man he'd given a ride to that day, but he wasn't injured or bleeding; Steve was sure of that. The old man had been wearing just a pair of shorts, and he'd have noticed a bleeding injury.

He could have left the cabin door unlocked the previous night. He remembered seeing the Coast Guard and local police talking at a nearby dock early the following day as he rowed his dinghy out to the tug. The police were taking notes as if preparing to file a report.

He looked again at the fire extinguisher and the wall around it. Nothing unusual.

On a hunch, he lowered himself enough to look up at the extinguisher from beneath. There it was, hidden in a recess in the base. A plastic Ziploc bag had been crammed up into the cylinder. He grabbed it, gave it a tug, and pulled it out.

Wiping away a film of brown-and-green algae covering the bag, he saw a small green notebook inside an inner bag. Steve recognized the type. It was a government issue, a three-by-five-inch pocket notebook with a cursive *Memoranda* on the front cover. He had used many like it himself before the advent of digital devices. They could easily fit into a back or inside coat pocket and were available to all branches of the military and federal government. Incredibly, the notebook appeared to be dry inside, and with it was a worn-down pencil. Careful notetakers always used pencils because ink would run and smear if it got wet.

At last, some of the answers to this crazy chain of events might be revealed. He placed the notebook in a pocket of his wetsuit top as carefully as if he were handling the first gold bar from a newly discovered Spanish galleon. Then he swam out of the cabin, glad to escape the gloom, and looked up to the surface.

His heart rate spun up as a shot of adrenaline raced through his body.

Kelly was gone. In her place were the twin pontoons of another float-plane. As he watched, there was a splash as something hit the surface beside the plane. The object was sinking rapidly to the bottom, not thirty yards from the tug. When it was halfway down, Steve realized it was a body.

In horror, he watched it fall, hoping and praying as it drew closer that he would not see Kelly's face. The body hit the bottom hard. With mixed feelings of relief and shock, he recognized their pilot. Blood was streaming from a gunshot wound to his head. An anchor had been strapped to his legs. His lifeless eyes were wide open in the underwater gloom with a frozen expression of horror. From the corner of his eye, Steve saw movement. He turned to see a bull shark thirty yards away, twitching its tail back and forth like a cat trying to incite panicked movement in its prey. The blood called the shark in, and Steve knew his friends would soon join him. He had successfully suppressed his neurosis of sharks in his dive to find the tug, but here they were. Of course they were—they had a score to settle with him.

Instinctively, he backed away from the blood-streaked body. The bull shark came closer, then sped up, took one of the pilot's arms in his mouth, and began to saw back and forth with his head to free it. It suddenly came lose and more blood filled the water. Lots more blood. Two more sharks appeared. In another few seconds, the three of them would go into a competitive frenzy to devour the rest of the body. Steve watched in horror, his breathing deep and rapid, trying to keep pace with his heart rate. He felt restricted breathing through his regulator, indicating he was almost out of air, and he was snapped back to the moment. Move your ass.

He looked at his pressure gauge. Top of the red arc—not good. Decision time.

He studied the surface. Steve had led these people right to the tug. They had Kelly, and they were waiting him out. It was obvious they would kill them both after they got the information they wanted, presumably the notebook. Then he and Kelly would join the other bodies on the bottom.

His only bargaining chip was the notebook. Watching his air bubbles, they would know exactly where he was, so he had to be extremely careful. He began to take even smaller breaths, exhaling a stream of comparably smaller bubbles in an attempt to conceal his position.

The seaplane they had flown in on was his only chance. He might be able to untie its anchor, let it drift out of gun range and escape on it, then make a deal with them later. If he tried to save Kelly now, they were both dead. He started swimming along the bottom toward the plane, carefully conserving what little air he had left. He would make a free ascent to the surface when he was under the plane.

But as he got closer, he saw the plane was half underwater, the fuselage filling rapidly. Apparently, after they killed the pilot, they'd scuttled the plane to hide any evidence.

Think, he told himself. Adjust. Make a plan B.

He immediately turned back toward the island, passing the tug and looking up to locate the other floatplane. He had an idea, but he was running out of both air and time.

He stopped directly under the plane and found a small piece of coral from the bottom. He slipped his tank, vest, and weight belt off, took several deep breaths, then carefully wedged the coral against the purge button of the regulator. A steady stream of air poured out of the mouthpiece as it dangled from the tank, and the bubbles rose straight up to the floatplane. Anyone watching for them would be convinced he was directly under them.

Satisfied, he swam off toward the island. When his lungs could no longer hold out, he started a slow ascent. As he approached the surface, the remaining air in his lungs expanded, giving him a few more seconds. Finally, he broke out into the clean, pure air as quietly and unobtrusively as possible. He couldn't suppress a gasp, but the swells had picked up, hiding him in their troughs.

The floatplane was less than fifty yards away. He saw a man standing on one of the pontoons, a machine gun in his hands, peering intently over the side. Clearly, he was waiting for Steve to surface under the dwindling bubbles and had taken the bait. Another man stood on the other pontoon, searching the surface but not looking in Steve's direction. He saw Kelly's silhouette inside the plane with that of a third man and had to suppress the overwhelming urge to go to her.

He took several deep breaths before letting himself sink below the waves, then dove deep and swam underwater for the tiny island, checking once to confirm that the now priceless notebook was still in his breast pocket.

17

Ray Ferguson sat in the stateroom of the giant catamaran and propped his feet up on the Swarovski glass tabletop. The bodyguard across the room sneered and shook his head in disgust as he turned away from the sight of another American pig.

Ferguson rattled the ice in his empty crystal highball glass and, seeing that no one would give him a refill, slowly got up and went over to the bar. He poured himself another generous serving of Double Eagle and looked out to the east end of St. Thomas.

This room, with its eye-shaped, heavily tinted windows, always reminded him of some scene out of that science fiction movie about Captain Nemo he had seen as a kid. He couldn't think of the name of the movie, but he remembered the inside of the submarine was decked out and overdone like this ship. He wouldn't be surprised if this crazy Russian, Chechen, or whatever the hell he was had a pipe organ in his cabin. These people had way too much money, and Ferguson needed to get as much of it as he could. He had already done well, but he needed more and would spend it much better than these overblown thugs.

He looked out on the crowded harbor of Red Hook. This was as close as he had been to United States soil since his elaborately orchestrated disappearance just a month ago.

He had been a DEA field agent. One of the best recruited from the military. He had risen to the top quickly. They had put him in deep cover early on, and he had done his job well, repeatedly uncovering evidence leading to the convictions of several big drug lords scattered around the world. He had been so good at it, he knew, because he was so much like the criminals he went after. Although he happened to have a badge, he thought just like they did.

But, in the end, it was a war he'd decided could never be won as long as there was a demand for the product—a demand that had not slowed but accelerated despite all of his efforts. America was still the greatest user of illicit drugs in the world, surpassing any other nation for quantity and quality. The government should legalize all of it. The taxes collected on drugs alone would solve a lot of the country's current economic woes.

Looking back on it, it was inevitable that after years of chasing bad guys and watching them being replaced by a multitude of other bad guys, after the divorce when his wife took more than her share of everything, including the kids he hardly knew, that he began to have a nagging feeling his life and his life's work were both worthless.

It was during that time he first began to think about going to work for the other side. The side that paid a lot more. He'd had offers before, of course, but from no one with the kind of money these people seemed to have. In a very short time, he would have enough to retire and live comfortably for the rest of his life.

He had traced a new source of heroin through the usual channels from the Middle East and then Africa, where all the big boys got their product. He had posed as a buyer from the States as he always had, a role he played so well not only from years of practice but because there was that big part of him that was indeed criminal. The shadowy Chechen source had been challenging to connect with at first, but he and Ferguson hit it off well in the end because they were so much alike. He had picked the exact moment to reveal himself when the stakes were higher than ever for both of them, and their relationship was solidified.

As Ferguson had foreseen, the Chechen employed him as an informant. He was brought into the fold in exchange for the information a man like him could provide about surveillance, hot spots, and areas of interest to the current administration in Washington. Within three months, the profits from their operation together had doubled. Good thing— they'd have killed him otherwise.

He had fabricated his own death at the hands of one of the Chechen's main competitors—a group of Nigerians who had become a real thorn in his expansion in Atlanta and the southeast. The DEA had taken the bait and bought the story in full, believing that the Nigerians had discovered his identity, killed him, and disposed of his body. It had all gone so well that the DEA had taken its vengeance on the Nigerians, eliminating that competition as well. Ferguson now had two million laundered and invested euros in Zurich, as well as a monthly stipend that beat the hell out of being a self-righteous DEA man.

But of course, there had been a few complications, which was why they were here in the Virgin Islands. For starters, he'd had to give up his partner. They had known each other in the military and came to the DEA about the same time. They had been assigned to the same region before finally becoming partners. That hadn't been so tough, though, he told himself as he drained his bourbon. The guy was so damn annoying. Always better than him in everything, a real boy scout, always trying to do the right thing, blah, blah, blah. With him, it was always black and white, good and evil, no in between.

Ray had always felt dumb around the guy, inadequate. So, in the end, yeah, it was easy to give him up to his new friends. He had collected way too much info on them, and they wanted him dead. He was ready to report on their whole operation and stop them cold, but he never got the chance. They caught up with him in San Juan. Ray had seen to that. He rattled his ice and thought about the last time he'd seen his partner and what he had said: "I think I may be onto something big, and I don't trust anyone but you, Ray." What an asshole.

But they'd never found his damn notebook. Ray had told them about it, how the guy was old-fashioned, never used a computer to store information, always wrote it down in that stupid little government-issue notebook with that stupid little stubble of a government-issue number two pencil. He kept that notebook with him all the time. Ray had emphasized how important it was to make sure they had the notebook first, then kill him, but somehow, they'd bungled it.

Now they were back to find the damn thing. It had most of the plan in it. That was bad enough, but it also had something that Ferguson, ironically, he thought, had only written down on a piece of paper because he didn't want to risk losing it on a digital device. Something the man from Grozny had given him personally when they met in Paris. And turns out Stodd knew Ferguson had flipped when they were still partners—just before he was killed. The fat prick had taken it from Ferguson's desk drawer. And they had to get it back—he had to get it back—or he wouldn't live to spend all that money.

He stopped staring out the Captain Nemo window and poured himself another drink, overfilling his glass.

18

For what seemed an eternity, Steve swam underwater, trying to put as much distance as he could between him and the floatplane. It was strange what popped into his head while his heart pounded and his muscles depleted the oxygen in his lungs. He suddenly thought of the time, years ago in Navy flight training, when instructors made the whole class jump one by one off a high platform into that Olympic-size pool and swim underwater as long as they could to simulate abandoning a burning ship with burning fuel and oil on the surface. There'd been a competition with another class to see who could swim underwater the farthest. Steve won it for his class when he doubled the length of the pool. The memory inspired him to keep going.

Finally, he broke the surface, gasping for air, and looked back at the plane. The men with the guns were still looking at the water, and one of them was putting on dive gear. Steve watched him disappear below the surface. The man on the opposite pontoon was talking to someone in the plane.

Steve took another deep breath and slipped below the surface. The island was close now, only thirty yards away. The sand bottom was speckled with coral rock outcrops from the island.

He decided to circle the small island to the other side, away from the plane. After another ten minutes of swimming underwater and cautiously surfacing for air, he reached the windward, much rougher side. Waves crashed into the algae-covered igneous rock, making it extremely difficult to climb out of the water. Only his wetsuit and neoprene swim boots protected him from the sharp rocks as he was slammed against them. Exhausted, he managed to climb out and away from the pounding waves.

The entire island was only two to three feet above sea level, and he had to stay down in a crawl so as not to be seen. He stole a look at the plane. The diver was still underwater. Good. He needed time to rest and think. It wouldn't be long before they had figured out what he had done if they hadn't already.

He couldn't stay here, yet there was nowhere else to go. The only conceivable hiding place was the Coast Guard hazard marker firmly anchored in the center of the island. Then he noticed a two-by-four-foot hinged metal door on one side of its square base, probably for access to the bank of heavy batteries that powered the marker day and night. He crept over and opened the creaking door, standing to look inside it. The base of the tower shielded him perfectly from the floatplane. The compartment was large enough for a man to hide in, but they were sure to search it. As he stood there thinking, he realized he was standing in a puddle of saltwater deposited in a shallow bowl in the rock by the crashing waves.

He stepped out of the puddle and decided to leave them a message.

Working quickly, he found the main power lead coming from the batteries to the lighted buoy. With a few hard tugs, he pulled the lead wire loose from its corroded bracket and then closed the door, leaving himself just enough room to work. Holding it by its insulated jacket, he touched the exposed wire to the metal door, jamming it into the hinge and electrifying the door and the entire metal buoy. Carefully, he stepped away from his handiwork. The trap was perfect. The door was open an inch or two as if someone had hurriedly hidden inside. The high amperage of the bundled batteries combined with the added effect of the saltwater footbath would give at least one of them a really bad hair day.

Better finish than they gave Joseph.

He returned to the windward side of the tiny island, using the buoy structure as cover, and slid back into the water with only his head visible. Now, he could safely catch a glimpse of the floatplane. The diver was back. All three men were looking intently at the island. His only option now was to swim back out to sea. With luck, he could wait until they finally left and, if he had enough energy left, swim back to the island. It wasn't much of a plan, but it was all he had.

He was about to push off when he saw the sailboat. It was small, under full sail, about two miles away. After studying it for a few seconds, he calculated it was on a course that would bring it a mile or so closer to the island. He decided it was worth a try to swim for it. He didn't dare hail it, of course. If he attracted the attention of the men on the plane, he and whoever was on the boat would die. But if he timed it just right, he might be able to intercept it.

He heard the sound of the plane's engine starting and, a moment later, watched it begin to taxi toward his position. They would beach the floatplane and be on the island in less than five minutes. He started swimming.

Keeping a pace that wouldn't tire him too soon, he still had to swim fast enough to intercept the distant sailboat. A fast endurance pace, he used to call it—when he was a hell of a lot younger. The island blocked any view of him from the floatplane, so he was able to swim on the surface without having to worry about being seen. As he settled into a labored but natural rhythm, his thoughts returned to the Navy and the last time he'd swum a mile.

It was during those first weeks of Aviation Officer Candidate School in Pensacola. Everyone enrolled had to swim a mile in their flight suits to qualify for the program. This was part of a rigorous agenda that included escaping underwater from a submerged helicopter mockup while blindfolded, treading water for thirty minutes in full flight gear and boots without a floatation device, and a variety of other nautical tortures the Navy thought necessary in enabling pilots to fly overwater missions, get shot down, and survive. It was easy for him, though. His enlisted Navy training had him swimming much farther distances. Although he had never gotten used to that damn helo dunker.

The training had steeled him, and one of the rewards had been the confidence to attempt the next to impossible without questioning or doubting himself. Crazy things—like swimming out to sea to catch a boat moving through the water at maybe fifteen miles an hour.

He raised his head to look at the sailboat. It was still on its original course but coming much faster than he had anticipated. He was in deep water now, at least half a mile from the island.

A squadron of flying fish broke the surface around him, gliding through the air, then folding their fin wings and slipping back into the deep water, escaping their pursuers. A hundred small mackerel were forced out of the water right in front of him, and he caught a glimpse of a blackfin tuna breaking the surface with a mackerel in its mouth. The school of mackerel showered down on him like living rain, and then they were gone. Steve was thankful for the distraction; he was getting dangerously tired now.

When he looked up again, the sailboat was much closer, and he adjusted his own course to rendezvous with it. He saw for the first time that it was towing a small dinghy behind it, and a young, topless woman was stretched out in the cockpit reading a book. Steve ignored the sideshow and concentrated on the sailboat, increasing his speed to the swimming equivalent of a sprint. If he missed the sailboat, he would be stuck well offshore and exhausted. At last, he was within yards of it—but he realized it was moving too fast, and he was going to miss it. He spent the last of his energy in a desperate attempt to reach it, but all he could do was read the name on its stern as it passed him by.

The dinghy trailed behind the boat by no more than thirty feet. With a final desperate kick, he lunged for the dinghy as it sped by, but his outstretched hand merely slid off the slick side of the high gunnels. The instant he realized he had missed his chance completely, and despair threatened to envelop his mind like an old familiar demon, his hand felt a rope and grabbed it.

A stern line from the dinghy had somehow found its way into the water and trailed behind. It snatched him along with it, and he was suddenly part of the conga line. He hung there for a while and let the boat drag him through the water, trying to hold on to his lifeline. Then, with one final push, using a last reserve of energy he had seldom tapped, he hoisted himself over the stern and into the dinghy. He quickly looked forward to the sailboat to see if the topless woman had noticed. He was sure his maneuvering into the dinghy and added weight would have had an effect on the small sailboat.

The woman looked up from her book at the set of the sails and scanned ahead as if something had happened, but she wasn't sure what. When Steve saw her start to turn around to look at the dinghy, he flattened himself in the bottom of the bow as best he could. The bow of the little boat was high up in the water because of the tow configuration, and Steve hoped it was hiding him from view. If he was discovered, he'd have to do some complicated explaining that probably wouldn't go well.

After a few minutes, nothing had happened. He raised his head. The woman had resumed reading her paperback, and Steve gave thanks to fiction writers everywhere. He lay in the dinghy, staring up at the cloudless sky and slowly catching his breath. He wanted to lie there in the sun and go to sleep, but with a great effort, he peered over the rail at the island.

The men were there now. They had taxied the floatplane up to the shore. One of them was walking up to the marker. Steve watched as the man, standing in the puddle of saltwater, grabbed the handle of the metal door. He convulsed wildly for what seemed like a very long time, unable to release the handle until he was finally thrown clear and lay motionless on the ground. His companion walked over, prodded him a few times, then looked at the floatplane.

The commotion had brought the third man out of the plane, and Steve could see him clearly for the first time. He was a small man dressed in camo-green infantry pants and shirt. He walked over to the dead man, looked around the island, and then motioned for the other to return to the plane. What happened next was crucial, and Steve watched with laser focus. The floatplane taxied into the deeper water. If they were going to get rid of Kelly, they would do it now. The plane turned around quickly, facing the wind, accelerated, and took off. It turned immediately toward St. Thomas, and Steve blew out the breath he had unconsciously been holding.

He lay back in the dinghy and thought of his next move, not the least of which was how to let the topless woman know she had a stowaway. After looking at the islands around him, he realized that the sailboat was on a perfect course to eventually pass near his cottage on St. John. He felt the notebook in his breast pocket and, after a moment of consideration, took it out. He was ready for the answers that were written on its pages. He opened the outer Ziploc bag and removed the inner sealed bag containing the notebook. Someone had been very meticulous about preserving its contents. He pulled the notebook out of the inner bag and opened it.

19

When Kelly first knew she was in danger, it was too late. She had been so intent on helping Steve locate the tug that she never knew the floatplane had landed, captured their pilot, and taxied over to where she was snorkeling. Her breathing through the snorkel, the sounds of waves crashing on the island, and her own splashing had masked the sounds of the plane's approach.

She felt proud to have found the tug for Steve, able to really provide some help in trying to solve the mystery surrounding the sunken boat. That feeling ended abruptly when she was snatched from the water like a fish in a net.

She watched in horror as the man in the green fatigues questioned their pilot at gunpoint, asking him repeatedly who knew of their whereabouts. Then, convinced that no one at the seaplane base knew their precise position, he made the pilot walk to the end of the floatplane's pontoon, where he shot him in the back of the head. Kelly jumped in her seat at the unexpected report of the pistol and the cold, inhuman efficiency of the murder. Still, she was unprepared for the look in the murderer's eyes as he turned to look at her as if she might be next.

Her heart sank, and fear began to well up in her as she watched the other men tie the anchor to the dead pilot's feet and shove him into the water. His body left a trail of blood that was swept away in seconds as if he had never existed.

She was trembling, doing her best to quell the absolute terror welling up inside her that threatened to make her scream uncontrollably. She tried at first to avoid the stare of the man in fatigues but then looked beseechingly into his eyes with an unspoken but desperate plea for her life. Adding to the uncertainty, he said something to the other two in a language she didn't recognize. She fought for control of herself as one of the men produced two plastic tie wraps and bound her wrists securely, then transferred her to their floatplane and tied her to the armrest in the back seat. It was more than a few minutes before she realized her life had been spared.

Gradually, she regained her composure and began to scan the surface for any sign of Steve's air bubbles. But the waves obscured them, hiding him below for the time being.

Now, flying over the southwest coast of St. Thomas, Kelly tried to imagine what had happened beneath the surface. Had Steve drowned, or had he managed to escape somehow? She watched a big commercial jet make its approach to the airport, bringing hundreds of people to the islands for a few days to spend their real or imagined disposable income. Seeing the jet made her question her judgment in staying to help Steve. The normal life she had known recently had gone off track, or she had been thrown out of it and was in freefall. She shoved the thought away. She belonged here—she was sure of that. Somehow, these people would be stopped, even if she had to do it herself. Being a Marine had given her the strength she needed now, especially the time she spent in Iraq, when, on any given day, she could have been captured by the enemy and put through unspeakable horrors as a woman.

No one in the plane spoke as they flew across the south side of the island. In another five minutes, they were over Red Hook, where the big yacht had anchored, but Kelly was surprised to see it was gone. They continued for some time to the northeast until arriving over a smaller island which, with its abundance of pleasure boats, sailing yachts, and inter-island ferries, Kelly surmised must be Jost Van Dyke. She had heard Steve and Doc discussing it as an island especially popular with the yachting crowd.

The mega yacht was anchored here now, off by itself as at St. Thomas. The pilot made a precautionary low pass over his intended landing site, looking for hidden obstacles or reefs just under the surface, then brought the plane around and landed. As they taxied toward the yacht, a small boat came out to meet them. They transferred to the ship with the floatplane in tow. In a few minutes, they were approaching a gangway on the starboard side.

Kelly had underestimated the size of the ship when she'd first seen it the day before. The sides of the yacht towered above them as they pulled into its immense shadow. She had forgotten that it was actually a catamaran, a dual-hulled design connected by a midsection that gave the ship better stability and much more room than a conventional monohull. A large crane was swinging out over the stern, and as she was pushed up the steps, she saw crewmen hooking up the floatplane with nylon straps as if in preparation to hoist it aboard.

She was hurried on board into the center of the ship between the hulls. One of the men held the back of her arm firmly and guided her into a large stateroom. He motioned for her to sit on a leather couch facing a wall of tinted windows. She could see the inviting white beaches of the island less than half a mile away and moaned inwardly that she was a prisoner here instead. The man in fatigues sat across from her and gave her a cold stare. His men stood guard around the room as if she might overpower them and escape. She glared back at him with contempt. Slowly, her fear began to subside and be replaced with anger. She thought of Joseph, his wife Martha, and again of the floatplane pilot. These men were the ones responsible for their senseless death and torture.

"What do you want from me?" she asked.

The man just stared back at her as if in a trance, his half-closed eyes sightless and bored, like an indolent lizard in the sun. A door opened at one end of the room, and Kelly noticed the guards, and the man seemed to tense. She didn't know what to expect from their reaction, and her fear returned instantly. She would not have been surprised if Satan himself were to walk in.

Instead, a short man in his late fifties strolled in as if he were the host of a dinner party. He looked directly into her eyes, and she was aware of an electrifying presence about him that she had experienced only a few times, usually around men of power.

She broke his gaze with some effort and saw a stunning blond woman trailing behind him. About thirty, the woman seemed uncomfortable in the room, as if she had been forced to be there. Kelly noticed with some relief that the woman's face seemed humane and sympathetic in the few seconds that their eyes met. Then the woman looked away and sat in a padded chair near the windowed wall.

A third person came in behind the woman, younger than the first man. Izod golf shirt and shorts. Probably American. He looked at her hard, but she glared back at him, and he, too, looked away and took a chair beside the woman.

The first man came over and sat on the small table in front of her, leaning so close that their faces were nearly touching. His languid movements reminded her of a jungle cat.

"I'll make this simple for you," he said with a Slavic accent. "Tell us everything you know about your friend Steve Remington and his little sunken boat." He paused for dramatic effect. "Or we will kill you, and your body will be thrown overboard and eaten by whatever swims below this ship tonight. Then we'll find your family and kill them all. No one will ever know what happened to you or why."

One of the guards in the room handed him an iPad, and he turned the screen toward Kelly. There was a recent surveillance photo of her mother holding a bag of groceries. The following few pictures showed her brother playing with his kids in their front yard, her sister standing in a line at Starbucks, and her father fishing off their dock on the secluded lake in Maine.

Kelly had no reason to doubt his words. This guy oozed evil. She could feel it. It frightened her like she had never been frightened before. He wouldn't hesitate to kill her or her family. But she was suddenly sure Steve was alive. And in her last glimpse of him from the surface above the sunken tug, he was holding something in his hands, studying it intently. She knew in her heart he had found the missing piece of information that would unravel this mystery—and it was also clear these people wanted it dearly. This was the one thing that might keep her alive.

She looked again at the woman across the room and caught her eye. The sympathy was there again, if only for a second before the woman looked away. Sympathy and something more. But then she looked back at Kelly and held her gaze with an expression that said clearly to please tell them what they want. Somehow, this gave Kelly the confidence she was grasping for.

"Who the hell are you, and what do you mean by kidnapping me?" she snapped at the short man in front of her.

She never saw him move until it was too late, but she felt the numbing sting of the backhanded slap across her face. She had been slapped only once, a long time ago when she was a child, and the humiliation of it stung more than the pain. She made an instinctive motion to fight back, but he anticipated it and caught her by the wrist with one hand and grabbed her hair at the back of her head with the other, a maneuver he had no doubt performed many times on women. He wrenched her head back, making her look up at him.

She whimpered, "You're hurting me," in a small voice, and instantly regretted it.

"Always the same, you American women," he said. "You want to act like a man, be treated like a woman, and behave like a child. You know nothing of your place and the proper way a woman should behave. Your sick country promotes your insolence through its perverted television shows and Hollywood movies. Your politicians court it to gain your vote."

She dared not speak again. His polished mask had been torn away. There was nothing but dark rage in his eyes now. Then he released her and sat back a little. As quickly as it had vanished, the mask returned, and he was once again the host at the dinner party. The transformation was sudden and complete.

"My name is Ruslan Malikov," he said. "This is my friend Mr. Ferguson, formerly of the American DEA. And this," he said, gesturing to the man in fatigues, "is, well, we just call him Treacher."

"Now that we have the formalities out of the way," he continued, "tell me what you know. For starters, why did you return to the sunken boat?"

Kelly looked at the woman again. She gave Kelly an almost imperceptible nod. Perhaps the woman had been brought into the room for just this moment, it occurred to her. But still, there was something else in the woman's eyes that gave her a shred of hope.

Kelly took a deep breath and let it out.

"Steve couldn't figure out why someone wanted him dead," she said. "Until one of the men you sent to the cottage told him you were looking for the boat, and we figured out it wasn't the boat you wanted, but something on it."

"And?"

"Just before you kidnapped me, I saw Steve holding something he'd found underwater—on the tug," she said, choosing her words carefully.

There was an instant reaction among the three men, and Kelly feared she might have said too much, even though she felt she was confirming what they already suspected.

"Now, see?" Malikov said as if speaking to a small child. "That wasn't so hard, was it?"

"Take her below," Malikov said. He stood up and walked out of the room. The woman and Ferguson followed, leaving Kelly alone with Treacher, who had the beginning of a sardonic smile on his thin, pale lips.

———

Malikov sat on one of the leather couches in his master stateroom, having a glass of some rare vintage wine he had already forgotten the name of. The 2,250-square-foot stateroom had its own deck perched on top of the mega yacht. It offered a nearly 360-degree panoramic view, broken only on the aft side of the room by the gilded glass-doored elevator that was off-limits to the entire crew except Treacher, who sat across from him drinking from a crystal glass, a bottle of Orezza mineral water nearby.

"Give me an update," Malikov said.

"We're doing a hands-off trial run tonight," Treacher said. "We're simulating the exact distance from the launch point to the target. We're even throwing in a few more acute turns than will be required for the actual run."

Malikov sipped his wine, waiting for Treacher to continue.

"It will be totally autonomous, capable of operating . . ."

"Yes, I know what autonomous means."

"Right. We are checking the accuracy of that tonight. The engineer we hired is very competent, and the system installed is state of the art."

"Yes. I know that," Malikov said. "Just let me know when the trial run is complete."

"Should be within the hour," Treacher replied.

Malikov, his conversation now complete, focused on an iPad he held in his lap. Treacher took his cue, poured himself another glass of the mineral water, and left the room. Malikov watched him depart and hoped they had thought of everything.

20

Steve finished reading the notebook for the second time as he lay in the bottom of the dinghy. He wanted to make sure he hadn't missed anything because he had more questions than answers. He drew a big breath, blew it out, and stared at the cloudless sky. A story was there in tiny, neat print covering all available space on each page. There were no blank pages, and at the end, on the inside of the back cover, was the writer's premonition of his own death. Because of the sheer number of words crammed in, he had expected a complete police report. Instead, he had a compilation of short notes jotted down hurriedly, sometimes hard to connect or understand, and sometimes in a code that Steve suspected was understood only by the writer. However, enough information was strewn throughout the pages to piece together at least half of the story.

The author of the notebook was a United States Drug Enforcement agent. His name, title, address, and telephone number were printed on the inside front cover, followed by "DEA-Miami, FL."

He looked at the name again. Frank Stodd. Steve surmised Stodd had hidden the notebook on the tug the night before he took the tug out of the harbor in San Juan. It was Stodd's blood on the deck by the fire extinguisher that morning, and the police never saw it, probably because they never knew to look there. Steve had arrived at the docks well after all the commotion that brought in the Coast Guard, so he hadn't given the dried reddish spot much thought at the time, but now the pieces were fitting together. The mysterious and ensuing attempts on his own life and the ruthless murders of those around him were all because this little notebook had been hidden by happenstance on his tug. Steve summarized the scribblings as best he could.

The entries dated back two years. Stodd had tracked a new flow of heroin from a variety of cities in the southeast. The source had originated somewhere in the Caribbean near San Juan. A suspect had been identified, and Stodd routinely passed his information up the chain at the DEA, but the reply he always got was that they needed more evidence to pursue the case.

Stodd called an old Army buddy he trusted, now working for the CIA at Langley, to see what he could find out. Then the story really got interesting.

The CIA did have a file on the guy. The file was incomplete, and they had learned most of what they knew from one of their field informants. She was Malikov's longtime girlfriend and was turned some years ago. She extracted a great deal of personal information through pillow talk and accompanying him wherever he went.

His name was Ruslan Malikov. He had been a fairly high-ranking KGB officer in the former Soviet Union. His early days as a military advisor in the troublesome Caucasus had introduced him to an American POW in one of the many camps the KGB routinely visited. He had turned the American major against his fellow prisoners. This American's name was the one they called Treacher now, and he was on a most-wanted list by most law enforcement agencies on the planet.

The relationship was the beginning of a long and successful partnership. The two had worked together for years in various Soviet theaters after Chechnya, including Afghanistan and Nigeria, where they cultivated contacts that made their heroin trafficking business one of the most lucrative in the world. They had amassed a fortune, most of it safely tucked away in so many far corners of the world that it drew no suspicion.

In recent years, they had refined their smuggling methods, which had always included offloading Nigerian freighters and delivering the heroin to US East Coast cities. There were problems, however—including newer and better radar coverage to intercept small boats heading to shore from the freighters.

The CIA had turned the information over to the DEA. The case was given to the Miami office, and Stodd's boss had assigned the case to him and Ferguson. Then the case hit a wall. The product was still getting through, but no delivery boats were being intercepted.

Shortly after that, Stodd began to suspect that his partner, Ray Ferguson, might have flipped. Ferguson was suddenly spending money he couldn't possibly have. Stodd reported his suspicion quietly to his boss, and a week later they were detached to San Juan to continue the case. Stodd decided to tail Ferguson whenever possible. He rented an unmarked panel van and parked it near the field office.

Two nights later, after checking out a parabolic microphone and binoculars from the office, he followed Ferguson to an upscale bar and parked the van, hoping to catch a glimpse of whoever he might be meeting. Stodd got a lot more than a glimpse. After a few minutes, Ferguson and five men appeared on the vacant deck outside the bar. Stodd identified Malikov and Treacher from the CIA file pictures. He also recognized US Senator Weloc from interviews on news channels. Of the other two men, one was a Middle Eastern man with a patch over one eye whom Stodd had never seen before, and the last man was a spook. Stodd had seen this man somewhere in his past, and he definitely belonged to one of the three-letter intelligence agencies in or near Washington. He had jotted this down quickly in the notebook, the handwriting hurried and incongruous with the rest.

Malikov would be paid two billion dollars upon the successful completion of the deal, half of it up front. The Middle Eastern participant referred to the financiers of the plan only in vague terms.

The last entry in the notebook read simply: "Must report this at once, think I've been made, maybe too close this time."

Steve closed the notebook and carefully returned it to the Ziploc bags. Stodd must have been spotted at the bar. There was no doubt they had pursued him to the docks and murdered him.

Steve put together what he knew. Someone was paying this Malikov guy two billion dollars for something. That's two billion with a *b*. A big *b*. That was much more than a whole bunch of drug runs. A US senator, a Middle Eastern man, a spook from God knows which agency, and two drug runners working together. And they wanted this notebook and were willing to keep stacking up a hefty body count to get it.

This thing was big, and he had a really bad feeling about it.

21

Kelly was taken down several stairs to a cabin with no windows. A heavy-duty hinge and lock had been secured to the outside of the door to make escape impossible. The guard pushed her inside and locked the steel door. She was in the forwardmost bow of one of the hulls on the ship's lowest level. The two walls opposite the door came to a point forming the bow, and the entire room smelled of mildew as if something wet had been stored there. She stood holding her elbows with her hands for a moment, trying to calm herself, then looked around for something they might have missed that could possibly help her escape. The cabin was tiny, with only a small bed, toilet, and sink. Except for a wall mounted TV, it made a perfect prison cell. It quickly became obvious to her there was no way out.

She turned on the television with a remote and flipped through the channels. At least half of them were in Spanish, broadcasting from San Juan. She was ready to turn it off when she recognized Joseph and Martha's house. A local news crew had drawn a small crowd of spectators as a young Hispanic woman delivered her live report in Islands-accented English.

"Police here say they have a suspect in the murders," the newswoman was saying. "He is identified as Steve Remington, who police describe as an employer of the victims."

Steve's photograph was flashed on the screen.

"There is a manhunt underway for Remington," the reporter said.

Kelly couldn't believe what she was hearing. Mesmerized, she watched as three uniformed police officers came out of the house.

"Here's Police Chief Haines now," the reporter said. "Chief Haines, do you have any comments?"

"We have just recovered shell casings from the scene, which we believe will prove to have come from the suspect's gun," the policeman said brusquely, gesturing for one of the accompanying officers to answer any further questions. Kelly watched as another uniformed cop came through the front door. The reporter approached him.

"This is Officer Cockerel, second-in-command of the St. Thomas police force," the reporter said. "Sir, can you give us any more information on these brutal murders?"

"As the chief said, we believe the fingerprints on the shell casings just recovered inside will match those of the suspect, Steve Remington. He was seen here yesterday with an unidentified woman, possibly an accomplice. If anyone has any information leading to the whereabouts of these two people, please let us know."

Kelly watched the rest of the slanted report in shock, which the young woman was unabashedly dramatizing. Steve was right to distrust the local police. Malikov had covered his tracks well. So, Haines and Cockerel were the dirty ones, probably others to a lesser degree. They had certainly paid a visit to the cottage and recovered Steve's shell casings from yesterday. At the very least, they had lifted his prints and transferred them to their own casings.

"Son of a bitch!" she shouted to the empty room.

The news gave way to a commercial, and Kelly turned off the television and threw the remote against the wall. Then she lay on the bed, her cheek now sore and bruised from Malikov's backhand, and stared at the ceiling, wondering if Steve was still alive.

22

Steve's next thought was to hail the woman in the sailboat in front of him, use her phone or radio to call the Coast Guard, and tell them what he had just discovered. But what did he really have? A notebook with half of the story. An extremely suspicious story, one that had a very nasty ending if allowed to go on, but an incomplete story just the same.

He thought of Kelly, alone and a prisoner on the boat or in some other location by now. They would kill her and dispose of her body at the first hint of any threat. He couldn't, wouldn't, let that happen.

He held the thought for a moment, but it was interrupted by the memory of his wife, dead for more than twenty years now. He rarely thought of Janice during the day; she usually surfaced in his dreams. Suddenly, he could see her sitting at her desk in the North Tower, the vivid image of an airliner growing larger in the window behind her. With an effort, he erased it, wondering why it had come to him now.

There was no immediate danger—Steve felt certain of that. Otherwise, Malikov and his men wouldn't be chasing him here in the Virgin Islands. There was still time to get Kelly out safely and notify the authorities. No use sounding the alarm prematurely. For now, at least, he refused to consider losing another person to another bunch of sociopaths. He would discuss this with Doc at the first opportunity, not only for the benefit of his advice but in case something happened to him. Doc would have his back, whether he welcomed the responsibility or not.

Steve heard something on the sailboat and cautiously raised his head to see an older man at the wheel. He watched him adjust the jib, then go to the auto helm, where Steve could see and feel him alter their course a few degrees. Their new track would take them clear of St. Thomas and out into the Caribbean. He looked off to the north and studied the islands, careful to keep his head down as much as possible. He was thankful for the long line the sailboat had paid out to the dinghy, making it difficult to see inside the towed boat. They were south of the gap between St. Thomas and St. John, and he could barely make out through the haze the Red Hook ferry in its crossing between the two islands. He estimated his distance to the southern tip of St. John at just under three miles. He lifted the dinghy's gas can. Almost full.

The man at the helm was adjusting the mainsail, perhaps wanting to squeeze a few more knots out of the boat. This was Steve's chance. Carefully, he pulled up slack in the tow line and untied it from the dinghy, leaving his arm strength alone as the sole link between the two boats. He waited, feeling the sudden pull of the sailboat—stronger than he'd anticipated—against the drag of the dinghy. He wondered how long he could hold the dinghy like this when he heard the loud crank of the mainsheet winch as the man tightened the sail.

Steve let go of the towline. Released of its burden, the sailboat picked up speed. No doubt attributing the sudden acceleration to his seamanship, the man at the helm said something to the sunbather, whom Steve couldn't see, and returned below.

When he was safely out of earshot of the sailboat, Steve lowered the dinghy's outboard motor into the water, squeezed the priming bulb, set the choke, and pulled the start cord. Nothing happened.

He pulled it again. Nothing. He was beginning to question the wisdom of his decision to leave himself stranded offshore in this small boat, with the wind and current pushing him out to sea, when he pulled on the cord a third time.

The engine caught. He quickly adjusted the choke as if trying to light a fire with his last match in a frozen wasteland. After a few seconds, the motor was idling nicely. He turned toward Cruz Bay and twisted the throttle handle wide open. There was no more time to lose.

23

The bar Doc's girlfriend, Sarah, owned was called The Channel, presumably after the Sir Francis Drake Channel, the main waterway that wound through the Virgin Islands. It was the Island version of an English pub a few blocks off the waterfront street of Road Town, Tortola. She'd made only a few changes after buying the place, preserving the charm dating back to its reconstruction after the fire of 1853 that destroyed most buildings in the small port town. The pub's stone walls still showed the fire's sooty stains near the ceiling and around the tops of the windows. The Channel made a good profit from the tourists and yacht people who wandered in but never got too busy or crazy to become drudgery.

Doc had met Sarah years ago when they served together in the British Army. She was a nurse then, and they worked together on a hospital ship in the Falklands. By chance, years later, he stopped at the pub shortly after coming to the islands, lured in by a prominent sign in the front window advertising his favorite beer. It was one of the most wonderful days in Sarah's life when Doc walked through the door.

They had often talked on the hospital ship, when cold South Atlantic winds were blowing across the Falklands, of how nice it would be to retire someplace warm. The notion had stuck in Sarah's head. After she retired from the nursing corps, she set her sights on the British Virgin Islands, never dreaming she would ever see Doc again. She'd had a crush on him then, and she still did.

Doc was sitting at the end of the bar with his back against the wall when Steve slipped in the back door through the kitchen and cracked the door to the bar a few inches. He looked past Doc and Sarah to survey the people sitting at the tables. They were the usual group of tourists and Islanders—no one out of place. He walked in and took a seat next to Doc.

Doc sat up suddenly, and Sarah was about to greet him when Steve put his finger to his lips in an effort to avoid attention.

"Where's Kelly?" Doc asked immediately.

Steve told him of the events of the day while Sarah poured Steve a beer from the tap. After Sarah left them to wait on a table, he explained to Doc about finding the notebook and what was revealed in it.

Doc was shocked. Like Steve, he had never imagined something of this magnitude. The involvement of a US senator and intelligence agency people, combined with the amount of money promised for the job, clearly pointed to a conspiracy of some kind. He took a long sip of his beer and lit a cheroot, exhaling the blue smoke toward the ceiling.

"You know we can't go to the police," he said, addressing the small cigar in his hand. "Telling anyone else right now would get Kelly killed. Besides, with no real evidence, the notebook and everything that's happened is just a work of fiction."

Steve nodded and he saw Doc relax a little. Doc was prepared to argue his point with Steve if need be. He was glad but not at all surprised his friend he knew so well had quickly reached the same conclusion.

"I'm going to get her off that boat," Steve said with an air of determination that left no doubt about the matter.

They began to formulate a plan. Doc already knew about the catamaran's new location through his intricate network of friends throughout the islands. They were a poor lot, and he gave them free medical help more often than not. It certainly wasn't easy to hide a boat like that just anywhere. Everyone in the community was talking about it.

"They're provisioning her right now for a trip," Doc said. "They put a nice dent in the fuel supply at West End topping her off before they left.

Now they're anchored off Jost Van Dyke, and everyone thinks they'll soon be underway, perhaps tonight or tomorrow."

"Destination?"

"Unknown. Nobody from the ship has talked."

"They wouldn't. Let's get going then."

As if on cue, a police Land Rover pulled up outside the pub. The local constable, in a white pressed shirt and mirrored sunglasses, stepped out of the passenger side. The driver got out as well. Both men, uncharacteristically, wore sidearms. They were responding to a request from the police chief on St. Thomas, who had called asking them to locate Steve and Doc and bring them in for questioning. The constable already knew they were in the area; several people had seen Doc earlier that day in and around the bar, and someone thought they'd seen Steve arrive earlier on the ferry from Cruz Bay.

Steve and Doc slipped off their bar stools and into Sarah's private office. She had just enough time to hide their glasses before the constable walked in. She knew him well, as she'd been paying him a monthly fee for operating the bar since opening it. It wasn't an exorbitant amount; he knew what she brought in and allowed her to run the bar without civil hassles. But she didn't like it. His arrogance oozed out of every pore. All he needs is a baton. Probably has one at home. Pompous ass. She wanted to slap those silly sunglasses off his face and stomp them into the floor.

He stopped and surveyed the room.

"Hello, Sarah," he said, flashing his best politician's smile. "I'm looking for your boyfriend and his friend Steve Remington. Remington is wanted for a double murder on St. Thomas and for the disappearance of a floatplane and pilot he chartered this morning. We want to question Doc too."

"Haven't seen them," she shot back without hesitation, unaffected by accusations clearly intended to rattle her.

"Oh, I think you have," the constable said, glancing at the bar, no trace of his smile left.

"No, I think they're down-island," she said. "Fishing," she added, following his eyes to Doc's smoldering cheroot in the ashtray.

She picked it up casually and took a puff, as if it were her own, but suppressing a gag response to the harsh flavor.

"Search the back room behind the bar and the kitchen," the constable told the driver. "I'll circle around back." He gave Sarah a hard look, drew his pistol, and walked out the front door. Tourists had stopped to watch as he walked around the building through a narrow alley to the back of the old building.

Sarah's customers were agitated as well. A woman she'd been talking to from Long Island sat with her mouth open, then got up to leave. Sarah offered them all a round of free drinks and they settled down.

The constable returned through the kitchen, his gun still drawn, more for effect than anything else. He met the driver, and they searched the back room and kitchen again to no avail. Suddenly angry, the constable turned to Sarah as they left.

"We'll find them, and you'll answer for your involvement," he said. They got back in the Land Rover and sped away.

Sarah smiled and had to restrain herself from laughing aloud. The tourists just stared at her, their mouths still agape. She went into the back room she used as an office and closed the door.

"You can come out now," she said to the empty room.

A well-concealed trapdoor opened in the corner of the room, and Doc and Steve ascended a short flight of steps from the small storage area below. It had been built centuries ago to hide the contraband of the day. Sarah had kept it a secret, thinking she might find a use for it one day, and at last, she had.

"Be careful," she said. "He's probably waiting around the corner watching the place."

"I'm always careful," Doc said and gave her a quick kiss on the lips before stepping out the back door with Steve. "By the way," he said as he left, "you've got rats."

24

It was well after dark when Doc steered the borrowed powerboat around the west end of the island of Tortola. Steve immediately saw the enormous catamaran miles away, anchored by itself in the deeper waters near White Bay on the southern coast of Jost Van Dyke. It displayed only the minimum required lighting for a vessel at anchor, which made the ship's dark silhouette appear ominous as it blotted out the well-lit festive bars and restaurants on shore.

A brisk, warm wind from the north was beginning to produce a few swells, but the catamaran seemed impervious to the elements as if in defiance of the world around it.

As they got closer, Steve could see the floatplane, still in the water on the starboard side of the catamaran. The crane from the ship hovered above it, ready to bring it aboard. A launch was tethered to the gangway.

They had been following other boats making the crossing from the port at West End Tortola to Jost Van Dyke—mostly power boats, going over to Jost for dinner and maybe an overnight. As they had discussed earlier, Doc adjusted his course to allow them to pass as close as possible without drawing too much attention from the giant yacht.

Steve knelt on the deck in the rear of the boat and checked his gear one more time. The Beretta was lost when the Lake amphibian had been scuttled, so he had picked up his Glock 19 at the cottage. It was enclosed in a double waterproof bag along with two extra magazines, a dive flashlight, and a change of clothes. At the last minute he threw in a burner phone Doc had given him, closed the bag, and stuffed the package into his backpack.

"It's going to be a bit of a swim I'm afraid," Doc said, leaning down to where Steve sat and trying not to raise his voice too much over the sound of the engine.

"Don't make it too far; I've already had my swimming exercise for the day," Steve replied, sticking his head up for a few seconds to gauge the distance to the catamaran. When he realized they wouldn't get any closer than two thousand feet or so from it, he grabbed one of the floating seat cushions nearby and put his arms through the straps.

"Good luck, and don't forget to write," Doc said with a grin.

Steve gave him a thumbs-up, took one more look at the catamaran, and slipped over the side, using as much of the boat as possible to conceal himself. He hit the surface hard and rolled across the water in a tucked position, coming to an abrupt halt like a water skier who had just taken a fall. He forced as much of his body underwater as possible while clinging to the cushion. Before the boat's wake washed over him, he was vertical beneath the cushion, with only his nose and mouth above water.

As planned, Doc had not slowed down or changed the pitch of the outboard engine. He continued on a straight-line course north toward a popular restaurant on Jost Van Dyke just a few miles away. They had agreed he would wait there for Steve to call. If Doc didn't hear from him in two hours, he would contact a trusted officer at the nearby Coast Guard station and tell him the whole story.

On board the catamaran, one of the three men on watch held night vision binoculars on Doc's boat. It had passed closer than the other boats between the islands, drawing some suspicion. Focusing on the type of boat and the driver, he never saw the drop-off. He made a quick note in the ship's log and sat back in his chair.

Steve waited until Doc was well out of earshot and looked at his watch. The water was warm and there didn't seem to be any activity on the catamaran. After five minutes he started kicking behind the buoyant boat cushion, balancing the pack on his back. There was a little current directly against him, and he moved slowly, trying not to splash the water or make any noise. Only a sliver of moon was out, already sinking beneath the western horizon. Perfect lighting. Occasionally a swell would lift him, exposing him momentarily. When this happened, he would stop swimming until the swell passed and he had been deposited in its trough. Another swell was approaching, and he had stopped swimming, anticipating it. He was no more than a few hundred yards from the catamaran, his body vertical in the water again, when something bumped him hard from below.

Shit. Not now.

He froze, feeling like a cricket on the surface of a pond full of hungry fish. His gut told him what it was, and seconds later, he saw a dorsal fin break the surface not five yards away. The fin was a perfect small triangle with smooth leading and trailing edges and a sharp apex. It remained on the surface, slowly carving an arc back toward him before diving and exposing the second, much smaller dorsal fin just in front of the tail. Fucking bull shark. One of the top five of the maneaters. He wondered if the thing could hear his racing heart or smell the fear that must be oozing from every pore on his body. Probably both. He remained motionless, trying to be an inanimate piece of non-edible flotsam as the next swell washed over him.

Steve knew swimming at night on the surface of the ocean was never a good idea. He also knew that sharks generally had poor eyesight and would often bump their prey before attacking, trying to draw blood and inciting fear before the kill.

He remained still, his heart pounding, making a tremendous effort to stay calm. He tried not to visualize the unseen predator in the deep water below him. Panic hovered just over the horizon, like a rogue wave bearing down on a ship. He started the deep breaths, taking them in and releasing them slowly in the yogic tradition of self-calming. After thirty seconds, he felt his heart rate and his breathing slowing. At last, with no sign of the shark and convinced it had lost interest, he cupped a double handful of water, soaked his face with it, then started again for the ship.

He had drifted away from the catamaran. Exhausted from the events of the day, he summoned a new level of strength and kicked harder, trying not to splash the dark surface and bring back the shark.

25

Doc kept the boat on a straight course for Great Harbor on the island's south side. Foxy's restaurant was a well-known destination for tourists and locals from all over the islands, and the nondescript powerboat would go unnoticed. He approached the harbor, slowed to a safe speed, and picked his way through the anchored boats to the short dock near the restaurant. It was barbecue night and Doc thought he'd grab a quick dinner while killing time. He tied up the boat, checked his watch and cell phone, then went under the palm trees to the deck underneath the thatched roof building.

Foxy was perched on a stool behind a microphone, singing his usual variety of songs and conversing with the drunken, sunburned crowd as they ordered more of his specialty rum drinks or gnawed on the barbecued ribs. Doc sat at a table in the back and ordered a beer, and Foxy nodded to him in a friendly manner. Doc had set his granddaughter's broken arm just a few months ago, and it had healed nicely. She was one of Foxy's favorites from a long, long line of grandchildren.

Doc finished his beer in time for the ribs to arrive. The waitress told him it was on the house. He smiled and waved thanks to the older man as he entertained the crowd with his lively interpretation of "One Love."

A phone call was made somewhere nearby, and within half an hour, a 42 Night Eagle cigarette boat arrived and docked on the other end of the bay. Chief Haines and Cockerel got out and jumped into a waiting taxi. Within minutes they were at the back door of the restaurant.

Doc was halfway through his dinner when the two policemen walked up behind him from the shadows of unlit palm trees.

"It's nice to have friends all over the islands," Haines said, stepping around in front of Doc. Doc moved to get up but Cockerel held him down from behind.

A man from the kitchen, the one who had called Haines, appeared. Haines gave him a few large bills, and the informant hurried back to the kitchen like a land crab scurrying back into its hole.

"We're in the British Virgin Islands," Doc said. "You have no jurisdiction here and I am a British citizen."

"We have a special agreement with our British neighbors," Haines said. "Come with us and we'll leave your girlfriend alone."

They walked Doc through the rear door to the cab. No one spoke during the short ride back, and Doc felt horrible for letting everyone down.

"Murder, is it?" Haines said, handcuffing him once they were back at the boat. "Didn't think you had it in you, but then again, they say we all do."

"You're making a huge mistake, you idiot," Doc replied. When he started to tell his story, Cockerel hit him hard from behind. The two of them dumped him unconscious into the boat, and in a few minutes, they had cleared the harbor and were racing toward the St. Thomas police station.

26

By the time Steve covered the distance to the catamaran, he had been in the water well over an hour. The combination of trying to swim against a current while keeping any splashes to a minimum made his approach painfully slow.

He stopped a hundred yards from the ship and looked for some concealed place to get aboard undetected. But the boat was completely dark except for a few cabin lights here and there. He swam quietly around to the stern and saw the retractable panel between the two hulls had been lowered to a few feet above the surface, as it had been when he first saw the yacht close up on the ferry with Kelly. He had assumed then that the front of the ship had a similar panel to provide a private area that might come in handy at some crowded dock. Now he knew it was likely added to hide something the owners didn't want anyone to see.

He decided to swim around to the bow and climb the anchor chain, when the ship began to move, pivoting around the anchored bow. He saw surface turbulence on one side of the stern. The boat was being pushed sideways by underwater thrusters commonly used in docking. He swam with the stern, keeping directly behind the ship. After it had swung around about ninety degrees the boat stopped moving, with the stern now pointing away from land directly out to sea.

Then a dim reddish light came on in the space between the hulls. He could see it through the narrow gap between the bottom of the giant panel and the surface of the water. Suddenly, the panel began to retract, like an overhead door being raised. His first thought was that he had been spotted and a speedboat full of armed men would come tearing out from behind the panel at any second. He let go of the cushion, prepared to dive below the surface. But, after an agonizing minute or two, no boat full of men appeared, and no deck floodlights or searchlights were turned on. The panel had been retracted halfway when it stopped.

Steve could make out a small docking area inside, with two men standing on it. He was still well away from the ship in the darkness, when he felt movement underneath him once again.

This time he knew it was no shark. A whale perhaps, but not likely, and nothing as small as what had bumped him earlier. This thing was much larger, heading toward the yacht. It passed just beneath him slowly, and the underwater current it created swept Steve's legs up and to one side as they dangled beneath the surface. Then he saw it and his suspicions were confirmed.

A streamlined periscope appeared first, not twenty feet in front of him. It had just missed him, and it crept slowly toward the catamaran like the raised head of a giant water snake stalking its prey. Then, slowly and silently, the small submarine surfaced between Steve and the waiting catamaran. Water slid off its flat black anodized hull as it crept along at a knot or two toward its berthing beneath the mother ship.

A hatch opened on top and one of the crew climbed out on the deck of the vessel and helped guide it to the dock.

Pretty slick, Steve thought, as he watched the sub being tied up. The catamaran floats around as a millionaire's plaything and gets within reach of the coast. Then the sub makes the final delivery. Its small size and diesel-electric propulsion make it virtually invisible from radar or underwater detection devices. He remembered reading about these minisubs while still in the Navy. Pretty good range on diesel power, then the engine could be turned off. The submerged vessel could travel on its batteries for quite some time, avoiding any SOSUS underwater arrays—the ineffective system during the Cold War that had never been good at detecting submarines running on battery power and listened mostly for engine noise.

The minisubs were ingenious and elaborate yet simple. And they worked. This one was probably returning from a drug delivery now, with easily enough space for high-priced heroin on board to make it cost-effective.

He watched the sub dock, followed by the lowering of the yacht's concealing panel. Just before it closed, he caught a glimpse of large cables being hooked to the top of the sub, no doubt to pull it out of the water. He wondered whether this was in preparation for the catamaran to get underway when he saw lights come on the deck with men moving purposely around on it.

He abandoned the idea of climbing the anchor chain and maneuvered over to the starboard side of the ship, still keeping his distance in the shadows. Drifting beside the lowered gangway was the floatplane. He swam up to it, using the plane as a shield from the ship and keeping in its shadow cast on the water by the lights on the deck. He climbed onto one of its pontoons to rest for a few seconds. It felt good to be out of the water; even when it was warm, the sea still robbed the body of heat over time.

When he had caught his breath, he tried the door of the plane and found it unlocked as he'd anticipated. Quietly he slipped into its tiny back seat and shut the door.

He took a quick inventory of his things, stashed the wetsuit under the pilot's seat, and had just loaded the Glock when a bright floodlight was turned on the plane from the ship. He heard men coming down the gangway and crouched below the windows in the plane's interior shadows as best he could.

Two men pulled on the lines securing the plane to the ship, and Steve felt it moving in the water. In a few more seconds it would be close enough to the gangway for them to jump across to it. He lay there holding the Glock across his chest like a child clutching a security blanket. If they opened the door and saw him, the deal was over.

He heard a shout from a man standing on the pontoon not two feet away. Steve's Russian was a little rusty, but he could have sworn he was shouting an alarm. He raised the Glock slightly, pointing it at the door where the man stood, and waited.

Then he felt the other man jump onto the plane, but their only interest was to attach the heavy nylon straps dangling from the ship's crane to several lifting points on the fuselage. He heard more shouts from the deck, and the crane began to lift him and the plane from the water. The two men jumped back to the gangway.

In less than five minutes the crane had maneuvered the floatplane to its resting place on the ship, a heavy-gauge padded aluminum cradle in the middle of the yacht's giant aft section, and more men secured it to the deck and cradle. The bright floodlight was turned off, and a few minutes later, Steve heard a door close, and the men were gone. He relaxed. He had only to wait for the right moment to leave the plane, find Kelly, and get the hell out of there.

27

Steve woke in a jolt as the big engines of the ship were started from deep in her hold. He had been overcome with fatigue. The past twenty-four hours had taxed him as much as he had ever experienced. Knowing he had to get some rest before he started making mistakes, the crew all over the ship around him, he'd set his dive watch to wake him in thirty minutes. With the Glock resting comfortably on his chest, he had fallen into a deep sleep. He woke minutes before the alarm, wholly rejuvenated.

Even on a ship of this size the unmistakable vibration of the diesel engines well below the decks could be felt throughout. The floatplane rattled in sync with the rumble. He heard shouts from below him on the main deck, then barely audible from the bow, the sound of the anchor chain being drawn up through its winch and deposited into the chain locker.

Steve had been evaluating the changing situation since being hoisted on board. The original plan of finding Kelly, getting her off the ship, and rendezvousing with Doc was no longer tenable. He hoped Doc would give him a little more time before going to the Coast Guard.

Chief Haines sat in his office at the Charlotte Amalie police station on St. Thomas scrolling through Doc's cell phone. Its owner was still unconscious in the holding cell. He focused on the only number called earlier that day.

"Do you think this is Remington's number?" he asked Cockerel, showing him the phone.

"Probably," Cockerel replied. "The phones were just activated today."

"Well, it's almost two in the morning," Haines said, looking at his watch. "If we call the number and someone answers immediately, they might be waiting for a call."

"Worth a try," Cockerel said. "If he does answer, we could get a better location on him."

Haines dialed the number.

Steve felt the phone vibrate in his pocket. He and Doc had purchased two throwaways from a tourist place in Cruz Bay. Doc probably wanted to know what was happening, but their plan had been that Steve would call him, not the other way around. If Doc didn't hear from him, he had his marching orders.

Steve ignored the call, but the vibrating phone worried him. It wasn't like Doc to change the plan. He would call him back as soon as possible, but in the meantime, he'd just spotted a crewman come out of nowhere and walk toward the plane. He ducked below the windows and waited.

28

Treacher's cell phone rang once, and he picked it up immediately. He slept only a few hours each night anyway, and he had been fantasizing about how he would torture and rape the woman they had captured before he slit her throat and dumped her body off the stern. He would have liked to do it in front of her boyfriend Remington, but the odds of that were decreasing by the minute.

It was the policeman from St. Thomas. Maybe he had good news.

"We have the doctor," Chief Haines said. "We caught him on an island near your ship. No sign of Remington, but we'll find him."

"You'd better or you won't see the final payment we discussed."

"No problem. We're getting ready to question the old man now."

"Call me on this number when you have Remington," Treacher said and gave him his satellite phone number, as the ship would soon be out of cell phone range.

He hung up and went to apprise Malikov of the situation. He knew his boss might be asleep, but he had orders to wake him if there were any changes. Treacher took the elevator to the master stateroom on the top level. To his surprise, the light was on behind the closed door to the bedroom suite, and he heard a muffled cry from the girlfriend. He paused at the door before knocking.

"Come," he heard Malikov say. When Treacher opened the door, Malikov sat in a chair reading something, probably putting the final touches on his planned coup. The girlfriend was holding a towel to her bleeding nose, and Treacher saw fresh marks on her torso and upper thighs where he had beaten her.

Treacher told him about the news from Haines. After a long, uncomfortable silence, Malikov said, "It's only a minor distraction."

Treacher nodded in agreement.

"If they had told anyone, we would have known it by now. It's too bad Mr. Remington couldn't join us, though. The police chief will find him soon enough. We'll hold the girl overnight just in case and dump her body when we are well out to sea."

Both men knew they were in no immediate danger of arrest. Their long-standing business model was to have contraband on board for the shortest time possible. It was the age-old smuggler's advantage—no contraband, no case against them.

"Any word on when we get the package?" Treacher asked.

"Our friends will contact us at the appropriate time. Until then, we proceed to these coordinates," he said, handing Treacher a slip of paper with the numbers on it.

"How did the test run go?" Treacher asked.

"Perfectly. It was completely hands-off."

Treacher knew it would be. The triple GPS system coupled to the sub's steering was accurate to within a meter. Hilbert, the electrical and computer engineer they'd hired had proven his worth. The sub was now capable of being programmed with a course, then submersing and surfacing without human intervention.

Treacher left Malikov alone and headed to the bridge. He gave the new coordinates to one of the men on the bridge and watched as they were loaded into the auto helm.

———

Back in his cabin, Malikov smiled to himself. In a few days, he would be back in his country and several billion dollars richer. America would be paralyzed with fear, and he would use the opportunity and the money to bring about his planned coup. He had already placed a massive order for a small but modern air force with an arms dealer.

In the east, a faint blue light was just beginning to brighten the starlit horizon. Dawn, the start of Ramadan, was only a few hours away. What a glorious week it would be for him.

29

Kelly slept on the bunk in the tiny room that was her prison cell. Several times, she had awakened with a jolt, not sure where she was at first, and then remembering, fallen back into a fitful sleep. Some small part of her was hoping that when she woke up next time, it would all have been a horrible nightmare.

She was dreaming now, a recurring dream like a familiar movie whose ending kept changing. Which version or different twist would she see this time? She was a girl of thirteen again, and her father was hugging her in their living room. He kissed her forehead, and as he drew away, she saw tears in his eyes—something she had never seen before in the dream.

She watched in disbelief as he told her how much he loved her, then turned and walked to the front door of their house. She couldn't see her mother but could hear her crying nearby. She saw her father pick up the same two suitcases that were always waiting there and walk out the door. He would not look back at her, no matter how desperately she wanted him to. She felt herself crying as she always did. No matter how many times her mind replayed the dream, the emotional trauma of that moment had lost none of its pain.

Her mind had worked out the details, of course. As she got older, she understood more about divorce. How some people just couldn't live

together for one reason or another. But the dream still surfaced occasionally, usually when she was most vulnerable. She watched the door close,
and her father disappeared. As always, the same overwhelming sadness
washed through her, and she knew the dream was over. But then there was
a knock on the door. This had never happened before.

She had spent countless months after her father left that night hoping
and praying her parents would somehow resolve their differences, and he
would come back, but it never happened. He had never changed his mind
and come home, thrown his suitcases down, and reconciled with her
mother. Kelly stared at the living room door in her dream, her tears subsid-
ing, full of hope that for once, the door would open, and the ending would
change.

She heard another sound at the door. The rattling of keys. She wanted
to let her father in, but of course, in that world, she was unable to move as if
paralyzed. She stared wide-eyed at the door, but nothing happened. It
didn't open. Her father didn't come in. She was suddenly angry at this cruel
new twist in the old dream and forced herself to reach for the door with all
her might.

But the scene changed, and she was awake. However, the sound of the
keys continued, and the door to her cabin opened slowly.

Several thoughts raced through her mind. The first and foremost was
that they had come to kill her now, or worse. She had searched, but there
was nothing to use as a weapon. A rush of adrenaline laced with an over-
dose of fear accelerated her heart instantly.

Slowly and quietly, like an apparition, a figure slipped through the
door, quickly closed it, and then turned on the light. It was the blond
woman from the meeting before. Kelly stared at her wild-eyed, but the
woman put her finger to her lips as if to say, "I'm your friend; be quiet, and
you'll be okay."

There were voices outside the cabin. The woman listened at the door
until two crew members walked by—their voices fading down the hall.
They hadn't noticed the open padlock or the hasp not closed. When she
was sure the men were gone, the woman turned to Kelly, sitting on the
bunk.

She produced a sandwich wrapped in aluminum foil and a water bottle and offered them to Kelly without speaking.

Kelly hesitated.

"Please take it," the woman said. Kelly noticed a Hispanic accent. She hadn't eaten in over twenty-four hours. She could see thick layers of meat inside a hoagie roll.

"Who are you? Why should I take anything from you?" Kelly said.

"Keep your voice down," the woman said. "If they find me here, they'll kill us both."

The woman kept glancing at the door as if they might be discovered at any moment. Kelly wondered with a little suspicion why this woman would put herself at such risk for someone she didn't know. Whatever was going on, it was obvious she was scared. Kelly took the sandwich. They were going to kill her anyway; if this was some trick, she might at least have a last meal. However, she examined the sandwich's contents suspiciously and then sniffed it. Somewhere, she had read, there was a poison that smelled like almonds. Nope, no almonds—just mouth-watering, thinly sliced roast beef on a freshly baked bun of some kind. She had never tasted better.

"My name is Maria," the woman said, "or at least that was the name I was given and have been using for the last twenty years. It is a very common Spanish name. There were over twenty Marias where I was raised."

Kelly was puzzled. The woman was striking. Tanned, naturally blond, good figure, intelligent, and apparently the girlfriend of an extremely wealthy man. Things many women would die for. But there was such sadness and desperation in her voice.

"Is this all about drugs and drug money?" Kelly asked, avoiding a question about the woman's origin, the Maria thing.

"No, I think it's much bigger than that," Maria said. Then, in a more desperate tone, "Don't talk; there's not much time. Most of the crew are still asleep but will be up soon. I don't know much. They don't talk about it around me. It has something to do with the submarine."

"The what?" Kelly said. "There's a submarine?"

"The ship carries a small one. Ruslan has been using it for some time to deliver drugs. You are maybe wondering why I am telling you this—why

I'm here," she said. "Everything I've told you is the truth. No one has sent me here. I overheard this plan and am trying to piece it together, but now I think they talked about it in front of me because they plan to kill me when it's over." She looked down at the floor as if embarrassed. "Ruslan has grown tired of me," she said quietly.

Kelly's intuition told her that this part of what Maria told her rang true. It was apparent the woman was in her own world of despair. Kelly saw what looked like dried blood in Maria's nose and the beginning of a bruise on one eye.

"I was kidnapped from my parents when I was barely two years old," she began again. "We were in Disney World in Florida. They grabbed me in the crowd when my parents were not looking. There is an 'industry' in the world to steal young girls, especially white girls with blond hair and blue eyes, easily sellable on the markets, and take them to other countries where they are raised like cattle until they are ready. I was taken to a small, remote village in Colombia. It was deep in the jungle, away from any main roads. I was kept there in a heavily guarded sort of orphanage with others like me until we were older."

"The other Marias," Kelly said.

"Yes. That name is hard to trace in Colombia." She hesitated, and Kelly saw her eyes tearing up.

"Sorry," she said. "I've never been able to tell anyone."

Kelly smiled encouragingly, and Maria took a breath and continued.

"We were educated in arts and sciences at this place. Some of us learned English, others Spanish, German, Russian, and Arabic. When we got older, they began to teach us how to please a man. They brought in professionals, and we learned quite well. Then, when we were barely old enough, we were sold to wealthy men throughout the world. Malikov bought me when I was seventeen. I've been with him ever since. We were told that our parents had abandoned us or that our parents were dead. They told us we were lucky to get an education and live a luxurious life with a wealthy man."

"How did you find out about all of this?" Kelly said. "I mean, about being kidnapped and all. You were only two at the time."

Maria smiled. "By luck and fate, I met one of the girls I had been raised with at the orphanage. We had been best friends. It was more than ten years since I last saw her, but I knew her instantly. She had been sold to a sheik about the same time I had been sold. We met again in Monaco, and as our owners became preoccupied one night with their high-stakes gambling, she told me how she had been approached by a woman who was a CIA field officer. The woman had traced my friend back to her kidnapping in Arizona when she was three, and that she would get her back to her parents and put her in protective custody if she would work for a while as an informant."

"And you did the same thing?" Kelly said.

"Yes," Maria said. "I met this woman later. She took my fingerprints and some of my hair. My parents had done the same before I was taken. It was part of a police protection package parents did for a worse-case thing."

"My parents did it too," Kelly said.

"She found my parents. They live in Florida. I can't wait to see them. That was a year ago, and now all this happened."

Maria could no longer hold back the tears, and they began to flow down her cheeks. "I can just remember my parents," she said. "The memory was always there, just suppressed. My mother was so loving, and my father held me in his arms. He used to hold me above his head, toss me up, and catch me." She smiled. "It would scare me, but I would tell him to do it again. How horrible it must have been for them," she said, controlling her tears and staring at the cabin wall. "They never knew what happened to me, if I was even alive. And they still don't know."

Then, with resolve in her eyes, she looked squarely at Kelly.

"But I'm going to change all of that. Ruslan is extremely preoccupied with his plan. I did overhear something about stopping in a few days. If we stop, we will be near land. That's when we'll slip over the side and get away in a speedboat."

"How will we get a boat into the water?" Kelly asked, picturing several boats she had seen secured in davits on the upper deck of the catamaran. It would take the crane to pick one up and lower it over the side.

"One of the crewmen on the boat, Yuri, is going to help us. He'll have the boat ready."

Kelly raised an eyebrow, and Maria added shyly, "He's in love with me. He'll be there, and the boat will be ready. It's my chance and yours too."

Suddenly, there were voices outside the door in the hallway. "I've got to go. Be ready when I come for you."

"Why are you helping me?" Kelly asked quickly.

"Because you are a prisoner like me," she said with a quick smile.

Maria listened at the door for a second, opened it, and then slipped through, locking it from the outside.

Kelly went over everything Maria had said in detail. Their escape seemed as fantastic as the rest of what had happened. How much could she believe? The kidnapping seemed genuine. Such stories—sex slaves and pedophile rings—were all too common these days as they were continually exposed in the information age. There was such real emotion in Maria's face and voice when she talked about it. At least the possibility of escaping, no matter how unlikely, gave her some hope. And hope was what she needed right now, like a man overboard that had just been thrown a life buoy.

30

From his perch in the back seat of the floatplane, Steve could look down on most of the ship as it plowed its way westward through the dark Caribbean waters. They were well offshore of the Virgin Islands now, and he looked over his shoulder to see the lights of St. Thomas sinking below the horizon. The seas were rougher here in the open ocean, away from any landmass to break up the swells generated by the wind and current. The ship rode gently up and down the three- to four-foot waves like a giant carousel horse. The catamaran's extremely wide and stable beam kept the boat from rolling about its longitudinal axis, left and right—unlike a traditional monohulled vessel—and negotiated the open water exceptionally well. Steve estimated that with its oversized diesel engines, they were making close to twenty knots. There was a sense of expediency in the pace, and he suspected they were trying to make a deadline.

He counted, as best he could, the number of crewmen passing below on the main deck, trying to estimate their onboard stations, but only a handful had appeared in the last hour. As he had suspected, the crewman who had surprised him earlier was apparently just making his rounds to get the ship underway. Completely hidden in the darkness near the top of the ship, Steve was confident he could leave the plane and explore any part of the upper decks, an advantage he couldn't have planned better.

He had called Doc an hour ago as they passed within range of the last cell tower on the ridgeline bisecting St. Thomas. The call had connected, and someone had picked up without answering. After another attempt, the phone went to voicemail, and he left a message, telling Doc to give him until dawn and then to go with the backup plan. On a hunch, he added, "Everything's quiet here at the cottage."

Sitting in the floatplane now, checking and rechecking his gear, Steve turned the calls over in his head. Something was obviously wrong, or Doc would have answered. Even if he did get the message, it would take a few hours to get the Coast Guard on the scene in the middle of the night. More than likely, it would be after sunrise, if at all. He had to assume he was on his own.

His main priority was to find Kelly and make sure she was safe. Then, one way or another, he would find a way off the ship, perhaps in one of the launches tied to the main deck. A bonus would be to get a call out on the ship's radio or steal a satellite phone before they left.

He took a deep breath, holding it for a count of ten while keeping his eyes shut, then exhaling slowly. He opened his eyes and looked around carefully. No one in sight. He opened the door to the plane in slow, silent motion.

The moon was long gone, but starlight reflected off the white-painted fiberglass-and-steel roof. Keeping to shadows the surface search radar domes provided, he tried to anticipate the pitching of the boat before each step. He moved a few steps at a time between swells, extremely careful to avoid transmitting any sound to the compartments directly below him. Though there were a lot of sounds audible in a ship's cabin while it was underway, even muffled noises from above would be noticed.

After a full five minutes to travel only a hundred feet, he was just aft of the bridge. He approached a side window and peered in through a corner. There were two men inside, facing forward and away from him. One sat behind the wheel, monitoring the auto helm and gauges; the second was beside him in the other padded pedestal chair with his feet on the dash. A soft green glow from the instruments illuminated their faces. Steve spotted an automatic weapon lying on a console nearby.

Leaving the window, he crept to the edge of the main cabin roof he was standing on and scanned as much of the roof and deck as he could see. There was no one in sight. He lay down carefully and, gripping the scupper along the edge, lowered his head and shoulders over the roof to look through the side window of the stateroom.

A man was sitting on a couch in the middle of the room. He looked to be in his mid to late fifties, with salt-and-pepper hair, well-dressed, Eastern European with perhaps some Middle Eastern blood, and well taken care of. He had the rough but polished look of someone who had grown up poor on the streets and fought his way to the place he'd made for himself. Definitely not the silver spoon in the mouth, never seen a hard day's work type. These guys were often the hardest, and Steve was sure he was looking at the boss.

He began to formulate a plan to hold Malikov hostage until they released Kelly and were safely away. Its simplicity grew in his mind until he was ready to slip down to the deck, open the cabin door, and go in. He had begun to lower the rest of his body when another figure came into view from the other side of the room. He'd been there all along. Steve just hadn't seen him. He said something to Malikov.

This was a type he was more familiar with and instantly recognizable as career military.

Steve could spot them in a crowd in any city in the world. They always had the same look—molded by years of discipline, lousy food, less than adequate living conditions, intensive training, and seasoned by perhaps no more than twenty-four cumulative hours of actual, terrifying, often horrific combat. Their faces had become hardened by this Spartan lifestyle, and they carried it with them the rest of their life. Their short regulation haircuts became a permanent part of their appearance long after they had left the military and its regulations were no longer in place. Even out of uniform, their clothes were neat and orderly, down to the laces on their shoes and boots from outboard to inboard. Steve had been one of them at one time. He had fit the mold when it was required of him, but since his retirement and relocation to the islands, he had started a renewal that was rapidly diverging from that past.

In fact, he found himself resenting any form of it, especially personified in the man he was looking at. This guy would never change and he had no intention of returning to what he'd been before. This guy was rare, even in the militaries of the world. He was one of the ruthless killers who thrived more on the suffering of others than on obtaining a military objective. He was the strong arm of this operation, Steve reflected as he watched him talking to his boss. He was the guy who had sent Bancroft to kill him on his uncle's tug. He had killed Joseph and his wife, their floatplane pilot, and kidnapped Kelly.

Steve unconsciously placed his hand on the Glock in its holster, but the military man turned, and Steve saw his sidearm in a belt holster on his left hip. The crewmember with the automatic weapon on the bridge was directly above the stateroom. Steve picked out a spiral staircase leading from the helm to a corner of the stateroom. The odds were against him. He decided against kidnapping the boss.

After this was all over, he had another job to do, and it involved settling the score with this guy in fatigues. Not now, though; got to find Kelly.

Slowly, he raised himself into a crouch, then moved stealthily across the roof to the next room.

A young blond woman was alone in this room, packing a small bag. These super-rich guys always had a beautiful woman around. He watched her place a thick roll of hundred-dollar bills in the bag, a small toiletries kit, and, to his surprise, a shiny nickel-plated automatic pistol the size a woman might keep in her bedside table for self-defense. He wondered why she would need a gun on a ship surrounded by armed men who worked for her boyfriend. She closed the bag and hid it carefully behind the bed under some pillows.

Steve maneuvered around the roof for the next twenty minutes, cautiously surveying each room below him. His search for Kelly was unsuccessful. Time was precious; each minute that passed took them farther from shore. He reasoned she was being kept well out of the way belowdecks. The fact that there were two separate hulls made his search even more difficult.

Frustrated, he decided the crew's quarters were his next best option. They would probably be forward in the hulls. The lower aft part of the ship was devoted to the mechanical and engine rooms.

He located the stairs leading belowdecks, slipped off the roof in a dark corner, and drew the Glock. This would be tricky, but time was running out.

As he reached for the door to the ship's interior, it suddenly opened. Steve drew back into the dark behind the opening door as a crewman stepped out and closed the door behind him. He looked right past the spot where Steve was standing but showed no sign of alarm. His eyes weren't adjusted to the dark yet. He went to the side rail, cupped his hands over a cigarette, and lit it in the breeze. He placed both hands on the rail and gazed out over the sea as it rushed by beneath him.

Steve looked up and down the side deck, saw no one, and approached the crewman from behind. He stuck the cold barrel of the Glock on the back of the man's neck. He got the reaction he'd hoped for. The man froze, dropping the lit cigarette from his mouth.

"If you want to live, tell me where the woman is," Steve said.

"No speak. No speak English," the man replied in a heavy accent. He had half-turned his head around, and Steve saw the terrified look on his face. Again, he repeated, "No speak English."

Steve recognized him now as one of the men who had been there when Kelly was kidnapped. He was part of the goon squad who did the dirty work with the psycho military guy, not just one of the crew who ran the ship. Steve would be more than happy to thin their ranks one by one if necessary.

In the darkness, the man drew a long knife from a sheath on his belt with his right hand while continuing to mutter and gesticulate with his left, turning a little more of his body to the left. Steve didn't see the move. It was a well-practiced maneuver the man had picked up years ago in Spetsnaz training—the turn while speaking, the frightened decoy look. The man had killed several times like this when someone got the jump on him from behind.

Trying to remember the right Russian words, Steve started to repeat his question when the man spun on the ball of his left foot like a power hitter, knocking the Glock aside with his arm. The move was lightning-fast, but Steve reacted to it instinctively. By long practice that had become a habit, he had kept his feet one in front of the other in times like this. Like a boxer, he could take a step back quickly if need be. He saw the glint of the knife, its polished steel blade slicing toward his throat. The blade missed him completely, slicing through the air inches from his face, the momentum of the swing spinning the man around to face him. Now, there was a genuine look of disbelief and fear on the man's face. Steve shifted his grip on the Glock and brought his full weight and the butt of the pistol squarely across the bridge of the man's nose in a sweeping forehand a Wimbledon player would envy. There was a sharp crack. The nose was broken, and the man was down. Steve stomped on his hand, and the knife came free.

"Is that the knife you used to torture my friend Joseph?" Steve said, pointing the gun at the man's face.

"No!" the man said in decent English. "It was not me. It was Treacher. He wants to do all that kind of work himself."

"Treacher." The psycho in fatigues still playing army man.

"Where's the woman who was brought here today?"

This time, he didn't hesitate. "She is forward, in the waiter's room."

"Which hull?"

"Starboard. Lower deck. The door with the padlock."

That would help. This might work yet.

"Get up," he said calmly, "and turn around."

"What are you going to do?" the man asked. "I've told you what you want—now let me go."

Steve spun him around to face the sea, picked up his knife, and shoved it back in its sheath.

"Here's your knife back," he said. "Let's see how you do with it on the sharks."

He grabbed the back of the man's belt and flung him over the rail in a surge of rage. He hit the water with a splash that was inaudible over the sound of the engines. Steve saw him surface well behind the ship in the foam of its wake. One less asshole to worry about.

He began to make his way forward along the starboard rail.

31

The secure satellite phone's steady buzzing ring sounded on the bridge, and Treacher was summoned.

"It's the policeman," the crewman on the bridge said. It was one of the calls the ship's security crew was to listen for. Treacher took the phone.

"You have something for me?"

"Yes," Chief Haines replied. There was a pause as Treacher waited for him to continue. The silly policeman seemed to be savoring the moment. This was likely the pinnacle of all his years working as a policeman on the island. Small bribes, the sale of seized property and drugs— no real money until now.

"Well?" Treacher replied impatiently.

"First, let's take care of business," Haines said. "The money we spoke of wired to me now."

Treacher felt his blood rise to the level of rage he knew so well. This man was going to die anyway; now, he would die a very long and painful death if he had anything to do with it.

"Of course. Give us five minutes. We'll wire you the money. Call us back when you confirm it."

"Very well," Haines said, and the signal was lost as he hung up.

It took just a few minutes from the laptop in his room, and the transaction was made from one of the small accounts they had in Zurich for just such an occasion. Two hundred and fifty thousand dollars.

Treacher smiled. He had bought lesser men for much more. Before he died, this policeman would transfer all of it back, plus interest. He closed the laptop, one of the two on board that would be jettisoned if they were ever boarded, a precaution he had implemented many years ago.

When he returned to the bridge, the sat phone was ringing.

"Yes?" Treacher said.

"You have a stowaway," Haines replied.

"What are you talking about?"

"Three calls had come into the doctor's phone within the last hour, all relayed from a cell tower on the westernmost side of St. Thomas. Their consecutive bearings and confirmation from other cell towers revealed the source to be at sea and heading northwest." Haines paused for dramatic effect. "I'm sure you never dreamed that an island policeman could be so clever or have the sophistication to track a call," he said. He had lobbied hard for the equipment a year ago under the guise of stopping crime, but in fact, it helped him keep tabs on local criminals who owed him money.

"The calls came from your ship. Remington is on board, or so it would seem," he added.

Treacher was surprised. He thought Remington might be bold and resourceful, but he had expected a confrontation before they left the anchorage at Jost Van Dyke. Once again, he had underestimated the man, but that had been the problem all along. Well, this was going to be easy now.

"What do you want me to do with the doctor?"

"Keep him alive and isolated. Don't let him talk to anyone," Treacher said. He would dispose of the doctor when he killed Haines and anyone else who knew what was going on. There had been too many mistakes already; he didn't want any more.

"I'll be in touch," Treacher said and hung up. Again, he let his mind wander as he choreographed a torture and rape scene with the woman while Remington looked on.

He reluctantly broke off his thoughts and turned to one of his men. "As silently as you can, gather everyone and have them meet me here immediately. Armed, with communications."

The man nodded, and as he left the bridge to get the others, he put on his headset and earpiece to connect him to the rest of the security crew.

Minutes later, they were all on the bridge.

"Where's Dimitri?" Treacher asked.

"Missing," his head sergeant replied. Treacher nodded. The man's absence confirmed Remington was on board.

"We've got an intruder. He's here to get the girl. There's nowhere for him to go. We'll start aft and work forward, one team in each hull. Check everything. I want him alive at all costs. Check your headsets and weapons."

Each man checked in, speaking Russian in a Chechen dialect. If they were overheard, they were unlikely to be understood. Each double-checked his MP5, and the two teams made their way aft to the engine rooms.

32

In the forward starboard hull, Steve stepped out of a recessed area he had hidden in.

He glanced down the corridor and saw the padlocked door. Moving toward it, he approached the door and inspected the lock. He would need something heavy to get behind the clasp and pull the screws out of the steel door. He knocked quietly and waited.

Steve heard movement inside the room, and a small voice call out.

"Kelly?" Steve said into the locked doorjamb, trying to keep his voice down.

"Steve?" Her voice trembled.

"Yeah. It's me. The Navy to the rescue. I'm going to get you out, but I've got to find something to break this hinge. Give me a minute."

"Okay," she answered. "Rescued by the Navy. I'm never going to live this down." But he heard her break down in sobs with relief, then quickly recover.

"Hurry!" she said. "These are really bad people."

"Right," he said. Suddenly, he saw movement out of the corner of his left eye. Without turning, he raised the Glock to waist height below his left arm and searched for his target. He saw a man with a machine gun and fired three quick rounds. The sound of the nearly continuous shot was deafening in the closed corridor, and it was accompanied by the man crumpling to the floor. An instinctive, lucky shot had found its mark.

Another man in a headset farther away held Steve in his sights behind a wall but didn't fire. They obviously had orders to take him alive, and capture was his worst-case scenario. He had nowhere to go. He was at the end of the hall with no portholes or doors on either side and no defensive position. He'd have to go out the way he came in.

Seconds later, a black-and-silver canister was tossed into the corridor and came rolling toward him, a trail of smoke hissing from its ominous head. He recognized it immediately. Flashbang grenade. Shit. A second later, the hallway erupted in the brilliant light of 7 million candelas and 170 decibels.

He'd managed to close his eyes and cover his left ear, but he instinctively held on to his only weapon with his right hand, leaving his right ear exposed. The eardrum shattered instantly, and he crumpled to the floor with the pain.

Someone was standing over him now. He felt a foot on his right wrist, his gun pried from his fingers.

Shock. You're in shock, he told himself. You've been here before. Just take it easy. The guy in fatigues who liked to play army was standing over him.

"Steve?" he heard Kelly shout from behind the door. "Are you okay?"

He tried to answer. He wanted to tell Kelly he was still alive. But he was unable to. He felt arms grabbing him, dragging him away. Blood ran to his head, trickling from his wounded ear, and he slipped into unconsciousness.

33

Malikov was seated at a small desk when Steve was brought to the main stateroom. He had just completed a large order on his laptop for numerous options in the world markets, especially those in the United States. The stock exchanges would soon be in a free fall. Oil, natural gas, and precious metal prices would soar. He was poised to make billions more by shorting blue chips whose put options were cheap, and call options for commodities were currently down.

When he had first been approached by the clients and began to formulate his plan, Malikov also began creating fictitious companies and entities through which to place his orders in the elaborate scheme he'd perfected with his drug money. His immense fee would be funneled into these companies, laundered through business transactions as fictitious as the companies themselves, and multiplied exponentially in the stock trades. Eventually, the funds would be liquidated, the companies dissolved, and his inside man in Zurich would completely erase any digital record of the transfers. This would be his real source of wealth building. He would become rich beyond his wildest dreams. Mere keystrokes to build fortunes and kingdoms—easy when you can predict the future. He pressed the enter button to confirm his order.

They dropped Steve on the floor at Malikov's feet like a disobedient child, and he dismissed all but Treacher and Ferguson. Steve groaned when his head hit the floor. Treacher produced a glass of water and, standing over him, slowly poured it onto Steve's face, bringing him around.

"Ah, Mr. Remington," Malikov said, his tone superior. "I just knew it was you who was responsible for all that racket downstairs."

"Please. Call me Steve."

"Okay, Steve," Malikov answered disdainfully. "Did you really think you could come on board my ship and take your woman off without being discovered?"

"Well, actually, yes," Steve said. He was fighting the sharp pain on the right side of his head every time he spoke, but he was determined not to let them notice.

"By the way," he added, "there'll be one less on your payroll this week. Knife boy went swimming a little while ago."

Malikov glanced quickly at Treacher, who confirmed it with a nod. The smile left Malikov's face. He seemed to ponder the loss for a moment, but his face showed no emotion, like a gamekeeper at the sudden loss of a dog from his pack of hounds.

"That's unfortunate. Dimitri has been with me for quite some time. It's hard to find good men these days, especially someone as gifted as he was."

"Guess he wasn't quite gifted enough," Steve said.

Malikov let the comment pass. But Steve saw a flash of anger in his eyes.

"I see you've met Treacher," he said, nodding in the man's direction. "He was a major in your army."

"You mean this asshole actually held a rank somewhere?" Steve replied. Then as Malikov started to tell Treacher's story: his recruitment, betrayal of his men, and subsequent promotion to Malikov's side, Steve cut him off.

"Oh yeah, now I remember, from the notebook. I don't need to hear it again."

"Yes, the notebook," Malikov said, winding up his short history of Treacher. "We'll get back to that." He stood and began a slow pace around the room, on his private stage again.

"After the fall of the Berlin Wall and the former Soviet Union, Russia fell quickly into the hands of gangsters and corrupt officials. They were always there, of course, but they became more powerful than ever while the crumbling government and military tried to manage as best they could as satellite states broke away. Two former KGB agents weren't really useful to them," Malikov said, nodding to Treacher.

He paused for effect like a lecturer wishing to hold the attention of his audience.

"Fortunately for us, our job at the KGB all those years had been to procure and funnel illegal drugs into the United States and its allies in a long-term Soviet strategy to weaken you."

"I wouldn't have guessed you were able to buy this little boat on the money you saved from your government job," Steve said.

"No, of course, you know that would be impossible on a military pension. We checked on you. Retired Navy commander, aviator, Gulf and Iraq War combat veteran. Interesting that you started out as an enlisted SEAL. That would explain your . . . skill set."

Steve half listened. His head was clearing, and he was looking around for a weapon while he had the chance.

"We still have our paid contacts at the FSB," Malikov continued. "And we know who your family is back in the States and where they live," he added for effect.

"So, you just stepped into the drug business and took the profits yourself?" Steve said, trying to keep Malikov talking about himself in an effort to buy some more time.

"Yes, it wasn't easy at first, but we managed. The selling of heroin to your countrymen has been very profitable. But all good things must come to an end. The same week that we were trying to recover the notebook from you, our submarine developed engine trouble on a delivery off the coast of Florida. Our crew had to surface in daylight to fix the problem. As fate would have it, one of your anti-submarine planes happened to be in the wrong place at the wrong time. We had to shoot it down."

Steve remembered the story; it had been all over the news. A P-3 had simply vanished on a routine flight. No survivors or wreckage had been found. There was renewed gibberish about the Bermuda Triangle, and then the story was dropped.

"We stopped all deliveries after that," Malikov continued, "and decided much more could be made on one final delivery. Enough to finance my life-long dream."

"Okay, I'll bite," Steve said. He had identified a few potential weapons, but they were too far away. Keep the bastard talking.

"I am not Russian," Malikov said. "I only worked for the Russians after my countrymen were allowed to repatriate after 1956. I am Chechen." He said this with pride, snapping his head up slightly. "I was born in a work camp in Siberia after my parents were deported by Stalin in the Second World War. He accused us of helping the Germans, even though they never made it to the Caucasus. That didn't stop him from deporting over half our country. Most did not return.

"I saw my family die one by one in the camps. Our Russian guards raped my mother and sister whenever they felt like it, my father was beaten to death in front of me trying to protect us. During the day, I was chained to a machine in a factory making bayonets for Kalashnikovs. At night, I watched the horrors of the camp unfold. For years, my family, those still alive, saved food for me so that I might survive to avenge them. My life's work has been dedicated to this ultimate goal. I was ten when those of us who survived that nightmare were allowed to return to Chechnya after Stalin died. I clawed my way up through the Russian military, eventually ending up in the KGB."

Malikov stopped pacing, and the twisted expression of pain and rage that had taken possession of his face was gradually transformed into a cunning smile.

"I watched events unfold during the Chechen wars of the last thirty years," he continued. "We had hope in Basayer, leader of our separatist movement, but he was assassinated by the Russians in 2006. Other resistance leaders were assassinated or bought by Putin—including the current pig, Kadyrov. It is past time for our independence. The money I make on this last delivery will be enough to equip a sizable army. We will join with our brothers and retake the Caucasus, creating a new, powerful, strategically located nation controlling the Russian land bridge to the Middle East. The oil fields of Azerbaijan and the uranium mines of Kazakhstan will fall under our control."

"You're forgetting about Mother Russia, aren't you?" Steve said. "They're not going to just let you waltz in and do as you please."

"Russia is entangled in Ukraine. This is where much of their food comes from, and it is Putin's primary objective," Malikov answered. "And we have very powerful friends in Washington, DC. Your Senator Weloc and his small group of friends in intelligence are with us. The disruption we cause in the Caucuses will be a convenient distraction for Ukraine. It will be coordinated by attacks from Ukraine with the medium and long-range missiles your country has recently supplied and aggressive NATO troop movements further east toward Russia. By the time Putin learns what we have done, we will have united our countries and formed a powerful nation. It is no secret, for example, that the US military has recently conducted exercises in the area." He was standing by a large map of the world now, and he gestured to the region for emphasis.

Malikov was silent now, and Steve felt the man watching him closely. It was inconceivable to him that his own country could be involved with this psychopath, but Senator Weloc was a well-known acolyte for the military-industrial complex, and he never met a war he didn't like.

"That's a nice little lie sprinkled with some truth," Steve said.

"Is it so hard to believe that the great United States might sacrifice its own people if the stakes were high enough?" Malikov said.

Steve didn't answer. There were questionable events throughout history where just such things had taken place.

Malikov clasped his hands behind his back and began pacing back and forth like a lecturer again. "In the last year, the Saudis have committed the greatest sin against your country. They have begun to sell their oil in exchange for Chinese yuan. Since the oil embargo in the early seventies, the Saudis have only accepted dollars for their oil. In exchange, the United States has protected them militarily, and the Saudis have recycled their dollars back into US Treasury bonds. Every country on the planet that wanted to buy oil from the Saudis had to have dollars, making the dollar the world's reserve currency and keeping it strong."

Since his retirement, Steve had kept up with geopolitics a little. He remembered the recent news about the agreement between the Saudis and

China. Oil was the weak spot in the Chinese armor. He remained silent, trying to buy time and regain his composure.

"And then there is Iran. An old problem for both the West and the Saudis. The Shias and Sunnis have been at odds since the time of Mohammed, and Iran is one of the few countries left in the world that is not in debt to the World Bank. In the past several years, Iran has used the Houthi rebels in Yemen to attack Saudi Arabia in strategic areas."

Steve realized that Malikov was enjoying himself. Maybe he hadn't had anyone with an equal intellect to talk to in some time, or maybe he was justifying what he was about to do. Whatever it was, he was glad for the delay.

"How easy would it be?" Malikov continued, "to blame an attack—a nuclear attack no less—on the Houthis, Hamas, and Hezbollah—all proxies of Iran? It would give the US another excuse to return to the Middle East, this time to occupy Saudi Arabia in significant force and invade and take over the rich oil fields in Iran. By their very presence in Saudi Arabia, they will control the Saudis, perhaps take over the country entirely, and cut off the sale of oil to China. As a bonus, Iran will no longer be a threat to Israel."

So that was it, Steve thought. They had a nuke of some kind and were going to use the sub he'd seen to deliver it. If they continued heading north, they'd be within launching distance of US targets within a few days.

"They'll never get away with it; Iran is a huge country," Steve said, trying to keep him going, though there were parts of the diatribe that rang true in a very disturbing way.

"Oh, of course they will," Malikov said. "The powerful corporate-owned Western media will be complicit, a special Washington commission will sanction it, and your military-industrial machine will provide the hardware. All at your taxpayers' expense. Besides, all the Iranian oil and natural gas proven fields are in the extreme western area near the Persian Gulf. The US and their allies would only have to occupy a fraction of the country.

"Together, we will sweep in to control the region, joining with our new American-backed friends in Georgia and the Armenians. We will reach out to Turkey in the end and form a powerful Islamic nation-state. Russia will be unable to fight on two fronts with its troubles in Ukraine. They will buy our oil rather than fight for it. They have bitter memories of the wars in our part of the world. It will all start in Chechnya, and that will always be remembered."

Steve stared at the man. This was not your run-of-the-mill ruthless drug runner. This was a true psychopath, bent on the deaths of millions of innocent people for vengeance and his personal gain. True World War Three material. Seemed like the world was full of them these days.

"Have you no compassion or mercy for all the innocent people you're going to kill?" Steve asked.

It was a rhetorical question, but it might keep him talking. They hadn't tied his hands. He'd been eyeing Treacher's pistol tucked into the holster under his left arm. Steve noticed an odd, glazed look in his eyes, bored from a lecture he had heard many times. That would help. He also noticed Treacher had a habit of putting all of his weight on one leg.

"Forgive me for not applauding," Steve said. "You've certainly done a good job of rationalizing your atrocities."

"We will merely be putting some of your misguided countrymen out of their misery." Malikov had come out of his rant and was once again calm and businesslike. "But now let's get down to the business at hand, Mr. Remington. You may have noticed somewhere in this silly notebook a long series of letters and numbers followed by the word *onion*."

"Onion?" Steve said. "No lettuce and tomatoes?"

Malikov's eyes narrowed in anger, the gentleman's mask removed again.

Steve had seen it neatly written on the top margin of one of the last pages. He didn't give it much thought at the time because he knew what it was, and it certainly fit in with drug smuggling and illegal activities. It was a series of fifty-six random letters and numbers followed by dot onion instead of dot com or dot net. A unique URL address for the Dark Web.

"Nope, don't think so."

"Oh, I think you saw it," Malikov said. "You're not a very good liar. We need that address, you see, because it is the only way to contact the most vital person for our success in Chechnya. A loyal friend and Chechen separatist I've known since childhood. He is one of the deputies of parliament and a confidant of the president, and he knows the president's daily changing schedule. This will be vital for our coup. I will simply replace the president over a weekend, but we must know precisely where he will be to make sure he doesn't have any chance to stop us until it's too late. He will also provide us with the names of those with us and those who will probably be against us. Mr. Ferguson was given the address, but our friend Mr. Stodd took it from him. Because the president has everyone close to him monitored, we have no other way to contact our man discreetly without compromising him.

"If you tell us where the notebook is and who knows of it, we will let you and the girl die quickly," he said, stooping over Steve on the floor. "Otherwise, it will be very bad for you. Treacher here is quite the animal when it comes to extracting information from people. And, oh yes, I almost forgot, we will let the doctor die quickly too."

Malikov didn't miss the faint look of surprise in Steve's eyes. "Yes, we have him, courtesy of the policeman on St. Thomas."

Steve felt hope kicked out of him. So much for plan B.

"And, as a bonus, we won't kill the rest of your family, your mother and sister, back in the States."

Feeling his anger rise, Steve calmed it quickly, aware that provoking anger was one of the most effective psychological ploys in extracting information. It would serve him no useful purpose at the moment. In a few minutes, they would take him somewhere for the first real physical test.

With a move that surprised the other two completely, he rolled to his right side and caught the back of Treacher's leg in a classic judo foot sweep. Treacher went over backward and crashed to the floor. Steve wrenched the pistol from its holster in one motion, flipped off the safety, and turned toward Malikov when something hit him hard in the side of his head, right on top of the ruptured eardrum.

The pain was unbearable, so much so that his brain decided that the body had had enough. As it began to shut down, he saw Malikov standing over him, wiping blood from his Italian leather shoe with a silk handkerchief.

34

The *Inshallah* cleared the final lock on the Gulf of Mexico side of the Panama Canal, received her clearance from the canal authority, and pointed her bow a few degrees west of due north.

It had been a typically long, uneventful passage from Jakarta with the usual load of rubber, clothing, and athletic shoes for Miami. These goods were produced at incredibly low cost in the South Pacific and loaded in bulk by the thousands of tons into the hold of the freighter. The run to Miami had become a monthly and very profitable enterprise for the shipping company.

The Americans, hungry as always for the many things they craved and could not produce as cheaply in their own country, had become the company's best clients. The much closer West Coast ports were saturated, however, and the extra trek to Miami paid half again as much for the same load. They would make good time on the return voyage because they would be dead empty of cargo. They were always empty on the return from America. It was cheaper to buy goods almost anywhere else in the world.

The captain gave the nod for full speed ahead as they cleared the no-wake zone and headed out to the open sea. The Gulf was like a lake compared to the torturous swells and storms of the mighty Pacific. A misnomer if there ever was one.

They had passed all the usual customs inspections and scrutiny. A bulky, tightly packed load like theirs offered many smuggling opportunities, but the drug dogs and electronic sniffers—essentially the same sonar echo devices geologists use to find rock cavities—had given his cargo the once-over and come up empty. Of course, they had found nothing. The captain had personally overseen the loading as he always did. As usual, the authorities were one step behind, because the smugglers knew what the authorities would be checking for and where on the ship they usually checked. Besides, an innocuous freighter like theirs would not be searched too carefully.

The search had been about as thorough as time and the customs resources permitted, but on the other hand they never checked in some places, like the ship's vast fuel tank. A four-by- eight-foot inspection plate accessed the top of the tank, allowing for anything worth smuggling to be lowered into it, submerged in diesel fuel, and never questioned.

It had been nearly a year ago, the captain reflected, when a well-known and popular cleric approached him. They had known each other as boys growing up in a small village in Malaysia. It took a few weeks of casual conversation at first, and then persuasion—the cleric seemed a little over the edge—but then he had no love for Americans either. He could easily deliver a package to their enemies—probably drugs, he assumed. Just as well, more poison for their sick Western society. He had become disgusted from his visits to Miami. Decadence and obscene behavior everywhere. He had grown tired of the money-grubbing whores who frequented the bars. They were all the same. Let them all burn.

He rechecked the rendezvous coordinates in the dual GPS. His ship was on course, surface search radar on, collision alarm set and synced with the navigation chart.

As he traveled aft of amidships toward his cabin, he passed the man the cleric had sent along. He didn't know the man, but he knew he didn't like him. Something about him. He had been seasick most of the voyage and had a hard time gaining his sea legs—probably because he only had one eye. The other was covered with a black patch.

The captain thought of his contraband deep in the fuel tank. They had lowered the package encased in the watertight black plastic container it

had arrived in. It was about the size of a large clothing trunk. He remembered that for such a small package, it put an unusual amount of strain on
the cable that lowered it.

After the fuel tank's inspection plate was carefully put back in place,
made to look like it hadn't been taken off in years, his loadmaster remarked
that whatever it was, the damn thing was as heavy as lead.

35

Steve had been through interrogation training twice before. The first time was years ago at the completion of his SEAL training, and the second was after he reinvented himself in the Navy and got his pilot wings. Both times, since he was an East Coast sailor, they sent him to the survival, evasion, resistance, and escape school, or "SERE," located deep in the wilderness near Jackman, Maine. So far away from anything, they used to say, that no one could hear you scream.

The base was set up like a POW camp complete with armed guards wearing enemy uniforms, carrying AK-47s, and flying an enemy flag. They beat you up and introduced you to different methods of extracting information, all very effective. The bottom line they wanted you to take away at the end of the grueling week was that you could never hold out information forever. No matter how strong you thought you were, trying to "John Wayne" your way out of things by stonewalling them was ultimately going to fail and maybe get you killed. What they did teach you were ways to survive without compromising everything.

Of course, it wasn't the real world at SERE school. As authentic as they tried to make it, they weren't going to put a bullet in your head at the end of it all. And Steve knew what was coming would be real physical torture, in addition to the mind games. His goal was to survive to fight another day. No one was coming to save them.

He was chained to a large pipe in one of the engine rooms with his hands above his head and his feet bound to the pipe as well, so that he was supported in an upright standing position. Based on the degree of numbness in his hands and arms when he regained consciousness, Steve guessed he had been there for some time. His head was roaring with pain, and all hearing was gone from his right ear. The room was stifling from the big diesel engine as it boomed along at full power. He noticed the sloped floor and the drain in front of him and grimly realized why they had chosen this place.

He gathered his thoughts and formulated a plan. The notebook was hiding in plain sight in the bookcase in his cottage. Malikov's minions on St. Thomas would eventually find it if they hadn't already. When that happened, once they told Malikov what he needed, it was game over. The best he could do was hold out and negotiate a deal to spare as many people who knew about this and their families as possible. Then tell him where the notebook was. Salvage what he could and maybe live to fight another day. It was all he could come up with. He would have to make it look real and not give in too early, but in the end, no John Wayne moment.

Steve hoped they would torture him before involving Kelly. His worse fear was they would bring in Kelly first thing and use her against him. But he reasoned that they'd be in no rush. He suspected Treacher enjoyed torturing others and would want to drag out the process as long as he could. That would be his weakness, and there were at least a few days' travel before they got close to the mainland.

He moved his hands and arms to keep the blood flowing, clenching and unclenching his hands. It seemed to be working.

A few hours later the door opened and two of Malikov's men stepped in and checked his bindings. Then Treacher walked in. He had stripped to just a bloodstained wife-beater, for special effect Steve assumed, and was carrying a small bag. He locked the door behind him, and Steve gave no sign of his relief. Kelly was not with them. Such as it was, his plan was working so far.

36

Still in his wife-beater, Treacher found Malikov outside on the main deck with both hands on the starboard rail watching the sunrise. They were still heading northwest toward the coordinates.

Malikov raised his eyebrows when he saw Treacher, his eyes wide with questions.

"He talked finally," Treacher said. "The notebook is in his cottage. Should I send the policeman to retrieve it?"

"Of course," Malikov said. "He can relay the URL address to us. Did Remington try to negotiate?"

"In the end," Treacher said. "I told him we would spare the families."

Malikov nodded.

"Let me know when you have the address," Malikov said. He turned back to see the sun beginning to show itself on the eastern horizon.

Two hours later, Treacher stepped off the master stateroom elevator and found Malikov sitting alone on the couch.

"We've got it," he said, handing Malikov a piece of paper with the address.

"Good. Now, it's time to take care of our policeman friend," Malikov said. "He's useless to us now, and we may not have time to deal with him later."

Treacher's face must have shown his disappointment in being denied the opportunity to personally deal with the pompous cop. Malikov laughed at him.

"See if you can contact the contractor we used several years ago in Negril. If he's still working," Malikov said.

"I can do that," Treacher said.

"We want all the money back before he's killed unless he's already spent it. And take care of the other one too—his second-in-command."

Treacher nodded. "What about the doctor?" he said.

"He's locked up deep in the police station. We don't do police stations. Too much publicity, too many cops. We'll deal with him later," Malikov said. "Anyway, it will be easier for the contractor and better for us if he does the job someplace more discreet."

That afternoon, a small man with glasses who looked like anything but the highly successful contract killer he was stood beside Haines as he transferred all of the money Treacher had sent him, plus all of his own money, to one of Malikov's many accounts. He used a small laptop the contractor had provided.

Cockerel sat at the table with him, his hands cable-tied to the chair behind him, his mouth gagged with a pink washcloth. Haines had a matching washcloth stuffed in his mouth. The washcloths were courtesy of whoever's waterfront condo they were in. Judging from how the place was decorated, the contractor figured it must belong to one of their girlfriends.

He couldn't have asked for a better setup. He'd followed them here from the police station and used the UPS uniform with a box in his hand to get the door open, then the dart gun with just the right amount of night-night to let them sleep for the time it took to drag them to the table and secure them.

When Haines was finished and trying to say something like they all do, he shot him in the middle of the forehead with the suppressed Beretta 71, two in the heart for insurance, and then did the same with Cockerel. He waited a bit, looked at his watch, then checked their pulse. Easy money today. It didn't always go this way.

37

Twenty-two degrees, fifty minutes north, and eighty-six degrees, thirty minutes west were coordinates on the earth's surface in the Gulf of Mexico just north of the gap between Cancun, Mexico, and the westernmost tip of Cuba. This was the busy shipping lane one hundred nautical miles wide that handled all trade between the southern United States and the Panama Canal, in addition to traffic to and from South American countries bordering the Caribbean.

After clearing the gap between the two land masses and allowing an appropriate standoff distance from Cuba, ships either turn east to negotiate the straits of Florida and access the East Coast of the United States or continue north if their destination is a port on the Gulf Coast.

In recent years as shipping traffic had increased, with the Cubans erecting offshore oil rigs in the area, passage through the gap had become increasingly treacherous. There were still a few spots, however, that were out of the main highway of ships, away from the multiplying oil rigs and, more importantly, over the horizon from prying eyes.

Those coordinates described just such a spot, and the captain of the Indonesian freighter bound for Miami had adjusted his course and speed with all the precision that modern navigational instruments and a lifetime at sea could provide. He had explicit instructions to arrive at the coordinates at a very specific time, offload the cargo, and continue to Miami. He would be paid a handsome fee when he returned to Jakarta.

It was just before two in the morning when the one-mile alarm went off on the bridge, indicating they were approaching the waypoint set in the auto helm. The captain had been watching the surface search radar for some time and could now easily see the giant unlit catamaran dead ahead in brilliant starlight on the calm sea.

The rendezvous time and location had been carefully selected based on the best intelligence available to Treacher from his contacts through Senator Weloc, primarily concerning the locations and orbits of various military satellites. The investigation following their attack would undoubtedly replay all recorded images from these satellites. But if everything worked as planned, the minute or so the two ships were near each other, a not uncommon occurrence, wouldn't appear particularly suspicious.

He had called his source in intelligence just an hour ago and had confirmed there were no satellites that could see them even if they were looking, which they weren't. As luck would have it, a high cloud cover had moved into the north, obscuring the view from that direction. Treacher finished his little cigar and flicked it over the side. He had been watching the approach of the small freighter for the last half hour through night vision goggles. Now it was close enough that he didn't need them.

Malikov suddenly appeared silently by his side like an apparition able to appear and disappear at will. Although he had grown accustomed to them, Malikov's sudden materializations always gave Treacher a bit of a start. He surveyed the catamaran a final time prior to rendezvous. His men had been through the drill many times on drug runs. One in the bridge with a sniper rifle and night vision scope. One on the bow with the grenade launcher. Everyone else with SAWs and a thousand rounds. It was enough to start or finish a small battle.

They had never had any real problems, and they weren't likely to tonight. He was told the captain and crew of the freighter were experienced and to be trusted, but even men such as these could do foolish things.

The freighter drifted in slowly. At the appropriate time, a single flood-light was shone on the aft deck of the catamaran to indicate the spot where the cargo was to be dropped. Treacher saw with satisfaction that the cargo was already on the deck of the freighter ready to be transferred. The two hulls kissed each other, and the cargo was lowered by a crane to the cata-maran with precise efficiency.

The freighter turned away, and Treacher thought he saw the captain waving farewell from the bridge. Then the freighter chugged away to the east.

Within minutes, the cargo had been removed from its case, and the case and lead shield were thrown overboard to sink to the bottom. Hilbert and the Russian bomb technician carried the olive-green backpack below to the sub.

38

Maria sat cross-legged in her cabin biting the last fingernail she hadn't already destroyed. Her once well-manicured, multicoated nails were now shredded nubs.

They had taught her in the school never to put her fingers near her mouth, let alone bite her nails. They had coated all the girl's fingertips with an incredibly spicy liquid from the time they were young, and they had all quickly learned this lesson the hard way. But her current preoccupation with the life-and-death situation she was facing had overridden all those lessons of the past and she had begun to nibble her nails obsessively. When she first realized what she was doing she could have sworn she tasted habaneros, and her eyes watered at the memory.

Now she sat on the bed and contemplated her increasingly complicated position. She had never anticipated this man Steve Remington attempting to rescue Kelly. He had come out of nowhere to spoil her plans of escape. The ship had been traveling at top speed for two days now and she didn't know exactly where they were, but she knew it wouldn't be long before they reached their target.

She had learned from her boyfriend that they tortured Remington and threw him into Kelly's cabin. She knew beyond a doubt the two of them would be shot in the head and dumped over the side at any time. They had placed a guard on Kelly's door, so there was no way she could get them out.

She couldn't bear the thought of Treacher getting his reptilian hands on Kelly. She sensed a strong, sisterlike attachment with her and knew that monster well enough to be aware he had special plans for her before she died. Somehow, without Kelly, her hopes of escape were slipping away.

With the tenacious resolve that her life had distilled in her, she got off the bed and slipped into something Malikov especially liked. She would plead for their lives, beg him at least not to kill Kelly, although she knew the cost would be tremendous. He would beat her and violate her in ways she knew all too well, yet she would live through it. She felt she had no choice. But it would be the last time, she promised herself. Steeling herself outside his cabin, she put a trembling hand on the door handle and went in.

Kelly wet the washcloth again with cold water and wiped the sweat from Steve's face. It was stuffy in the cramped cabin, but she didn't think he had a fever. He was sweating from the closeness of the room and the tremendous task his body had undertaken in its innate attempt to heal him.

He had been unconscious since they brought him in the day before and she couldn't stop worrying about him. She had cleaned him up as best she could. She was horrified after they had first dumped him in her room. His face was badly bruised and swollen from the beatings they'd given him, and two of the fingers on his left hand appeared to be broken because they stood out from his hand at an odd angle. She dared not touch them for fear of doing more damage or causing him more pain, so she just continued sponging the sweat off of his face and neck, her tears falling on him like the first drops of an approaching storm.

There were burns too. Several of them on his torso. They'd used some type of heated rod on his skin. A yellow suppurating substance oozed from the edges of the cauterized wounds.

Eventually Kelly replaced her tears with anger. She found it to be a powerful substitute. She began to dream of the chance to even the score, and how she might do it.

His breathing was much more regular now, not the rapid shallow breaths that had so concerned her the first few hours after they brought him back, and his pulse was slower and stronger. All good signs, but the longer he slept the more she worried. When he'd sufficiently recovered, he would wake up. She desperately hoped it wouldn't be too late.

She'd been nursing the water bottle Maria had given her, trying to get Steve to swallow some of it. They hadn't been fed at all, in itself a bad sign.

She knew they were likely to be killed. The military had been a good teacher, but those times she felt her life was threatened in combat had come and gone relatively fast. This long, drawn-out waiting was really pissing her off. She resolved to go down fighting if they gave her even half a chance. On the brink of her life's untimely end, she felt more invigorated and alive than ever. She felt stronger, forever changed.

Steve moaned, something he hadn't done in two days. After a few more seconds, when he opened his eyes, she put a hand to her mouth to keep from shouting out her relief.

39

Malikov washed his face at the basin in his cabin in the predawn hours and looked at his reflection in the mirror. Maria had been very persuasive. She knew his dark sexual side and had used it cleverly to her advantage. Sometime in the throes of ecstasy, he had agreed to spare Remington and his girlfriend, another lie that rolled off his tongue as effortlessly as they always did to get what he wanted.

He smiled at himself and the memory of the past night. Of all the women he had known and that his money could buy, she had been the best. He had gone a little too far this time, like red lining one of his Ferraris he knew he would sell—driving it one last reckless time as fast as he dared at the very edge of control. The memory made him glance down at his torn knuckles. So stupid of him to hurt himself instead of using the tools. Still, it had added something different when he was hurt, too.

She wouldn't suffer any permanent damage if she lived, he reflected—but that was out of the question. He had known about the clandestine escapades with her boyfriend on the ship's crew for some time, which made the past few hours all the more pleasurable.

He knew she was angling for something when she knocked on his door, and he had played along, letting her think she was in control. He had something special planned for her and her boyfriend. Something that would make Maria's final few minutes of life unbearable, a just reward for her betrayal.

As a final gesture to Maria, even though she did not deserve it, he had told Treacher to torture Remington no further. They would all die together. He had seen the disappointment on Treacher's face, and he laughed out loud now at the mental image, admiring his reflection in the mirror, how good he looked when he laughed.

He heard the main engines throttle back and felt the ship begin to slow.

Since rendezvousing with the Indonesian freighter, they had traveled at the best possible speed. Still, for Malikov, their journey to the target had taken an excruciatingly long time. He was eager to get on with it and fulfill his destiny.

He watched the sun peek out over the horizon. Perfect timing. It would be the biggest day of his life, with many, many more magnificent days to come. Finally.

Hilbert was sweating profusely in the cramped interior of the mini-sub. He was watching the bomb technician make the final connections that would detonate the nuclear device shortly after the sub surfaced well inside Galveston Bay. There was enough air circulation to keep him from sweating, but the realization of what he had become a part of was devastating. He never would have signed up to be part of some terrorist attack, and to his credit, he told himself, he had no idea there was a weapon of any kind involved, much less a fucking nuclear weapon.

He had planned to get off the ship before they left the Virgin Islands. After all, he had done his job, and they were satisfied back there, but the creepy Treacher guy insisted that he stay on board, and that was that. Looking back on it now, he wished he'd jumped off the ship and swam to shore before they left. Had a few Painkillers at the Soggy Dollar. Too late now.

Hilbert stared at the bomb. As a kid, he became fascinated with nukes and learned all he could about them. He even thought about majoring in nuclear physics.

This was what they called a backpack nuke because it was small enough to theoretically be carried as a backpack on the battlefield. When the Soviet Union dissolved in the late eighties, the story was that as many as a hundred of its suitcase nukes were not accounted for. One Russian general had, in fact, come forward years later on *Sixty Minutes* and confirmed this and that some were sold to the highest bidder.

This one was two kilotons. The bomb technician had translated the yellow stenciled Cyrillic on the bomb for him. The equivalent power of two thousand tons of TNT. He was sorry he asked. Everything in a half-mile radius would be vaporized.

He felt something rumble deep in his gut and thought he was going to be sick.

40

The catamaran was a motionless steel island on the water. The sea had been calm since they stopped, and there was only a two-knot breeze from the northeast. Perfect conditions for what they were about to do.

They were just outside the twelve-mile territorial limit of the United States, a few miles east of the main shipping lane into and out of Port Arthur, Texas. Malikov and Treacher stood on the bridge while their men scanned the horizon with surface search radar and high-powered marine binoculars.

As anticipated, there was the usual oil tanker traffic off to the west, queuing up to enter the Sabine Pass and disgorge their loads, but nothing to the north, east, or south. Not even a fishing charter. Malikov smiled at their good fortune. This was perfect for launching the sub.

The sub crew was making the final preparations for its course, carefully rechecking the waypoints. The bomb would be programmed in such a way as to arm itself and detonate only after the sub had surfaced inside the estuary of Lake Sabine. Its final destination waypoint, programmed into the GPS, would put it adjacent to Motiva Enterprises, one of the largest oil refineries in North America, owned by Saudi Aramco. This would ensure immediate destruction of surrounding refineries as well, and forecast wind from the east would carry the fallout inland over nearby Houston for maximum radiation casualties. In addition to the psychological shock, Malikov wanted to be sure the operation was carried out to the complete satisfaction of his clients to guarantee being paid in full.

At last, Hilbert climbed into the small top hatch of the sub and gave the signal for it to be lowered. Acting as helpers for the launch, the sub's two crew members, now permanently displaced from their jobs, came alongside in an inflatable dinghy. Once the sub had settled on the water, they quickly unhooked the two steel cables that had lowered it.

The sub moved out from under the catamaran slowly; once it was clear, Hilbert climbed back out of the top hatch. He closed it, securing it with the watertight wheel, and the dinghy picked him up.

This was the moment of truth that would determine whether the sub performed as it was supposed to without a glitch. Malikov watched silently, his jaw clenched. They had practiced this fully automated maneuver over and over with the two crewmen on board. It had performed flawlessly and entirely hands-off each time, but now that it was for real, Malikov felt a dread of superstition creep in. He glanced at Treacher, who had his familiar bored lizard going.

The sub continued ahead for a short distance as if it were merely going to meander in the direction it had been launched. Then it slowly turned to its new commanded heading and sank below the surface. The whole crew watched in complete silence for another minute until it was completely submerged.

They all sprang into a frenzy of preparations for their escape. It would take a little under two hours for the sub to reach its destination. They had slowed its speed to conserve battery power and ensure the operation's success. Malikov could hardly control his excitement. He felt jubilant. By the end of the day, he would be well on his way to his destiny as ruler of Chechnya.

He signaled to Treacher to lower the big speedboat stowed on the deck near the floatplane. It would take the two of them and the remaining crew ashore to a waiting van, then to a private airfield where his chartered Gulfstream jet was waiting. By the time the bomb went off, they would be well out of the country.

Malikov returned to his private stateroom and picked up the burner sat phone. He dialed a number just outside of Washington, DC, listening to its encryption device go through its series of check tones.

In a historic house on an exclusive horse farm in Virginia, Senator Weloc answered the call. In the room with him was a small group of unelected government intelligence men and women that many would call part of the deep state. People who aided officials like Senator Weloc to carry out operations that were crucial, in their minds, to national security and the interest of a select handful of people with most of the money and power. None of them, except for their mouthpiece, Senator Weloc, would ever see the light of day publicly.

"Yes?" Weloc said.

"The package is on its way. Don't forget our deal."

"We won't," Weloc said, and the line went dead.

Malikov put the phone down, discarding it like an unwanted toy. "Now for some long overdue, unfinished business," he said to the vacant room.

41

The three of them were bound with heavy-duty cable ties to a handrail in the stateroom. Kelly sat on the floor, her hands suspended above her head. Steve sat slumped over next to her. He had briefly come around and spoken to her in the cabin the day before, then slipped back into unconsciousness.

They dragged his limp body up to the big stateroom that morning, and the bright sunlight had started to revive him. The sudden brightness had hurt her eyes at first, but now she watched the crewmen scurrying back and forth and realized with a terrible certainty the ship was being abandoned. Then they brought in Maria, literally kicking and screaming, and tied her beside them.

Kelly's heart sank. In the depths of the last few days after Steve was dumped in her cabin, she had clung to the thought of a rescue by the girl and her boyfriend. The panicked thought rose to the surface of her mind that they would all be shot at any moment. She could no longer suppress the tears. They flooded her eyes and blurred her vision, and she cursed herself for her weakness.

A switch was thrown somewhere below, and the main generator was shut down. A second later, the lights and air conditioning went off. Outside, she heard the engines idling on the speedboat. She had seen them lowering it into the water. This is it, Kelly thought. We're going to die now.

Then Malikov and Treacher walked into the stateroom. They seemed nonchalant and in no particular hurry as if this were something they did every day. Malikov had an unemotional, detached look as he approached Maria and held her face up with his hand under her chin.

Treacher nodded toward the open door, and two men brought Maria's boyfriend, Yuri, into the cabin. They held him in front of her, a terrified look on his face. Maria gasped aloud at this new turn of events.

"I've known all about you and your little friend for some time, my dear," he said, slowly drawing his pistol from a shoulder holster under his jacket. "Did you really think I was going to let you live? I treated you so well all these years, and this is how you repay me?"

"You promised me you would let us live." Then a look of defiance came over her face. "I'd rather die than live as your slave again," she said, giving him a cold, hard stare.

"And die you shall," Malikov answered. He turned and shot her boyfriend in the forehead. He fell straight back into a sitting position in one of the plush leather chairs in the room, a neat hole in his forehead and a dark mass of blood covering his shoulders and back.

Maria screamed and turned away, expecting to be next.

Instead, Malikov holstered his pistol and turned to Kelly, hardly glancing at Maria, whose life he had manipulated once again.

"I've decided to leave you alive as the boat sinks around you," he said.

Kelly was flooded with emotions. Relief at not being dispatched like Maria's boyfriend but intense fear from the horror scene that popped into her head, of watching and feeling the boat fill with water around them, helpless to do anything about it. Malikov studied her face and was pleased by his decision.

"We must dispose of the evidence, you see," he said. "We've set small charges in each hull," he continued in his theatrical manner, "precisely placed to blow small holes without doing too much damage. The ship will fill with water and go straight to the bottom, and if they ever find her, they will trace her registration back to one of my rivals in the drug business. Someone else who deserves a little 'payback,' as you Americans are so fond of saying."

Kelly remained silent, and Maria stifled a sob.

"She has served me well," he said, looking around the cabin and then at Maria. "But like all beautiful things, it must come to an end."

The bomb technician appeared from below and gave a nod. The charges were set. Malikov turned away from them like a predator that had suddenly lost interest in its prey. He left the room quickly. Kelly could see the crew outside on the deck boarding the speedboat.

She tried to rouse Steve. She shook him as hard as she dared and thought she saw his eyelids flutter in response, but he still would not wake up. She stood, twisting her wrists around until she faced the handrail and studied it for a minute, looking for a weak point. It was made of heavy-gauge stainless steel tubing, joined to the wall in several places with brackets and bolts. She strained against the wall, putting her foot against it while holding the handrail.

Nothing happened. The spot had been well chosen.

"Help me!" Kelly said to Maria. When Maria didn't respond, she repeated her request as a command.

Slowly, Maria came out of her stupor, and they both began yanking furiously at the rail. The wall the rail was so firmly attached to was made of solid mahogany, one of the most beautiful and hardest woods. It had probably come from an old tree deep in some rain forest, dried for years, then sealed with multiple layers of shellac. It might as well have been made of steel.

Next, they tried to break the cable ties. Their wrists began to chafe and bleed as they struggled frantically against the heavy-duty plastic. It was thick, and the ratcheted locks of the ties were made to hold a thousand times the force the women were now feebly applying to it.

They pulled again in unison with all their might. Kelly knew that in their fanatical despair, they were exerting many times their normal abilities. Yet all they accomplished was nearly pulling their arms from their sockets and further flaying their blood-soaked wrists.

Kelly noticed movement through one of the stateroom windows. The speedboat bobbed in the waves at a safe distance like a scavenger waiting for a wounded animal to die.

The explosions were muffled belowdecks like distant thunder. Two of the big glass windows cracked, and the women were knocked to the floor with a shock wave that shook the whole ship. As she fell, Kelly saw Steve's body rise off the floor, suspended as if in slow motion, and then slam into the wall.

He was suddenly awake.

42

Steve struggled to his feet too quickly and doubled over with the pain in his head, but he managed to stay on his feet while clutching the rail as if he were learning to walk again. He fought to stand up straight with tremendous effort, then forced his head to clear and his eyes to focus. He couldn't hear out of his right ear, and that side of his head throbbed with every quickening heartbeat. Then he remembered where he was and what had happened, and his anger fortified him.

Kelly was saying something to him with a terrified look on her face. But she was shouting into his right ear; he couldn't understand what she was saying. It was too much information at once, and she was talking too fast. Her eyes were wild. Another woman standing beside her was nearly hysterical. He had seen her somewhere before. They were all tied to a rail in what he recognized as the main stateroom. Then he heard through his good ear and saw at the same moment that water was pouring into the room.

The ship listed sharply to one side, then righted itself as the distribution of water equalized. The holes had been blown in precise locations to allow the vessel to fill and sink upright, minimizing the chance that one of the hulls would trap enough air to keep the ship on the surface. A rush of adrenaline surged through Steve's veins as he comprehended their situation.

They had tied him to the last bracket holding the rail to the wall. "Pull with me here!" he shouted. With their combined effort against the single bracket, they might possibly break free. It was their only chance.

The women instantly slid down as close as they could to Steve and the last bracket. He glanced through the broken window and saw the speedboat accelerate away. He made a mental note of the boat.

The water now covered their ankles and was rapidly rising.

"On three!" he said. "One, two, three!"

They yanked in perfect unison with all their combined strength. The bracket moved a little, but the bolts held tight. He called out the cadence again; this time, the bracket appeared to separate from the wall a fraction of an inch more. It was working, but it would take them hours to break free. The ship listed to one side again, and the water inside the cabin was suddenly up to their calves. At this rate, Steve thought, the ship would sink in minutes.

43

Treacher was at the helm with Malikov by his side as the oversized cigarette-style speedboat skimmed across the warm gulf waters like a giant flying fish. A few thunderstorms lingered overland from the previous night, and an onshore breeze had picked up and churned the surface waves to a moderate height. The boat, made for pounding the water at extreme speeds, occasionally leaped from one crest to the next, its twin screws spinning freely in the air for a second before the boat slammed back into the water.

Malikov gave a nod to Treacher, and he covertly pushed the red engine kill switch on the side of the throttles. The engines died, and the boat settled abruptly into the water like an amusement park water ride braking suddenly at the end of its run.

Before anyone could say a word, Treacher barked out an order.

"All of you, get back there and see what the problem is."

The seven remaining crewmen instantly obeyed, followed quickly by the bomb technician, Hilbert, and Ray Ferguson. They knew all too well the consequences of being stuck on the water within the kill zone of the bomb. Malikov stayed at Treacher's side while Treacher feigned an attempt to restart the engines, his other hand still depressing the kill switch.

Then Malikov opened a storage locker while his crew crawled over the engines on the stern. He and Treacher drew two suppressed MP5s from the locker, their thirty-round magazines fully loaded.

With one coordinated movement like a pair of misguided, synchronized dancers, they turned to face the group on the stern.

"Never mind," Treacher said, "we found the problem." He wanted them all to stand up so the rounds would not hit the engines. They had done exactly as he had anticipated, a look of complete surprise on their faces.

The assault created its own lethal symphony. The muffled report of the rifles, the rounds slapping into the crewmen, the empty shell casings hitting the deck, and the fall of the bodies as they hit the water off the back of the boat. Only one fell inside. It was Ferguson. He had made a lunge at Treacher at the last second. He and Malikov lifted him, still alive, and tossed him in the water, where they finished him with the rest of the rounds in their magazines.

The bodies floated for a minute, then sank below the surface, a spreading cloud of blood calling the ever-ravenous creatures of the sea to a banquet.

Treacher started the engines quickly and pointed the boat again to the north.

They were still six or seven miles out, but they could just make out the slight rise of the low land on the horizon. The handheld GPS pointed unerringly to their clandestine landing site.

44

Steve looked around frantically for another option. He needed some kind of tool to cut the thick cable ties, or they were all dead. Scanning the area around him, he spotted the only item remotely within reach. On the wall to his left, away from Kelly and Maria, a small fire extinguisher hung in its bracket. The red cylindrical body and silver metal handle suddenly gave him an idea. It would be a long shot, but it may be their only hope.

Supporting his weight the best he could, Steve stretched out his left foot. Try as he might, he couldn't reach it. The toe of his shoe missed the extinguisher by just an inch or two.

Suddenly, the ship listed to starboard at an acute angle, and Steve feared for a moment that it might flip over on its back. But then it began to right itself, with more water surging through the shattered cabin windows. The starboard hull had flooded faster than the port hull, momentarily causing the lighter side to rise. And in the sudden movement of the ship, the extinguisher had been unseated from its mount. Now, supported only by a single hook below its handle, it swung toward him like a pendulum.

But as they continued to return to level, it began to swing away from him slowly. In a few more seconds, it would be out of reach again.

Stretching the entire length of his leg and pinioned arm, he lifted the heavy extinguisher with the top of his foot with all the strength he could summon. He held it there, cradling it against his shin. If he dropped it, it would be lost in the rising water, and he wouldn't get a second chance. It was a precarious balance at best, and the ship was in constant motion in the waves as it slowly returned more or less to level. Kelly looked on as he struggled to drag the extinguisher toward him through the water, pinning it to the wall beneath the handrail.

There was a loud bang as one of the bulkheads gave way below, and they could hear water rushing in somewhere nearby. It would be only minutes before the ship reached the critical turning point where it could no longer support the weight of the water filling its hulls. It would sink rapidly to the bottom, dragging them with it. Kelly was silent, staring intently at what Steve was doing, but Maria was sobbing uncontrollably, the floating body of her boyfriend nearby, and her cries the only sound above the nightmarish roar of rushing water.

Steve worked the extinguisher toward his tied hands, trying to keep it balanced and against the wall. When it was mere inches away, the ship shuddered violently as another main bulkhead gave way, and the cylinder began a slow roll away from the wall. Just then, Kelly's left foot caught it and kept it from toppling any farther. She had maneuvered behind Steve to back him up, and now, pushing against it with the bottom of her foot, slowly slid the extinguisher up the wall to Steve's hands.

He grabbed it and immediately forced the upper handle between the railing and the cable tie binding his left hand. He turned the cylinder sideways to expose the sharper edge of the stamped metal handle, then forced it down as hard as he could, hoping to cut the restraint. His cut and bleeding wrist took the brunt of his efforts at first, but then the plastic tie began to bend. Encouraged, he continued to force the handle back and forth across the tie in a sawing motion. Finally, he broke through it, freeing his left hand.

Kelly gave a delirious cry of relief. Steve hurriedly performed the same operation on his right wrist, cutting the tie in half the time now that his left hand was free. He waded across the room in hip-deep water to the bar, remembering a drawer he had seen Malikov open that contained a small, serrated knife he'd used to cut a slice of lime for his drink. Steve found the knife, then sloshed back to the women and cut them loose.

They were rubbing their wrists, shaking their arms to restore circulation, when the boat settled abruptly, and water began to fill the stateroom at a new and alarming rate. The final stage of the doomed ship had begun; there was no time to lose. As if in the slow motion of a bad dream, they waded as fast as humanly possible through water that was now up to the women's shoulders toward an exit that would lead them to the upper deck near the bridge, then to the roof of the stateroom. Soon, it would be the only place above water on the ship.

Below them, the hulls were nearly full of water. They were about to become giant sea-filled anchors that would drag the vessel to the bottom like an anvil tied to a wine bottle cork. The placement of the charges to sink the boat upright might actually have given them more time in the end. If either of the hulls had filled before the other, it could have dragged the rest of the ship under by now.

As they reached the roof and emerged into the bright morning sunlight, Steve looked around wildly. There was no dinghy or small boat anywhere. The deck-mounted life rafts in their hard-shell cases were all below water level.

The ship settled again violently as the last air escaped from its hulls. Only the connecting area between the hulls was keeping the catamaran temporarily afloat. Its limited buoyancy would soon give way.

Then he saw the floatplane, still secure in its cradle on the far end of the roof.

Kelly followed Steve's gaze, and a look of relief erupted on her face. Maria saw it too and grabbed Kelly's hand with a cry of joy.

"We're not out of this yet," Steve said with urgency as they ran across the roof of the stateroom, water lapping its sides. "It's tied down. We have to release it before the ship goes under."

Then Steve saw the sharks, and he froze.

Called from the depths by new smells of a dying ship and the blood of Maria's boyfriend Yuri, a quartet of bull sharks and a huge lone hammerhead swam along the length of the submerged hulls. A few of the bull sharks turned in quick circles and twitched their tails impatiently, waiting for the feast. The catamaran settled again another few feet, and the roof they were all standing on was underwater. Every fiber in Steve's body told him to move, but he stood in place as if chained to the deck.

Kelly and Maria ran ahead of him toward the floatplane. They turned to look at him, their eyes wild in disbelief.

"Steve!" Kelly shouted. We've got to get to the plane. What are you doing?"

Steve didn't answer because he didn't hear her. He was in a dark chasm deep in his soul, staring at the sharks. His mind was replaying a distant memory of a mission with his SEAL team gone bad—when half of them had been attacked by sharks. The same day, he should have been home.

And then he heard a voice with no face telling him this was not his day to die. It was a voice he had not heard in over twenty years. His dead wife, Janice.

The hammerhead swam across the newfound water on top of the roof near the floatplane, its belly scraping the boat and its tall dorsal fin and tail almost entirely out of the water. Its eye on the end of its grotesque head pivoted to look at them as it swam by.

"Get to the plane and start untying it," Kelly told Maria. Then she turned back and covered the distance to Steve in an instant.

"Steve," she said, her hands on his shoulders, trying to make him look at her. "It's okay. We've got to get to the plane."

Steve was transfixed, watching the hammerhead. Kelly followed his gaze. The shark was approaching to swim near them, the water where they stood not yet deep enough to attack. When the shark was close enough, Kelly kicked it in its eye as hard as she could. It raced away quickly, colliding with one of the bull sharks in its escape.

Steve was looking at her now and shaking his head. "This is not my time," he said. "Not today. Let's get the hell out of here."

They sloshed their way to the floatplane, still above the water in its cradle. Maria had only managed to get one of the four tiedowns loose. Frantically, silently, consumed, and intent on their purpose, they worked on the ratcheted tiedowns that held the plane.

As the water reached them, they scrambled on top of the plane's pontoons. The ship went down under them in the next second, the last of the trapped air inside it exhaling in one giant dying breath and shooting a plume of water and air vertically that rained down on them like a blessing. There was a horrifying moment when one of the tiedowns attached to the plane snagged on its cleat in the cradle and violently pulled the pontoon down in the water, but it gave way, releasing the plane and popping the pontoon back out of the water like a bathtub toy. They stood there for a minute perched on the starboard pontoon, panting and listening to the muffled sounds of the ship's bulkheads collapsing under the increasing pressure as she sank.

Around them were just a few remnants on the surface. A bobbing ice chest half submerged, a few pieces of paper, apples from the galley, and a very thin oil slick. The shock of their narrow escape overwhelmed them all. Steve found himself hugging both women, and everyone started talking at once, grateful to be alive and given a second chance. There was no sign of the sharks. They had followed the ship to the bottom to pick through the wreck.

Steve had not forgotten the sub, silently speeding toward its target with its payload of nuclear destruction. "Everyone in the plane!" he said.

"Do you know how to fly this thing?" Maria asked.

"He was a pilot in the Navy," Kelly answered her. But she knew it wasn't the flying that might be a problem. It was taking off and landing on the open ocean with its never-ending swells and troughs that could do in the uninitiated. Steve had explained this all to her when they chartered the floatplane and pilot in Charlotte Amalie. Maria, however, accepted Kelly's reassuring answer with relief. A pilot trained by the Navy would certainly have been taught to take off and land a plane on the water.

But Steve had never flown a floatplane before, though it had been on his list of things to do for a long time. He had more than three thousand hours flying a wide range of aircraft in the Navy, most of them infinitely more complicated than this one. He tried to remember what a bush pilot friend had once told him about open ocean takeoffs and hoped he could get the thing airborne if need be. But perhaps that wouldn't be necessary.

He found the key and switched on the ignition. The DC gauges sprang to life, the ammeter indicating a fully charged battery. He flipped through frequencies on the outmoded analog radio dial until he'd selected the VHF guard frequency of 121.5, an emergency frequency continually monitored by the military, air traffic control, and most aircraft.

"Where are we?" Steve said.

"Near Port Arthur, Texas," Maria answered. "I overheard that much."

He switched on the cockpit speaker. "Mayday, Mayday, Mayday!" he shouted into the handheld microphone. Nothing.

He repeated the international call for help. Still nothing.

He was puzzled. Aircraft flying overhead and air traffic control with their network of powerful receiving towers monitored this frequency continuously, all the more so in the advent of 9/11. Someone should have heard him this close to shore. But there was also no sidetone in the speaker, and he couldn't hear himself transmitting. It was like shouting in a concrete vault underground; no one was going to hear him. He concluded that either the damn thing was inoperable or possibly worked only when the engine was running.

"We're not transmitting," he explained. "We'll have to get the engine started and try again."

Kelly looked at him and nodded.

"How long ago did they launch the sub?"

The women agreed that about an hour had gone by.

"It's running on batteries in order to remain silent and undetected," Steve said. "If its speed has been slowed to four or five knots to conserve power, that gives us another thirty to forty-five minutes, assuming ground zero is near the refineries."

"Maria, did you overhear anything about when the bomb would go off?" Kelly asked.

"No, nothing. I'm sorry. They were very careful not to tell me anything or even speak of it around me in the last few days. My boyfriend knew nothing, either. They were all paranoid that word would get out."

Steve turned the engine over, and it started. He tried the radio again, this time listening through a Telex headset he found hanging from a hook behind him in the cockpit. He turned an overhead speaker up as a backup.

Still no response.

"Everybody strap in tight," he said. After a quick check, he opened the throttle, kicked the rudder over, and headed the plane as close as he could into the wind, studying the growing swells on the open water.

"Whatever you do," he remembered his bush pilot friend saying, "don't fly into the crest of a wave when you take off. It'll ruin your whole day."

That was consistent with everything the Navy had taught him about ditching at sea. Land parallel to the swells, not into them—easier said than done, of course. By taking off parallel to the rolling swells, one automatically acquired a crosswind because the swells moved with the wind. The more crosswind, the less lift across the wings to help get the plane in the air.

"Is everyone ready?"

The women gave their belts one last cinch and nodded.

Steve opened the throttle until the needles on the engine gauges were at maximum power. The floatplane responded, creating a hurricane of spraying water behind it. Keeping the control yoke back, he tried to anticipate the swells to prevent the pontoons from digging into the water and flipping the plane over. The swells had grown to over five feet, easily enough to bury the small plane if it plowed into the face of one, so he tried to apply just enough rudder to stay inside them as they swept across the surface.

In the distance to the west, he noticed a line of thunderstorms several miles away. He would be able to avoid them, but he'd have preferred one less complicating factor right now. The plane was accelerating as he held it firmly in the troughs of the swells.

At last, the plane seemed to rise a little, then settle as if it had lost its nerve. This must have been what they called getting up on step, the water-to-air transition between takeoff and flight or flight and landing, when you weren't quite flying, and you weren't a speedboat either, as his friend had said. Just a little further, and they would have enough speed for takeoff.

Then Steve saw the crest of a wave, twice as tall as any of the others, approaching at a right angle to his direction of travel against the prevailing troughs and swells he had been paralleling. Probably created by the storm miles away, it loomed across his horizon only a few hundred feet ahead like a moving mountain range as the plane skimmed the rough surface of the trough.

There was no time to check his airspeed and nowhere else to go. He waited until the last possible second and smoothly pulled the yoke back until it was almost in his lap while simultaneously opening the throttle as far as it would go. The needles leaped into the gauge's red warning areas. If they were allowed to loiter there, the engine could come apart or seize up. The plane made its final transition between water and air as the rogue wave was upon them.

In that instant, Steve remembered a lesson taught by his first training instructor in Pensacola. The seasoned instructor had demonstrated a minimum airspeed takeoff in the T-34C primary trainer. Though he'd rotated the plane well below its normal takeoff speed, the trainer had nonetheless wallowed into the air somehow. "Put that in your back pocket," he said. "It's not in the syllabus, but I like to show it to my students. It might save your ass one day if you're running out of runway. Of course, if you're below stall speed, you'll crash and burn, but you were going to do that anyway."

The floatplane left the water, shaking off spray like a dog bounding from the surf. The yoke trembled ever so slightly in Steve's hands, hinting at the start of a stall. He relaxed it a fraction of an inch and held his breath. The pontoons cleared the rogue wave by less than a foot, its angry spray blowing off the crest like claws, just missing its prey.

They were flying. He stole a glance at his airspeed. It was hovering well below the green, safe airspeed band. So as not to anger the Gods of physics any further, he pushed the nose over a bit and picked up airspeed. He closed the throttle enough to bring the needles out of the red and started a gentle climb when he'd built up enough speed.

She was right. He was not going to die today. Today, he was going to stop a madman.

45

They climbed to twenty-five hundred feet, heading northwest toward Galveston Bay, still at least ten miles away. Malikov had positioned the catamaran as close to the bay as he dared without arousing suspicion. The sub could easily make the short one-way trip.

Steve found that the plane handled nicely now that it was actually doing what it was designed for and not plowing through waves twice its size. He tried the radio again. Still nothing. He cycled the power switch and reset the frequency, volume, and squelch, all to no avail. They had plenty of altitude to transmit and receive. The VOR navigational receiver swung around and locked on a coastal beacon directly in front of them. Its distance-measuring equipment, or DME, read a slant range of fourteen miles. That must be Port Arthur.

Although it was only a rough estimate, he did another mental calculation of where the sub should be. He was sure it would surface once in position, begin a short countdown, and detonate. An underwater explosion would be devastating to the area, but it wouldn't have the total destructive power and psychological effect of a surface blast, shockwave, and subsequent mushroom cloud. In the silence of the cockpit, he half expected to see a brilliant flash in front of them at any moment. Even if he got a warning out in the next few minutes, he wondered what could be done on such short notice.

He glanced at the DME indicator on the VOR receiver. The distance had closed to thirteen miles. He knew that deep inside a windowless air-conditioned building somewhere nearby, they were being closely watched. The Aircraft Defense Identification Zone, or ADIZ, had been intensified since 9/11. All aircraft were tracked on radar as they approached US waters. If they reached the twelve-mile international limit without being identified, they would be intercepted.

It had been some time since Steve had flown regularly. His last two years in the Navy were taken up in a non-flying job in the sandbox—as his colleagues in the military referred to Iraq and Afghanistan—working special envoy missions for the Pentagon. His piloting skills had become a little "rusty" as they say in the aviation community, but his baptism by fire on the takeoff had knocked the rust off with the intensity of an industrial sandblaster. It felt good to be flying again, even under these circumstances.

Somewhere in the back of his mind, he kept working out the radio problem, beginning to think like an aviator again. A broken antenna would do it, but he remembered seeing it intact and undamaged when he first stole onto the plane to hide, a rectangular vane firmly attached to the bottom of the fuselage. In fact, he had made a mental note of it at the time as a possible emergency communication source. All the rest of the plane's instruments were working fine.

He could see the shoreline now and corrected to the right for what looked like some smokestacks. It was easy to guess where the channel was. There was a line of ships of all sizes, oil tankers mostly, coming and going through it. They flew over an anchored supertanker, with a smaller tanker parked alongside, taking in crude fuel for one of the mega refineries. As they got closer, he saw a long bridge spanning the bay a few miles inland, and in the perpetual summer haze, he could make out the refineries inside the bay.

His mind returned to the radio. Everything depended on it. If he couldn't get it working, he would have to decide whether or not to break off the attempt, dive to a low altitude just above the water to avoid the shock wave as best he could, then fly upwind at the greatest possible speed. It would have been easier if he had been alone. Then there would be no question that he would have continued straight ahead in an attempt to warn someone.

Then the answer hit him like an epiphany. Circuit breaker.

Frantically, he scanned the cockpit. Kelly and Maria watched him but could only look on with bewildered expressions.

"What is it?" Kelly said.

"Look for a circuit breaker panel," he said.

"Oh shit! Of course."

Individual circuits providing power to the aircraft's electrical components were protected from faults and overloads in much the same way circuit breakers function in every wired building in the world. A momentary surge past the amperage a breaker was rated for would "pop" the breaker and open the circuit, removing power from that circuit and everything it powered until the fault was corrected or the breaker was reset. Try as they might, though, they could not find the panel.

Then Maria said, "I think it's in there," pointing to a small door above Steve's head. "I've seen the pilot from the catamaran open it before."

Steve opened the panel. A flood of relief washed over him. There they were—eight circuit breakers in a horizontal row. One of them, the second from the right, clearly showed a white collar against its black background, a visual indicator that it had popped. The letters VHF COMM were stenciled beneath it. He pushed it in.

The radio came to life. There was talk on it, but the squelch, turned up too high, was drowning it out. The frequency was still set on 121.5, VHF guard. Steve rotated the squelch knob, and a loud voice suddenly boomed from the speakers above their heads.

"Unknown rider. Unknown rider. At twenty-five hundred feet AGL, bearing one hundred and fifty degrees from Sabine Pass VOR at ten miles, tracking three five zero degrees. This is Air Force Coastal Defense Control on guard. You have entered US airspace. Respond and reverse your course, or you will be intercepted."

It was the best words they could have hoped for, and Steve picked up the microphone.

46

In the computer screen–lit underworld of the windowless high-security Houston Air Traffic Control Center, in a special military room with "USAF Coastal Defense/Det 151" stenciled across the door, the tech sergeant on duty was staring intently at a blip on his screen. It designated a low-flying aircraft that had brazenly penetrated the ADIZ a minute and a half ago and failed to respond to his repeated calls on all frequencies. Not really an unheard-of event by itself. It happened a couple of times a year when some clueless private pilot forgot to check-in. Back in the day, it wasn't such a big deal, but nowadays, no one took any chances with unidentified aircraft that could potentially be loaded with bombs or filled with fuel, like the events of 9/11.

What made this particular sighting unique was its sudden appearance on the screen. The sergeant had worked at this site for over three years, and he had never seen a target appear out of nowhere like this one. Every other time, he had spotted unidentified targets, from the surface to high altitude, long before they got close to the twelve-mile limit, thanks to a tethered radar balloon directly south of the center and an integrated system that alerted the controller a new target had appeared and needed to be identified. The balloon, permanently held in place by an eighteen-thousand-foot steel cable, was on station twenty-four hours a day. The system shouted warnings when an aircraft was well offshore so controllers could identify and approve it to continue into US airspace. Targets never just appeared suddenly this close to shore.

Working with its sister balloons strategically positioned along the coast with overlapping radar coverage, there were simply no aircraft that suddenly appeared without warning. With the permission of the officer of the watch, the sergeant had initiated the first step to scramble a fighter intercept. He'd just given them the go-ahead when he heard a response, finally, from the unknown aircraft.

Usually, in such cases, this was the voice of an inexperienced private pilot, scared or embarrassed or both, returning from a party weekend somewhere like Cancun. But this voice was different. The pilot spoke in a deliberate, confident, direct voice but said some crazy things. The sergeant's first thought was that it was either a hoax or a clever diversion.

The officer of the watch was now by his side, talking to intercept fighters from the nearby Air National Guard base.

"Bandit 7 is wheels up. ETA three minutes," he said to the sergeant, referring to the two F-16s launched minutes ago.

"He's saying something about a submarine," the sergeant responded. "He penetrated the ADIZ three minutes ago."

"Turn him to a heading of one eight zero," the officer said calmly, studying the radar screen in front of them. He could see the intercepting fighters now, moving across the screen from the north at just under the speed of sound. A ground stop had been issued at major airports in the area, halting all takeoffs. Another private plane transited the area at thirty-five hundred feet parallel to the coastline, which would conflict with the intercept flight.

"Bandit 7, climb to angels five," the officer commanded the intercept flight. He and the sergeant watched the target on the radar, representing the two fighters immediately climbing to five thousand feet to avoid the private plane. They struck past a Beach Bonanza carrying a very surprised retired couple seconds later.

The Unknown Rider was still tracking north toward the coast, not responding to their order to turn south. The officer of the watch told the sergeant that if the Unknown Rider didn't turn around pretty soon, they might have to shoot him down.

Steve held the microphone and stared ahead intently. He could make out the shoreline now and the bridge spanning the bay. The women sat silently. Steve knew they were coming to terms with the uneasy fact that they were approaching the source of mortal danger rather than turning away from it and fleeing for their lives.

"Cessna NP587X," the sergeant replied as if he were a recorded message, "you are in violation of the United States ADIZ. Turn around to a heading of one eight zero and head away from land."

Steve saw the F-16s now, appearing ahead of him as small dots, then filling his windscreen the next time he blinked. He held his course for the entrance to the channel, now only five miles off the nose of the floatplane. The jets passed in front of him, speed brakes extended to slow their speed and to create as much wake turbulence as they could to deter the float-plane. They split left and right of him as they passed, displaying the array of missiles tucked neatly below their wings. Steve noted the Texas Air National Guard emblem on their tails.

He climbed another five hundred feet to avoid their wake turbulence, then spotted smoke plumes of the giant refineries deep inside the bay. Looking more closely, he also saw a docked cruise ship with black diesel smoke rising from its stack as it prepared to get underway.

When the officer of the watch first heard Steve mention the word *submarine*, he knew that in the extremely unlikely event the crazy man in the Cessna was indeed telling the truth, the situation was well beyond his area of expertise. The F-16s had confirmed a single-engine floatplane with three passengers, not armed, but after the events of 9/11, the plane itself was a potential missile. He knew he could not let them reach the coast. In fact, he had only another minute or so before they were too close to the shore-line for the wreckage to fall harmlessly into the water.

Then he remembered the naval officer from a nearby base that had come around several months ago. The officer was an older, overweight, gruff passed-over lieutenant commander that no one liked very much. He had made the rounds to all the coastal centers with the self-important message that he was on assignment with the Navy on a special-interest project involving submarines. If they saw or heard anything unusual, they were to contact him. "Anything, anything unusual at all," he had stated emphatically.

The officer of the watch picked up the direct line to the Navy and made the call.

A petty officer answered the phone and spit out a long-winded greeting naming the facility the caller had reached, the division and department, and his name, rank, and title.

"I need to speak with Lieutenant Commander Ross," the officer of the watch said impatiently. "It's extremely urgent."

The petty officer groaned inwardly. Ross was never around much. In fact, he hadn't seen him yet this morning, and if today was typical, the fat slob would come dragging in just before lunch, hungover as usual.

To his amazement, Ross walked through the door that very moment with a mug of coffee in his hand.

"Sir," the petty officer said, "there's an urgent call for you."

Ross never got urgent calls. He was long divorced, his kids grown, his parents dead. He sprinted across the room quicker than the astonished petty officer would have thought possible and grabbed the phone.

He listened to what the ADIZ officer said, then put him on hold. He dialed a number and said with crisp precision, "Launch the ready alert for Port Arthur; report to me when they're airborne," then he returned to the other line.

"Can you put this guy on speaker?" Ross asked the ADIZ officer.

"I can do better than that," he replied. "I'll pipe him directly into your line. But we don't have much time here. We're going to have to splash him soon."

47

For the last several months, the faint, occasional sounds of an unidentified engine and propeller acoustic signature had been detected and monitored by the Navy's Integrated Undersea Surveillance System (IUSS). The system's computer algorithm identified a diesel-electric submarine as the probable source. The mystery sub had made most of its appearances along the Southeast Atlantic coast.

IUSS is an elaboration of SOSUS or Sound Surveillance System, an array of underwater microphones developed during the Cold War to track Soviet submarines. Since the mid-nineties, however, narco-submarines had become a more compelling concern to the Navy and DEA.

Lieutenant Commander Ross had observed their evolution from death-traps for ferrying cocaine from Colombia to Mexico to sophisticated home-made semi-submersible vessels able to dive to depths of thirty feet or more to avoid detection.

When the latest IUSS contact near the Florida Keys coincided with the mysterious disappearance of a P-3 and its crew, it was Ross who connected the two incidents. Because an Admiral friend owed him a favor, the Navy reluctantly agreed to explore the matter further. Several P-3 Orions had been strategically placed along the coast and been on alert for the last few months. Armed with two MK-46 torpedoes, expressly designed for submarine warfare during the Cold War, they were ready at a moment's notice for the call they had just received. They were from the same squadron as the one lost off the coast of Florida, and they were out for blood. Ross's call was to the crew at Ellington Field, just minutes away.

"The P-3 is airborne, sir," the petty officer said. Ross nodded.

"Tell them buster speed for Port Arthur and stand by," he said, returning his attention to the other line and knowing that the P-3 would accelerate to its maximum redline airspeed of four hundred and eleven knots to meet the threat.

Steve was making a slow turn now back to the south. He had no illusions about the F-16s' intentions. He watched as they set up a classic attack pattern between him and the shoreline. He wanted to assure them he was not hostile. He knew the drill. If he got any closer, they would blow him out of the sky. They had probably already received authorization.

In spite of that, he deliberately shallowed his turn for a moment, and the new perspective of the entrance to the bay confirmed his guess of the sub's intended track. A line of tankers streamed in and out of the bay on a titanic two-lane highway. Their course took them down the middle of the dredged channel and under the center of the bridge to the refineries. He imagined the little sub with its horrific cargo dutifully driving beneath the tankers like a remora in a giant pod of whales.

"I think the sub will enter the bay right down the middle of the channel, then surface and detonate near the refineries," Steve said into the mic as he finished his turn.

Ross needed to quickly evaluate who was flying the floatplane. There were too many ways this could all go sideways if it was a hoax, a lie, or a decoy of some kind. He pushed the transmit button on the mic to talk to Steve.

"This is Commander Ross," he said. "Identify yourself."

"Steve Remington."

Ross paused, staring into space as if searching his mind for a memory of that name. He felt like he had heard it before somewhere in his career.

"Ever in the military, Mr. Remington?" Ross asked.

"Navy," Steve replied. "Retired."

"Persian Gulf?"

"A few times."

"What commands?"

"With the teams, then on the *Kennedy* with VF-14, then as an LSO on the *Nimitz*."

"Were you in the Iraq War?" Ross asked on a hunch.

"Briefly, on a mission just before the war started," Steve said. "I was with SEAL team Six then."

That was it. Ross had been attached to a Marine amphibious transport ship during the war. The ship had taken on a SEAL team for a critical mission just days before the war started. The mission was to take out a key command and control bunker that defended the southern half of Iraq from air attack.

Ross remembered the determined, hard-looking Remington as one of the two survivors who returned from the mission.

"What was the name of your mission with SEAL Team Six?" Ross asked for a final verification.

"Sir," the petty officer interrupted, "the P-3 is approaching the target area, awaiting your orders."

Ross held his index finger in the petty officer's face. This was crucial. The name of the mission was still classified, and only those who were there would know the name. It would prove Steve was who he said he was.

There was a pause. Ross feared Remington had not heard him. They were running out of time.

"Did you hear my last transmission, Mr. Remington?" Ross said.

"Five by five," Steve said, indicating he had heard it loud and clear.

"The name of the mission was Spearpoint."

"I remember you," Ross replied. All eyes in the command center were on Ross now. The senior managers of the center had entered the room minutes ago.

"We've got a good handshake," he said, indicating they had identified the Unknown Rider as not hostile. There was a collective sigh of relief in the room.

Steve gave Ross a short, detailed brief of the situation with the sub.

"Have the P-3 lay a pattern of sonobuoys across the mouth of the channel," Ross said to the petty officer. "Tell them the sub is unmanned, so there won't be any maneuvering. It will detonate once it reaches the surface."

The petty officer's jaw dropped open involuntarily.

"And one more thing," Ross said. "Tell them the sub is a hostile terrorist threat and that they are weapons-free."

48

The P-3C was loaded with two MK-46 mod5A anti-submarine torpedoes in its bomb bay, and on the ordnance stations under the wings, four five-hundred-pound Mk-82 iron bombs with Snake Eye tail configuration for low-altitude release. The bombs were initially intended for use only as a last resort to prevent a submarine from surfacing to launch its missiles—a carryover from the Cold War and the threat of Russian ballistic missile submarines in an era not so long ago. But for patrols involving suspected drug smugglers, the Navy equipped its planes to defend against surface fire.

The real weapon was the MK-46 torpedo. Dropped near its underwater target, it would listen, then seek out the specific acoustic signature it had been programmed to destroy. The mod 5A version the P-3 carried today was improved for shallow-water performance. It was time-honored and deadly accurate. Once it acquired a submarine, it would accelerate to over fifty knots and deliver its hundred-pound PBXN-103 high-explosive warhead straight into it. The optimum delivery altitude coincided with the best altitude for the magnetic detection device—or MAD boom—on the tail of the aircraft. Lower was always better, but the weapon needed a minimum of two hundred feet to fully deploy and arm before it hit the water.

The F-16s were called off and put into a holding pattern at five thousand feet. Steve climbed a little higher and, to his great relief, saw the P-3 approaching along the coastline at an altitude he estimated at just a few hundred feet. He watched as it laid its pattern of sonobuoys across the entrance to the channel.

Each sonobuoy, spit out from preloaded tubes on the belly of the plane, immediately deployed an underwater microphone called a hydrophone to a specified depth. The sonobuoy tube floated like an elongated cork on the surface, popped up a small antenna, and then began sending its information back to the P-3 overhead. The plane's onboard computer processed the information from each buoy and presented it in a graphic display. If a suspect frequency was detected—the frequency of an electric motor drive or subsurface propeller, for example—the target location could be triangulated based on its bearing from each buoy, then tracked and, if necessary, destroyed.

While the usual collection of fishing boats, shrimpers, and tankers went about their business below, on board the P-3, the two sensor operators—highly trained enlisted men—sat at the heart of the plane's listening center studying a visual screen depicting the various frequencies picked up by the sonobuoys and listening to the unique sounds of their targets. The ambient noise of all this surface traffic concentrated in the shallow bay was overwhelming. Compounding the difficulty was that the sensors didn't know exactly what type of sub they were looking for and, therefore, which frequency band to search in.

They did have the "mystery" sub's contact frequency that IUSS had identified in the Keys less than a year ago, but that had been produced by a diesel engine, not the quieter hum of an electric motor drive, which now powered the sub. The senior sensor operator shook his head. He had never worked in a crowded bay like this, with so much interfering noise. Finding and tracking a sub in the open ocean was hard enough—even distant shipping noise well over the horizon could interfere with the intricate process. This was like trying to hear through a cell phone in the front row of an AC/DC concert. They were running out of time, and they knew it.

On a whim, the senior operator powered up an older analog processing device still on the plane, although seldom used these days in the digital world. It had saved his bacon more than once in his thirty-year career. He controlled it with a well-worn rotary dial at his station, rotating it to match the mystery sub's frequency. The antiquated processor looked at a narrow band of very low frequencies, like that of a specific propeller shaft. No matter what was powering the sub, the propeller was still turning, and buried in the IUSS recording, under the diesel engine noise, was the specific frequency of its prop.

And there it was, as weak as the hum of a mosquito in a flock of seagulls, but it was fading fast. He locked onto it.

"Definitely an underwater contact," the operator said into the open interphone communications system.

"Electro-diesel motor," he added. "I'm sending it to you now, TACCO."

The tactical officer, or TACCO as he was called, quickly gathered the sonobuoy data on the screen before him. Each buoy was represented by a symbol based on its location in the pattern, and each drew a bearing toward the frequency the senior operator had located. Where the lines crossed on the screen was the target's exact location.

When the position and course were plotted, the sub was pinpointed north of the buoy pattern, already well inside the breakers and in Sabine Pass, course three-four-zero degrees magnetic, speed five knots and slowing. It was entering Sabine Lake near the refineries, slowing as it neared the final waypoint on its programmed course. Soon, it would begin its ascent to the surface.

Steve could only watch the show from above. He had positioned the floatplane in a holding pattern near the bridge, but he had no secure radio to keep up with the P-3's progress. He called the operations center for information.

"Still trying to acquire the target," was all Ross had time to say.

He thought about turning the floatplane upwind and hauling ass. They had to be minutes away from detonation, though, and there was no turning back now. Besides, it looked like the P-3 had found something.

He watched the plane make a tight turn over the channel. It flew over the center of the bridge, clearing its highest point by only fifty feet, and dropped a single buoy in the middle of the channel on the north side. It splashed into the water, narrowly missing a tanker, and Steve guessed it must be close to the sub's location. Then he noticed the big cruise ship had left the dock, its giant props clouding the water behind it, and was bearing down on the buoy less than half a mile away. Traffic was backing up on the bridge as some cars stopped to watch the show while others drove around them as if nothing unusual was happening.

Unlike the initial buoys dropped in the search pattern, which were merely passive microphones, the last one was an active buoy that could be commanded to send a sonar ping toward the sub to acquire its exact location and depth rather than a triangulated estimate. Active buoys are typically used just prior to weapons drop or to agitate a target, and this one revealed that the sub had nearly stopped. Its position as ground zero would obliterate the area, leveling the refineries and surrounding structures and tossing the cruise ship and tankers around like pool toys. The upper prevailing winds would then carry the deadly nuclear fallout inland, contaminating most of Houston, as the second half of Malikov's plan called for.

The TACCO called the pilots. "Target has stopped and is ascending."

"Bomb bay doors are open. Master arm is on," was the answer from the cockpit. The patrol plane commander, or PPC, was sitting in the left seat and flying the plane. He was also the mission commander and coordinated the crew in prosecuting the target.

The TACCO selected the torpedo from his console, glanced at the current depth of the sub at fifty feet, and set the torpedo's depth at thirty.

After the PPC dropped the last sonobuoy, he had turned and crossed back over the bridge to the south in an oval-shaped pattern. Now that they knew the sub's exact position and that it had stopped, he wouldn't be able to fly back over the bridge and dive to release the torpedo within the optimum airspeed and altitude parameters required; the sub was too close to the bridge. And there wasn't time for another run.

He took a good look at the center span of the bridge, which was tall enough to accommodate some of the largest tankers. There was only one thing to do. He would have to fly under the bridge. There was just enough room if he put the big four-engine turboprop right on the water as he passed under it. He told his copilot and the flight engineer what he had in mind. The copilot in the right seat looked at him dumbfounded, then managed a slight nod in agreement. Without a word, the flight engineer disabled the low-altitude warning horn as if this were something he did every day. The PPC turned the P-3 back toward the bridge and eased the plane down to the waterline, the four giant Hamilton props so close to the surface that they sucked up salt spray like miniature waterspouts and threw it in all directions.

They were on the attack run now. The whole crew was electrified and focused on their mission. No one spoke. Everyone knew from countless hours of practice exactly what to do.

The PPC tweaked the airspeed to within the exact parameters for the torpedo drop. After passing under the bridge, he would ease the plane up to two hundred feet. The bridge loomed ahead, and he made a final correction with the rudder to pass exactly through the middle span. There was a moment when it felt like they had flown into a tunnel, followed by the glimpse of some startled fishermen in a boat beneath the bridge. Then they were through, and the plane was climbing back up to two hundred feet.

The sensor three operator, manning the scope that monitored the MAD boom, was standing by. As the plane flew directly over the target, the scope would provide a final confirmation when the tail device picked up a change in the earth's magnetic field triggered by the metal submarine. This would produce a spike on his scope like a sudden heartbeat on a flat-lined EKG screen.

The TACCO put his finger on the release button, his eyes glued to his tactical scope.

Five seconds, four . . .

The PPC held his course to the target. It would take them directly over the cruise ship, which was trying to stop dead in the water on the other side of the bridge. He was in danger of hitting the radio tower on top of the multi-decked ship if he didn't change course immediately after weapon release.

One second to target. The TACCO released the torpedo. Through the viewing window above the bomb bay, the onboard ordnance man watched it release perfectly and fall straight to the surface, as it was supposed to, its arming wires detaching and falling beside it in a perfect arc.

"Weapon away," the ordnance man shouted over the ICS.

A second later, the sensor three operator called out, "Mad man, mad!" as the anomaly device spiked his graph.

The PPC yanked the P-3 up and abruptly to the right to avoid the cruise ship. The ordnance man, still looking through the bomb bay window, saw a number of passengers, uncommonly close on the deck of the cruise ship, waving as if this were all part of their entertainment.

The senior sensor operator was monitoring the high-speed whirl of the torpedo's dual propellers intermixed with the pings from the active buoy and the deafening background sound of the reverse engine props of the cruise ship.

"Torpedo in the water," he said calmly. "Torpedo has gone active."

The P-3 crew gave a collective sigh of relief. The weapon had been loaded and dropped correctly within its parameters. There were many things that could have gone wrong. Now, even though the torpedo had been dropped right on top of the sub, it still had to begin its run, acquire its target, then turn and intercept it.

"Torpedo has acquired the target, range two hundred yards," the sensor operator said. On board the submarine, its electronic arming device, ingeniously hooked up to the fathometer, was counting down the ascent to the surface. It would begin its sequence at ten feet and detonate at zero. A true doomsday machine, it waited patiently and impersonally in the cold dark silence of the sub, impervious to the distant but increasingly louder whine of the torpedo approaching at high speed.

"Distance is one hundred yards, depth of target twenty-seven feet," the sensor operator intoned like a sports announcer.

After clearing the cruise ship, the PPC had maneuvered the P-3 back around in a tight circle. If the torpedo didn't do the job, there would be no time for another one to be deployed to intercept the sub. They would have to drop the five-hundred-pound iron bombs and hope one or all of them would do the trick. He closed the bomb bay doors where the other torpedo was located and told the TACCO to arm the wing stations where the iron bombs were mounted. But with no bombsight or guidance for the bombs on board, only luck would give them a direct hit.

"Roger that, Flight," the TACCO replied, moving a selector on his panel. "Wing stations are activated. Your pickle is hot."

A small red button on top of the yoke, the pickle, as pilots had long called it, gave the pilot the ability to drop the bombs at will. He consciously moved his hand completely away from the button as he began the run. He didn't want to drop the bombs too soon.

When he was about half a mile from the bow of the cruise ship, he returned his hand to the upper part of the yoke and poised his left index finger over the bomb release button. They had dropped a smoke marker on the sub's position shortly after the torpedo drop. He saw it clearly, bobbing under the bow of the cruise ship. If he had to release the bombs, at least one of them would hit the cruise ship.

"Range to target fifty yards," the sensor operator continued his narrative. But this time, there was some inflection in his voice, echoing the tension of the crew.

"Depth of target twenty feet."

In the next few seconds, several things happened at once.

There was an enormous explosion underwater, less than thirty feet from the bow of the cruise ship and just under the surface of the water. Then it appeared the ship was backing away quickly as if a giant was pulling at its stern. Several spectators on the bow were thrown overboard by the blast. The sensor operator called out, "Torpedo impact with the target," and the PPC withdrew his finger from the bomb release button and turned off the master arm switch.

The P-3 turned and overflew the site seconds later, and the sensor operator, shifting his attention now to the active buoy, said, "Target is breaking up and sinking to the bottom."

A huge cheer went up on the P-3.

Circling offshore with the F-16s overhead, Steve heard the report on guard frequency that the target had been destroyed. He relayed the information to his two female companions, and all three of them cheered fanatically in the cramped cabin of the Cessna.

The P-3 started a slow climb to a higher altitude, and the F-16s retracted their flaps and started back to the north.

"There's one more thing," Steve said into the microphone after their celebration had died down. "The people responsible for this are getting ready to fly out of the country from an airstrip somewhere east of here. We should send the F-16s over to stop them."

There was a silence on the other end of the line, and Steve knew Ross was talking to the F-16s on a discrete military frequency he couldn't hear.

A minute later, Ross replied: "The F-16s are low on fuel. We'll alert their base to send another flight, but there will be a lag time."

"By then, these guys may be out of the country!"

"We'll track them from here—they won't get away," Ross said evenly.

Steve thought about this for a few seconds. It was true that they could easily spot a jet takeoff from a small field and head out over the Gulf. They would put a ground stop on all takeoffs in the area. But that wouldn't stop someone determined to take off anyway from a small out-of-the-way municipal field. Steve could see how, in a worst-case scenario, Malikov would slip away. A confirmed visual sighting from the air would reduce the odds of that happening.

"I'm heading to the east now," Steve said. "I'll need you to point out the most likely airfields a small jet could take off from."

"We can do that," Ross said. "The F-16s say the next flight will be airborne in twenty minutes."

"This thing will be over in twenty minutes," Steve said. He glanced at his fuel gauge, tapping it out of superstitious habit to try to will it to suddenly show a few more gallons. Just under a quarter of a tank showing. It would be close.

49

The coastline east of Port Arthur, Texas, was punctuated by small inlets and estuaries. Flying due east, Steve could easily see as he climbed that a likely place for Malikov to have gone ashore was directly off his nose. The speedboat would have enough range to go anywhere within a fifty-mile radius, but Steve was sure they would head for a suitable airport upwind and outside the immediate blast range of the bomb.

Maria had overheard Malikov and Treacher talking late one night when they thought she was asleep. They had agreed that they would wait for the explosion and the ensuing pandemonium and confusion, then take off after the bomb had taken out air traffic control facilities near Houston. Steve assumed that by now, they were wondering what had gone wrong and would be anxious to escape.

His assessment was accurate. After killing the crew, Malikov and Treacher had raced to the Cameron Inlet east of Port Arthur, were picked up by a prearranged van, then shuttled to a private field near the coast, where they met their pilots at the fixed base operator terminal. They arrived at their chartered Gulfstream 650 in plenty of time to watch the fireworks and aftermath of the explosion.

Confident of their success, they were already drinking champagne in front of a television when CNN broadcast a news flash. Not the news flash they had been toasting, but a dramatic story about what was believed to be a thwarted terrorist attack near Houston. Details were sketchy, but an amateur video from the cruise ship showed the P-3 dropping its torpedo, followed by the underwater explosion. The two watched in disbelief as the short video sequence was repeated. Then the news moved on in its never-ending loop to a story about a politician caught in a bribery scandal, followed by the arrest of a sex offender.

"We must leave immediately!" Malikov shouted to the pilots, and preparations were expedited by the ground crew to ready the plane for departure. But when they boarded, the pilots informed them of some maintenance irregularities that had to be checked and signed off before they could depart.

Malikov hurled his glass against the cabin wall of the jet, shattering the crystal, then exchanged glances with Treacher. He got up and walked down the short aisle to the cockpit.

———

Now approaching Cameron Inlet, several miles offshore, Steve tried to compute the remaining time he could stay in the air. Before he could conclude his mental calculations, the radio blared on the discrete frequency he'd been given.

"Steve, there's an airfield off your nose that might handle a small jet." It was Ross's voice. "It's the only one around with a long enough runway. Turn left ten degrees."

Steve acknowledged and took up the new course. It pointed him farther down the coast than he had guessed, but Ross was convinced it was the right place because a chartered Gulfstream had landed there a few hours earlier.

The authorities had been notified. The local sheriff's helicopter was airborne and fifteen minutes away.

"And, Steve," Ross said in a small voice. "The F-16s have been told to stand down. Air traffic control has orders to let the Gulfstream takeoff and leave the country."

"What? Why?" was all Steve could say, but it was obvious that the powers that be wanted Malikov to escape without legal questioning.

"I know," Ross said. "Echoes of 9/11. I'm sorry, man."

"We'll meet later," Steve said, ignoring the insanity of the moment. "I can't let this asshole get away." He turned the VHF radio off.

He studied the fuel gauge again. It had dropped by half, indicating about an eighth of a tank left. Checking his fuel flow and doing the math, allowing for some error in the gauge, Steve concluded that he might run out of gas before he could get there. He was going to continue anyway.

He studied the sea's surface and saw whitecaps forming as the now gusty winds of late morning blew the tops off the rising swells. He was confident he could land in the water if need be, performing the tricky takeoff maneuver in reverse. However, he knew the floatplane was made for the calmer waters of bays or protected inlets, not open ocean swells. But he was taking this chance without hesitation, fueled by his growing hatred for the men responsible—for what they had done in the past, what they had tried to do, and what they would certainly continue to do in the future.

It was clear to him that even if local law enforcement apprehended Malikov, a high-placed phone call would allow him to be released and escape in his private jet if he didn't stop them himself.

Kelly watched Steve tap the fuel gauge again. She knew nothing about flying but could easily read the gauge on the dash between them. It was clear to her that they were nearly out of gas. Even though she trusted Steve as she had not trusted anyone else in a long time, she began to fear he was caught up in a single-minded determination to "finish the mission" and stop Malikov at any cost.

They had been incredibly lucky. First, the narrow escape from the catamaran, then the harrowing takeoff at sea, followed by the flight to Port Arthur and the destruction of the sub. She had experienced enough excitement and adrenaline rushes in the past week to last three lifetimes, let alone the last few hours. She glanced at Maria in the back seat, and her eyes reflected the concern also building in Kelly. But after looking for a place to land, she realized they would at least need to make it to the shoreline a few miles ahead—Steve had just told her that a first-time water landing in the rough seas that had come up in the past hour would be their last choice. She could see inland for a few miles, and no airport was in sight.

She glanced at Steve. He was staring straight ahead with a concentrated, single-minded detachment that she guessed had seen him through more than one hurdle. She was about to say something to him, something like, "It's okay now; it's over. You've done all you can. We should land now!" But then, to her surprise, he told them both to put on their headsets so that they could hear one another talk over the noise of the engine. They had discovered the headsets just a few minutes earlier. He showed them how to use the transmit button attached to the cord of each headset.

"Can you hear me?" he said after they'd fitted the headsets over their ears.

They both said they could.

"Good. Here's the situation. We've got just enough gas to make it to the field where Malikov is hiding. I know we've all been through a lot, but my gut tells me Malikov will get away if we don't try to stop him. We can land at a field before then if I can find one and let the authorities take over—if you guys have had enough. It's up to you."

Kelly had been ready to plead with him to do just that—land the damn plane. For once, let someone else risk their lives. But suddenly, like the last key piece put into place in an intricate mosaic, she felt a transformation had taken place within her. She was no longer the person she had been just a week before.

It was Steve's offer to sacrifice the pursuit of Malikov that did it. Her mind made up; she turned around to face Maria, not knowing what to expect. Neither of them spoke. At first, Maria's fearful expression was unchanged. But then, whether from Kelly's look of determination or the thought of her life of virtual slavery, the murder of Yuri, and Malikov getting away, she adopted the same resolve. They gave each other the same knowing look. No longer the scared deer-in-the-headlights look that had passed between them so often in the last few days, but a determined look more like Steve's. Yet with a feminine slant that women understood and men could only guess at.

Kelly raised an eyebrow at Maria as if to say, "Well, what do you think?"

Maria simply pushed the transmit button on her headset and said, "Let's go get the son of a bitch!"

Both women smiled at each other, and Kelly keyed her mic and said, "You heard the lady."

———

Steve stole a glance at Maria, who gave him a slight nod, then his eyes rested on Kelly, who looked squarely back at him—one eyebrow cocked up at an angle and a devilish smile on her lips. A smile like a pirate.

"How will you stop them once you've found them?" Kelly asked.

"I'll think of something," he replied grimly. "We'll have to burn that bridge when we come to it."

In truth, he didn't really know. He had no real plan and no weapon. He knew only that he had to find them and at least try to delay their takeoff. Several ideas were going through his mind, none of them any good. Then the engine began to sputter and lose power.

50

He began to climb, trading airspeed for altitude to increase his glide range as he'd been taught in his early days of Navy flight training until it had become instinctive. Those early basics came flooding back to him now. Reaching an indicated airspeed just above stall, he lowered the nose just before the engine quit altogether.

He glared at the lying fuel gauge, still indicating an eighth of a tank, then went through the motions of trying to restart the engine, but he knew it wouldn't help. After a few tries, it became obvious they were completely out of gas. He would have to dead-stick it in for a landing.

At a higher altitude now, Steve saw the airfield just inland along the coast. His primitive aviation brain told him he could make it. He turned the radio transceiver back on and switched to the default UNICOM frequency used by small uncontrolled fields.

The women tried not to panic. Neither of them said a word for fear of distracting Steve from saving their lives yet again.

The propeller stood at attention now. The prop brake was holding it in place, decreasing its drag. The sound of the wind rushing past them as they began a shallow, slow descent toward the airfield sounded like a suppressed, high-pitched scream.

Still barely above stall, Steve executed an extremely shallow turn, losing as little airspeed as possible, until he lined up with the longest paved runway. He made a quick calculation based on his altitude and estimated distance to the runway, then eyeballed the glide path to touchdown.

They would just make it. He was relieved that despite the drag of the floats, the Cessna, empty of the weight of its fuel, had a decent glide ratio.

He found the release for the wheels that would pop down at the last minute under the pontoons and allow him to land on the hard surface. They were a little over three miles out when Steve saw the Gulfstream taxiing toward the runway. It had appeared from a hangar near the end of the field and was facing them on the taxiway next to the runway. In a few seconds, it would turn the corner and take the runway. He knew it was them, but he really needed to be sure.

At that moment, the jet transmitted on the UNICOM frequency Steve had switched to earlier. "Gulfstream November Tango taking the runway, departing to the south."

It was Treacher's voice—no mistaking it. And in a few minutes, they could be gone forever.

He made another shallow turn, maintaining airspeed just above the start of stall buffet, and lined up on the jet. He tightened his seatbelt and shoulder harness and told the women to do the same.

"Hold on and strap in tight. This may not be one of my best landings."

51

The trick was to clip the jet on the ground so as to render it incapable of takeoff and, more importantly, to salvage from the attempt some type of crash landing he and his passengers could walk away from.

Since he'd never landed this particular plane, he had only a guess as to the exact location of the bottom of the pontoons relative to his seat in the cockpit. In addition, there was the annoying fact that he had never crashed a plane into another, deliberately or otherwise. He gave his plan less than a fifty percent chance of success.

It was defining circumstances such as this, throughout his life, that had led Steve to some of his best decisions, as well as some of the worst, but overall, he had learned to trust his instinct. And this one just felt right.

He could see Treacher now in the left seat at the controls. He made a slight correction with the rudder and lined his right pontoon up as best he could with Treacher's face.

The last thing Treacher saw as he looked up from his takeoff checklist was the floatplane filling most of his windscreen and descending on him like an oversized bird of prey. The pontoon crushed the Gulfstream's metal canopy and shattered its triple-layer windscreen. Treacher's head was crushed as the jet's fuselage folded in on him instantaneously.

The floatplane yawed violently to the right on impact as it bounced off the windscreen. Steve instinctively yanked back on the yoke and tried to straighten the nose with the left rudder pedal. Now traveling more or less sideways, the left pontoon skimmed a few feet above the length of the jet's fuselage until it struck the vertical stabilizer of the tail section, shearing off part of the tail and rudder on impact. Still applying full elevator, Steve managed somehow to keep the plane flying, more or less, for a few more seconds. The collision with the tail had pivoted the tattered floatplane back to the left, allowing it to crash straight ahead instead of sideways. What remained of the pontoons and struts collapsed as they struck the narrow taxiway behind the jet. The plane skidded on its belly and turned slowly to a stop, pointing back at the Gulfstream about a hundred yards away.

Steve still held full left rudder in and the yoke full back for at least ten seconds after they'd come to a stop. He was frozen in that position, his brain trying to process what had just happened and that they were all still alive. Finally, he relaxed his grip on the yoke and released the rudder pedal. Only then did he realize the sounds he'd been hearing in the background were the women's hysterical sobs of relief.

The jet, with no one at the controls and the engines still running, began to taxi itself, creeping forward like a blind and wounded animal. It continued off the taxiway and onto the scrubby, sandy ground until its nose wheel encountered a drainage ditch between the taxiway and the runway, and the jet stopped abruptly. The entire plane was now cocked up at an odd angle, its rear end hanging over the taxiway pavement.

Suddenly, the cabin door was thrust open, and the two pilots, who had earlier been forced from their seats by Treacher and held captive by Malikov, leaped to the pavement and sprinted from the plane. A moment later, Malikov appeared in the doorway and stumbled to the ground. As he got up, Steve saw the assault rifle in his hand.

There was nowhere for him to go, no limo or armored car to pick him up and race him to safety, no minion to act as his human shield. It was at least half a mile to the nearest building. Steve was sure the man had seldom found himself as exposed as he was at this moment. Then he looked directly at the floatplane, and their eyes locked. Never had Steve seen more hatred in a stare.

The sound of sirens had been growing louder, and a fire-and-rescue truck soon appeared, followed by several police cars, which fanned out in a semicircle around the jet as Malikov opened fire on them.

The firemen scurried to cover behind their truck. The police, however, were more than ready to return fire, having received a report terrorists might be at the scene.

"Stay down!" Steve warned his passengers. It wasn't just the gunfire. He'd noticed a trail of fluid following the contours of the taxiway pavement and spreading out from the jet like a giant flattened snake. Tracing it back, he saw a widening pool underneath the right wing of what could only be jet fuel. He'd done more damage than he realized. Flying debris from the crash must have pierced the fuel tank.

The police were firing wildly. Malikov opened up again with the assault rifle, and one of the policemen, a woman, was hit. Her partner, newly inspired, took deliberate aim at Malikov and fired once. The bullet struck below his right knee, and as he went down, Malikov sprayed the pavement around him.

A spark from a ricochet was all that was necessary to ignite the jet fuel in the ninety-eight-degree heat. The plane was engulfed in a fireball. Steve saw Malikov on fire, and then, as the fuel in the full tanks of the plane ignited a split second later, he saw him vaporized in the detonation that followed.

As the shock wave spread out at the speed of sound, it lifted the police cars and set them back down again. The fire truck was moved a foot or two, and the Cessna was buffeted wildly. It spun around 180 degrees to face the shallow waters of the brackish lake nearby.

A fitting end, Steve thought, though perhaps a little too merciful.

He stared at the beauty of the serene lake now directly in front of him, its water shimmering in the late morning sun. The women were out of screams, and no one made a sound in the Cessna. As he watched the water, a mullet jumped not far from shore, for whatever reason a mullet jumps, as if nothing unusual had occurred.

EPILOGUE

Pirate's Smile lay at anchor on the calm waters of the protected bay. Her refitting and restoration now complete, along with the traditional naming ceremony that had followed, she hardly resembled the run-down inter-island trawler she had been in a previous life.

Somewhere in the distance, a thunderstorm rumbled, momentarily lighting up the predawn sky to the north. The stars were reluctantly giving up their place on the celestial stage as the first signs of the sun, yet to make its appearance, began to turn the sky purple, orange, and yellow. Just above the sea's surface, the crescent moon cradled Venus in an intimacy that would not be repeated for another year.

Steve was dreaming again. It was one of those rare lucid dreams when you know you're dreaming, somehow conscious of the fact that this is not normal, everyday reality; more like a movie you'd written, directed, and are starring in yourself.

He was sitting on the beach in front of the cottage, watching the first rays of the sun peeking over the horizon. He could feel it's warm touch on his face. He was holding a fishing pole.

Then a dolphin surfaced in the shallow water before him—an impossibility because he knew the water was much too shallow to allow such a large mammal to swim there.

Yet there it was. He dismissed it as an inconsistency in his dream, but then the dolphin spoke to him in a woman's voice. A calm, strong voice he knew immediately. It was the voice of his wife again, then it was Janice, sitting cross-legged there in the clear shallow water by the shore, the waves gently lapping around her. He recognized the bathing suit she wore as the one from their honeymoon at this very spot.

Tears flowed, burning his eyes as he caught his breath.

"Catching anything?" she asked, smiling.

He tried to answer but couldn't. There was so much he wanted to say to her, but his dream hadn't given him a speaking part. All he could do was shake his head, dumbfounded.

"You've been busy," she said. "You need to get some rest. It's going to be all right now."

Then she was the dolphin again, her eyes holding his, swimming away from him in that dolphin backstroke like one of the trained ones at Sea World, a perpetual smile on her face.

"We'll meet again," said the dolphin, still in his wife's voice. "Get some rest."

She disappeared below the surface, and a gentle rain moved in across the bay, erasing any sign she had really been there.

A peace came over him then, a warm embracing peace he had not experienced for as long as he could remember yet recognized at once.

Then something was tugging at his arm. The arm holding the fishing pole. He looked at the line, but it was slack, and the rod wasn't bent. He felt the tug at his arm again and opened his eyes.

Kelly was there, sitting on the side of the bed. It was morning, the sun shining through the cabin window. Her hair fell over her shoulders and cascaded down her front. She was smiling, holding a cup of coffee for him.

"You were having a dream," she said, studying the tracks of tears on his face. "Are you all right?"

"Yeah. I think so," he said, taking the coffee, returning her smile weakly. He walked with her up the short flight of stairs to the main deck.

He noticed the deck was wet from a recent shower. Well, of course it was.

He looked over toward the cottage and saw Doc asleep again in his chair below the palm trees.

Then he looked toward the mouth of their little bay, and there, just inside the reef, heading out through the gap into the open ocean, a dolphin broke the surface, its gray dorsal fin glinting in the morning sun.

"It's going to be a beautiful day," Kelly said, following his gaze.

"It is," he said, putting an arm around her waist. "It's going to be a very beautiful day."

ACKNOWLEDGMENTS

I'd like to thank all my friends and family along the way who helped me begin to think of myself as a writer, even though some had never read a word of what I had put down. Lifelong friends like Chuck Perry and Fred Dunlea, who somehow thought I could do it.

To everyone I've met at Severn River Publishing: Andrew Watts, Amber Hudock, and my "handler" Megan Copenhaver—whose professionalism and timely expertise kept this project going smoothly. Also, to those at Severn River I haven't met who were in the trenches and behind the scenes and made this book a reality.

I'd especially like to thank my developmental editor, Randall Klein, who was instrumental in helping me "kill my darlings" and polish the story to a brilliant shine. My copy editor, Lisa Gilliam, whose comprehensive knowledge of the written word kept me from sounding like a fool sometimes.

And to my readers, thank you all for taking the time to enjoy this story. I look forward to giving you more adventures of Steve Remington and Kelly Phillips—whatever they may be.

ABOUT THE AUTHOR

Andrew Scott Jackson grew up in a small town south of Atlanta and earned a degree from the University of Georgia. After graduation, and with no real direction other than wanting to learn how to sail and see the Caribbean, he bought an open-ended ticket to St. Thomas, U.S. Virgin Islands, walked the docks, and got a job as a deckhand on a 78' Rhodes Ketch charter boat. That experience and the people he met along the way cemented a lifelong interest in writing.

He returned to the States, joined the Navy to learn how to fly, went through Aviation Officer Candidate School, and flew the P-3C Orion during the last Cold War with the Russians. His deployments covered the globe, including the Western Pacific, Indian Ocean, Eastern Africa, the Mediterranean, and Iceland, prosecuting Russian submarines and keeping tabs on Soviet Battle Groups. He retired from the Navy in 2006 while concurrently flying for a major U.S. Airline as an International Captain.

He enjoys writing about exceptional people with real flaws and dreams thrown into extraordinary situations requiring a baptism by fire to survive and succeed. When not writing, his passions include salt and freshwater fishing, hunting, and improving his tree and wildlife habitat farm in Georgia, where he lives.

To find out more about Andrew's books, visit:
severnriverbooks.com/collections/andrew-scott-jackson

Made in United States
North Haven, CT
13 July 2025

70642611R00152